Biker's Ritual

BWWM Dark Motorcycle Club Romance

Rebel Barbarians Motorcycle Club

Book Three

Jamila Jasper

ISBN: 979-8-3303-0735-7

Thank you to my Patreon subscribers for your support with this book. I could not have done it without you. www.patreon.com/jamilajasper

❀ Created with Vellum

Rebel Barbarians Motorcycle Club

Biker's Surrogate

Biker's Servant

Biker's Ritual

Biker's Enemy. (Book #4)

Biker's Property (Book #5)

... and more

Description

Southpaw shows up at Reaper's doorstep with a screaming, crying black woman who claims that Reaper owes her a life-changing debt.
He wants nothing to do with the skinny, tall, dark-skinned black woman who fights like a hell cat.
He especially hates the strange effect she has on his arousal.
Reaper has no choice but to keep this woman in his Texas condo.

This woman's body belongs to him completely according to the motorcycle club boss, Southpaw...
And if the boss says Reaper can't get rid of her,
She has to stay.

He never said she had to stay tied to the bed but after 24 hours with Tamiya, he has no choice.

Forced to care for a vicious, violent black woman who hates his guts, Reaper takes his desires for control, revenge and retribution to new extremes.

Everyone has a past... and Reaper's past secrets are darker than normal.
He might be the most depraved and unhinged psychopath Tamiya has come across.

She's the one woman who understands him the most... and she wants him dead.

It doesn't matter how much he does for her,
Or how many times he gets on his knees...

Tamiya knows what she wants from the dangerous, muscular biker.
To end his life.

*You are not too damaged for real love. For the readers who have been through hurtful or traumatic pasts – **you are not too fucked up to find love.***

If he won't do it, another man will — willingly, lovingly & passionately.

*Here's to manifesting your **happily ever after…***

The female lead in this book is named after my lovely patron, Tamiya. A supporting character, Katrina, is named after another Patron.

Click here to subscribe:
www.patreon.com/jamilajasper

Blackwood.

Gideon "Reaper" Blackwood

Rank: Co-President
Patched In: September 2017

Book III

Rebel Barbarians Motorcycle Club Alpha Chapter Charter

Edition II

The democratic organization of the Rebel Barbarians Motorcycle Club permits club operations within 100 miles as the crow flies from the old Route 66 highway on the traditional Rebel Barbarians bike route.

Club headquarters decided by committee are located in the basement of Hollingsworth's Chicken Basket, run by Deb Hollingsworth-Shaw.

Section I Purpose

Our club monitors and protects the safety and purity of families and associates of the Rebel Barbarians. Members share a passion for patriotism, respect for authority, a desire to protect tradition, and maintain the sanctity of the American race across the Midwest.

Section II Membership

Eligibility: *Eligible members must be over 18 years old, white American* males, & receive three references from active members. A preference for: No women. No homosexuals. No niggers. No spics. No immigrants.

Eligibility will be assessed on a case by case basis determined by connection to active club members.

Once recruited into the Rebel Barbarian's organization, initiates receive their first brand or tattoo prior to a year long initiation.

After the year-long initiation, recruits may become permanent active members, requiring them to pay 15% of their legitimate earnings to the club and 30% of illegitimate earnings. New recruits participate in an 18 month initiation ritual into the organization and during that time, they must follow a strict code of conduct, show respect towards the organization, and demonstrate loyalty to the motorcycle club.

Club members must have several years of riding experience assessed by the club officers and their membership must have the support of active due-paying members. Junior club members have 5-10 years of membership, senior members have 10+ years of membership.

Recruitment: Recruitment period begins every year in Pontiac, IL club headquarters with the annual July 4th summer barbecue followed by the charity ride for veterans with leukemia and local food banks. The recruitment period ends on Labor Day when all potential recruits must put in an official bid with the club officers.

Potential recruits must meet the requirements for eligibility and dress in club colors during the recruitment period to signal loyalty to the organization. Once becoming a "recruit", said recruits must spend 18 months in service of the club before becoming full members.

Code of Conduct: If you're gonna start a fight, make sure you finish it. Never let another man speak ill of your club or brothers. Never touch another rider's old lady. Never cheat a club member. Never touch another man's bike. Never sit on another man's bike.Get drunk. Fuck. Fix bikes. Have fun.

Section III Club Structure

Officers: *The current officers of the Rebel Barbarians are as follows.*

Co-Presidents - Southpaw, Hawk, Reaper, Cash

Enforcer - to be determined.

Treasurer - to be determined.

Meetings: *Quarterly meetings are held at NEW South West outpost in Tucumcari, Texas, and they are presided over by the club president. Attendance is mandatory unless you are serving a prison sentence, the military, or an equivalent commitment.*

Rank:
Recruits - Fresh recruits are the newest members of the club. Barring special circumstances, recruitment lasts 18 months before graduation to "newbies"

Newbies - Recruits who survive their 18 month trial period with the club participate in the initiation ritual to become newbies. The newbie period lasts five years.

Juniors - 5-10 years of club membership.

Senior members - 10+ years of club membership

Officers - Elected club officers hold the club leadership positions

Junior Officer - Officers appoint one family member to apprentice under them for their position in the club however, the final decision on officers relies on a club election.

⅔ quorum must be reached for all club elections pertaining to membership & officers.

Section IV Rules & Regulations

Riding Rules: Fuck pigs. Stay armed. Shoot if you must. Never ride alone. Never ride without club colors.

Club Colors: All riders must wear a Rebel Barbarian's MC patch dependent on their rank and position within the organization. All club tattoos must be prominently and proudly displayed.

Club Dues: All active members pay club dues of $250/month to maintain club membership. If dues are unpaid for over 90 days, they fall into collections.

Section V Amendments

All amendments must be decided by a 75% member vote and there must be a quorum - over ⅔ of all membership present for any voting to take place about matters pertaining to the club.

Section VI Dissolution

In the event of the tragic end to the Rebel Barbarians, all club assets should be liquidated and proceeds split up amongst the four founding families. S. H. R. C.

PART ONE

CHAPTER ONE
REAPER

I stay up all night waiting for judgment but it never comes. My legs are crossed on the Apache blanket as I watch the darkness fall over the desert, but my body refuses to feel the cold, even as I see my breath coming out of my mouth in disturbed, cloudy puffs.

I can still breathe.

THE DARKNESS BEGINS to shift from that impossibly blue-black to a soft, morning-gray. I haven't moved in hours and I can't get the disturbing pictures out of my head.

I WATCHED the blood burst from the woman's chest and mouth as she fell backwards against her boyfriend, who gladly let her take a bullet for him. Mom told me the folks out here were abominations and that Satan would bring his scourge for them.

Am I the scourge of Satan?

· · ·

HUNTER GAVE me his last pack of American Spirits before he fled south with the Shaws and the Hollingsworths. His twin brother, Steel, fled the scene too, promising me that everything would be okay. Ruger, dad, and myself are the only ones still out here in the early morning hours.

The twins burned the bodies last night in the desert beneath rock formations that tourists would destroy if they ever learned about them. Utah is one of the country's prettiest states. Too bad I'll never come back here.

I burn through all the cigarettes and I still can't push the image out of my mind. I can hear dad and Ruger talking about what to do with me. Like I'm fragile.

"He killed men in Iraq," dad says. "He handled it just fine. He'll come out of this."

Ruger is one of those men so committed to being a country boy that his exaggerated drawl gives his voice a different accent from the rest of us.

"Uncle Lyle," he says softly. "He ain't ever killed a woman before."

"Shut up and get him some liquor. We have to move him."

DAD PUTS his hand on my back.

"Get up. We're going home."

"I can't go back to Salt Lake."

"I meant our home," he says. The new place.

WE LIVED all over when we were kids but the only place that ever felt like home to me was Arizona. Running guns out of Salt Lake City for dad didn't bother me, but I couldn't never get too comfortable in a city where half the women I met wanted to drag me to church or get me to quit smoking and drinking.

· · ·

EVENTUALLY, dad gets me off the ground and folds up the Apache blanket for me. Out of all his sons, I look the least like Lyle Blackwood. He has round features and a large, bulky body. I've always been lean with high cheekbones, pale skin and eyes like the Arctic. I suppose I have mom's features, except for my hair. Dad's hair went white long ago but when he was my age, it was the same pale shade of blonde.

"Come on, Gideon," he says. "You can't sit here and rot."

ROT. Like the woman I shot and witnessed buried in a shallow grave. My father helps me to my feet. Ruger gets too close to me. I love my cousin, but liking him has always been something I had to force upon myself. He puts his hand on my shoulder in an effort to comfort me that I'm certain will fail before he even opens his mouth.

"It doesn't really matter, Gideon," Ruger says. "She was just a nigger."

I glare at him. Only an idiot like Ruger could think that would make me feel better. Doesn't matter what that woman was. I told her to stay out of the way. I tried to give her a chance... My jaw tightens and I take out my anger on the only person I can.

"Shut the hell up, Ruger."

Before I escalate the situation, dad steps between us putting one hand on my shoulder and another on Ruger's back.

"He's only trying to make you feel better," dad says. "We'd better head home. Ruth has been calling, wondering where we are."

My youngest sister Ruth has been going through hell since mom went to prison. Dad wasn't meant to be a single parent and the only help he has right now is my aunt, who helps herself to his wallet and the contents of his fridge more than she does anything for Ruth. If it's not about getting the girl into church or criticizing her for immodest clothing, our aunt does nothing for her.

"Did you tell her we were in Utah?" I ask, although the question is stupid and only escapes from my lips as something to fill the space. I would have said anything to avoid letting my mind wander to the images that refuse to disappear.

"I didn't," he says. "Now stop fussing and come on. You're fine. Everything is going to be okay."

I SHOULD HAVE KNOWN dad was just saying that to make me feel better and calm me down. Everyone thinks I'm crazy as fuck because of what happened that made me leave the Army — bad conduct. Lost my benefits because of what happened. But like dad said to Ruger. I did my therapy. I left that fucked up part of my past behind me.

I turn my bike down Ironwood Drive first and before we get to the large wrought iron gates at the end of the cul-de-sac, I can tell dad has other plans for me today aside from allowing me to rest from our four hour ride from the middle of the Utah desert to Sedona, Arizona.

My twin brothers leave my spot empty, but Jairus and Jotham clearly got here first. My aunt's grey Volkswagen Jetta blocks our neighbor's driveway and there are a couple more bikes belonging to other family members who are part of the club.

Shit...

AUNT KATIE EXPECTS US, so she leaves the front door unlocked. I walk inside the house and I hear my little sister scream.

"GIDDY!!!!"

She's the only one I still let call me that. I hear her clomping down the hallway like a horse, then I hear my aunt yelling her name but it's too late to stop her. Ruth comes whirling around the hallway like she's racing and smacks into me at full force. She squeals as her arms wrap around me and jumps up and down as she squeezes my stomach.

Her warmth and her excitement do nothing to move me at first. I can't even hug her back. I feel like hugging my little sister will contaminate her with my crimes and immorality. But her excitement to see me is so goddamn infectious.

"Gideon! Gideon! Gideon! You're home!"

Her jumping up and down and skinny little arms around me gets me to hug her back. Dad walks in the door and Ruth pulls away from me, running to give dad a hug. She has always been his favorite. Ruger grunts as he walks inside and heads straight for the kitchen to talk to his mom on the phone. She's in prison with my mom for an entirely different crime. And she's been in prison much longer.

They have a tense relationship since she spent most of Ruger's life in prison and their reunion doesn't take long to descend into arguing once they're in the same room. Dad sends Ruth upstairs with a stern voice after a brief greeting and then with a stern tone, he commands us all to the basement.

Most of the family was already waiting for us there, so dad must have arranged this family meeting seconds after I pulled the trigger. Blackwood club members as far as ten hours away are sitting in the basement. They must have driven all night to get here. Dad shuts the door to the basement once we're all accounted for and walks to the center of the room.

"Good morning everyone," he says. "Something happened last night and we need to take care of it. Make sure it never comes back. *Never.*"

He doesn't fill anyone in on the details, just what needs to be done. Vehicles and clothes burned. Alibis established.

At the end of it all, we promise to take the secret to our graves and pray together as a family for my freedom and my soul. When our family meeting ends, Harlan Shaw calls dad with bad news.

They arrested Ryder Sinclair on the highway with the murder weapon and he's going to prison on a weapons charge.

CHAPTER TWO
TAMIYA

Five Years Later

Months Before The Blue Blood Knights "Incident"

I hate this job. Every day, I pray that my boss drops dead and then over lunch, I pray for forgiveness for the earlier prayer. I figure if some bad shit is going to happen to me, I want to give God the opportunity to punish me between 7 a.m. and noon. But I need this job because it's the only job that allows me access to the internet all day for me to do some research.

I'm the secretary for my town's worst private investigator. My boss, Rebecca Knight, only takes cases for women, which would be all well and good if she wasn't terrible at dealing with clients. She's in the back with the first person to walk in all week – a blond woman with a bob carrying a baby and sobbing her eyes out.

I sit at the big computer with access to all the software and complete my job as secretary, writing down all the information the blond woman tells me to. Eleanor Pearson sounds like she has her hands full — and not just with the baby. She cites as her "reason for visiting" a suspicion that the father of her baby emptied their joint account to spend the money they were saving to buy a new trailer. She smells like cigarettes and she looks pissed off. Her baby daddy fucked up. I nod along as she tells her story and give her the required spiel about how Rebecca won't rest until she solves the case.

(The truth is, Rebecca has a Xanax problem and her dad's enormous settlement from the US Army that she inherited is the only thing keeping this business afloat. I unofficially became her accountant after the business almost shut down last year, but that's not currently relevant to the Eleanor situation.)

Once I check her in, I dial Rebecca's extension and she tells me to send Eleanor back to her. She sounds relaxed, which is a good sign. It's better that she sees clients after she takes her pills rather than when she's on a detox.

Eleanor bounces her pretty baby girl on her hip and whispers something about "killing that idiot father of hers" before trotting to Rebecca's office. The noise machine between the front desk and Rebecca's office drowns out their conversation. Rebecca used to be a cop and there's a part of her that *does* take this seriously.

ONCE ELEANOR DISAPPEARS, I head back to my *real* work - my research. It's the only reason I kept this shitty job after all these years. It's been three years since I started working here and gained access to all the special software private investigators use. When I told my best friend, Katrina, that I planned to conduct my own research after high school instead of going to college, she asked me how I expected to become a private investigator when I was barely passing my high school classes. I asked her why her parents named her after a hurricane, a joke she heard literally a million times in high school.

But she made a good point. But I didn't have to become a private investigator to access all the dope shit they can. I just had to become a *receptionist*. Rebecca Knight goes to my church and she's only four years older than me. Our parents know each other and fate worked out to send me here... *to investigate the death of my estranged sister.*

My parents act like she never lived, like she did something so terrible that they can't even say her name anymore. She ran away from our hometown when I was just fifteen years old. I never remember her living with us, but she was a part of my life growing up enough that I feel her absence. I feel the weight of the silence around her name.

I don't know why they won't even mention her or entertain the idea that she might be dead. Technically, she's a missing person, but we all know the truth. We're her family. We can feel it.

Damara is dead. And nobody seems to give a shit.

DAMARA WAS mom's kid from her first marriage and seventeen years older than me. I can't get her off my mind lately. Maybe it's my recent birthday filling me with existential dread. I don't know what it is, but her absence has been haunting me like a poltergeist from *The Shining*.

The last night I saw my sister, I obviously didn't know it would be the last. I was basically a baby compared to now. Even back then I knew she wasn't perfect, but that didn't stop me from putting her right up on a pedestal. That night, there must have been something different about her, but no matter how many times I call the memory up, nothing sticks out to me. Damara sat there all calm and smoked a joint that was laced with something on the porch and told me that *love* was the most important thing and when it came down to it, I should be willing to die for the man I loved.

I just thought she was high.

NOW, I wonder if her boyfriend killed her and went on the run, or if something else happened.

I USED what little memories I had of that last conversation with her to try and track her down, but for years I turned up nothing. No trace of her. Rebecca's various investigative software has only led me on one goose chase after another. And well... there's my unofficial investigation service I sell on social media where I help women track down the men who ghosted them. It's light work, especially when I use Rebecca's old modeling pictures to catfish them.

Rebecca doesn't know about that though, and clients have really dried up lately for my little side hustle.

Despite the noise machine, I hear Eleanor emit a strangled sob and wonder if Rebecca is working some magic she's previously suppressed. *Maybe this will be the client to turn things around for her.* It's going to buy me more time to research.

I start by checking my "research email address" that I created just for the sake of keeping track of this seemingly useless project. I know if my sister were alive anywhere in the world, she would have found a way to contact me.

If she's dead, she's been murdered. It's the only explanation that makes sense.

For the first time in weeks, a new email sits unopened at the top of my inbox. This one isn't spam — at least I don't think it is — and it doesn't look like it's from any of the dozen or so people I emailed before looking for information — detectives, reporters, that sort of thing.

Nope. This email says it's from Coco Melon Cranberry. It doesn't even sound like a real name, but a character from a fantasy novel or something. The subject line reads: **Information about Damara Keturah Simmons.**

Tremors attack my hands instantly and the words crash into me, destabilizing me as I sit there trying to process the taste of bile at the back of my throat and the possibility contained in those words. Something tells me it's just a prank. I have posted *everywhere* on the internet

— including True Crime forums and all kinds of places where weirdos might lurk and want to play a cruel trick on me.

BUT... *They used her middle name.* How would they have known her middle name if they didn't know her? It's not like her middle name was "Ann" or "Mae", something common and easy to guess. I have to sip so much water to calm myself down before I open the email.

The email address is an obvious throwaway too, but the content scares the crap out of me because whoever sent this email clearly knew what they were talking about and this is the first time in years I've had anything close to a lead.

*YOUR SISTER WAS INVOLVED with a man who went by the name 'Voltaire' but his real name was Nathaniel Davis. This was a dangerous man who deserved what happened to him. I'm sorry for your loss but if you know what's good for you, **stop looking into this.***

ALL THAT CAN COME out of this is pain.

STOP WHAT YOU ARE DOING.

JUST STOP.

THE EMAIL ENDS. No signature. *Just stop.* The chill runs straight through me. I reply immediately.

WHO ARE YOU? How do you know this? Please, I want to know more.

. . .

— TAMIYA.

IF THEY KNOW this much about Damara, they must know my name. I want to keep this personal in hopes they reach out again. Nathaniel Davis. *Voltaire*. It makes sense. She always called him 'V'. I searched every database I could for every name I could even think of beginning with the letter 'V', chasing down one "intuitive" lead after another, always finding nothing.

HIS NAME NEVER STARTED WITH 'V'. That was just his nickname.

HER BOYFRIEND WAS CALLED Nathaniel and judging by this email... he might be the reason she's dead.

THIS WAS a dangerous man who deserved what happened to him.

I TYPE his name into the National Crime Information Center and as I click 'SEARCH', Rebecca's door flings open and Eleanor screams loudly, "You ignorant bitch!"

Great. Another client lost...

"I thought I was clear that my consultation fee was—

"No, I already *paid* a consultation fee. You are a *scammer*, Rebecca. That's why your business is flopping. You *scam people.*"

Rebecca doesn't even argue, but Eleanor doesn't stop cursing her out. I remove one of my AirPods to get a better listen.

"You little... If Jenny wasn't here, I would curse you out. That's why everyone in this town talks about you, Rebecca. I said I didn't care if you had a pill problem, but maybe I should have!"

Eleanor storms off and Rebecca doesn't even follow her. This time, she doesn't even leave her office. Eleanor doesn't look at me as she walks out, but I look at her, just in case I have to perform some last minute customer service like holding her earrings before she two-pieces my boss.

I get paid well.

I KEEP my cursor hovered over the 'X' button in case Rebecca comes out seeking some last minute therapy about the situation. I mostly just nod and agree with everything she says until she gets 'exhausted' and goes rattling around in her desk for more pills.

She used to be a good detective, I heard. Something fucked her up — I don't know what.

REBECCA AGGRESSIVELY STOMPS towards the door before slamming it shut. *Yes...*

I LOOK at the page in front of me with details uncovered about Nathaniel Davis. My missing sister's boyfriend.

Chapter Three
Reaper

TUCUMCARI

Shortly Before The Blue Blood Knights Incident...

Dad burned to death after a biker shot him in the chest twice. I identified his body in the morgue. The body didn't look like Lyle Blackwood. *Doc.* He had no lips. His skin blackened like soot from the fireplace. *This isn't dad.*

"Yeah. That's him."

I didn't cry until I got home from Amarillo.

The shit I went through in the army prepared me for loss. I've lost friends of mine growing up and you can't be part of a club like ours without losing friends and family to the road. I never expected to lose him like this. I thought if there was one loss in this world that could drag the tears out of me, it would be his.

I didn't expect to feel this deep, unyielding pit inside me. Tears might flush it out, but the tears just wouldn't come.

I sat at home, waiting to feel something, waiting for the time I call mom every day. She already knows he's dead. We gave Jairus the job of telling her. I didn't know what the fuck I would say to her when I picked up the phone.

But at least hearing her voice forced emotions out of me. I shed a few tears for the man who raised me when I hear my mom's grief on the phone from her prison cell. She loved that man. She would have gladly taken his place. Her grief forces me to think about love. Family. A wife.

I don't think there's a woman alive who loves as hard as my mother.

Brexlynn Blackwood grew up deeply involved in the biker lifestyle, harder than dad ever was, and she left no stone unturned. After I described my dead father to her in excruciating detail, we prayed. I hung up. Then it hit me. He's gone. And this shit is all going to be mine to deal with.

You can't handle this shit, Gideon. You're crazier than a fucking coconut.

When Southpaw calls me out to Tucumcari, I pack my shit up and wire over all the money necessary for me to settle into my place out there. Southpaw helps with the basics, but I'll need whatever money I can get my hands on for expenses, groceries, and parts for the bike.

I don't fight his instructions to head out there. Shit, I've got nothing better going on than club business and I could use some time to myself. Maybe I'll sleep better if I stay out of Missouri. I don't want any reminders of dad or the shit we've gone through.

The house in Tucumcari is small – thank goodness. I never liked big houses and all the work required to keep them clean. It's just a two bed, two bathroom home. I keep my boots and a rifle near the front door, and spend most of the day watching television in the living room on the couch my brother Jairus brought out here for me.

I have a queen-sized bed in my bedroom, but nothing else except the Bible on the nightstand and three more guns stashed around the room, just in case. Ever since the night we don't talk about, I sleep with several guns in my room. Sometimes I wake up in the night sweating while I shiver from the cold and my finger on the trigger of one of my pistols.

Third time that happened, I stopped keeping the guns loaded. The last thing I need right now is more trouble. I already can't sleep. I have the clubhouse project to keep me busy and work...

RUGER CALLS me about a week out from the clubhouse completion date. Once that's over, Hunter and Wyatt will come down to give everything a final inspection. I built our solid oak meeting table myself and engraved the brand new club rules into the hardwood meeting room walls in cursive. Dad made sure we were all good with our hands before we enlisted.

You idiots will need skills when you get back... providing you get back with all your fingers and toes.

"You get out of bed today?" Ruger asks after I reluctantly pick up the phone to answer his call. The fact that Ruger is the one checking up on my mental health makes me even more tense.

"Yes," I say, my voice growing immediately tense. I don't need anyone in the family thinking I'm falling apart. It's bad enough everyone saw how I reacted after everything that went down on the night we don't talk about.

"Did you eat? Take a shower? Feeling any better?"

I snap at Ruger preemptively. "I don't need you playing therapist. What are we doing today?"

"It's not club business," he says. "We have a client."

Good. I need some extra money. I spent a lot of what I had on dad's funeral, put a couple grand on mom's books because she got in trouble with some 'crazy illegals' on her block who allegedly want to 'take her appendix out'. She had to pay some gang for protection.

"What kind of client?"

Ruger had better not be fucking around. The promise of extra money gets me out of bed. Dad prepared us well for life. We all enlisted and it was well-known that we all would. He taught us all different trade skills so we could work once we left the Army. The real, official family business has nothing to do with the skills dad taught us so we could maintain regular employment.

Jairus and Jotham co-own a mechanic shop. I build cabinets, tables, whatever folks need. Ruger works at a warehouse loading pallets for a food company. Tobias works the land out in the mountains with his family. He barely rides anymore and all he does is preach to his wife and kids when he isn't forcing them all to raise chickens, ducks, or whatever his new animal obsession is.

"The kind of client that pays well," Ruger says. "Our supplier won't want us taking the risk and bringing guns all the way to the border."

I laugh. "The border? We're not selling guns to Mexicans."

"We're not. We're selling guns to Texans."

I'm glad I don't have to explain to Ruger that we only do business with white people. I don't know any clubs operating out of Texas, especially not close enough to the border for Ruger to have any concern.

"Bikers?"

He pauses, like he's nervous about what I'll say. I hope he isn't bull-shitting me.

"No," he says. "We're better off not asking them any questions about their intentions."

In our line of work, he's right that it's the best choice. It's not like I've gone out to look for work or even put a sticker on a truck out here in Texas. I've put my heart and soul into my work for the club, but it's time for me to get a little extra cash.

"Okay," I say. "Send me the details. I'll assemble the team."

Ruger pauses and then I hear strange sounds coming from the other end of the line. I want this call to be over, but the twisted sound coming from Ruger's end sounds a lot like a sob. I exhale slowly, waiting for him to say something or identify the strange groan coming out of his mouth.

Yeah. It's a sob. "I miss him. I miss Uncle Lyle so goddamn much, Gideon..."

"We don't need to talk about this."

"How can you stand it?" he says, ignoring my efforts to change the subject completely.

"Stand what?" I grunt.

"He's gone, Gideon. Don't you feel anything?"

"OF COURSE I FEEL SOMETHING, you fucking idiot. He was my father. But we still have shit to do."

I HANG UP ON RUGER. He'll send me the details when he has them. I call the twins and let them know I need them to ride some guns down to the Texans. We have a meeting point that doesn't get regular visits from cartels or border patrol traveling immigration routes searching for folks who crossed from Mexico and are making their way on foot to God knows where. The twins ask if they can bring help.

"Only family."

Their plan is to get the supply from Ruger before driving down to my place. After a couple nights here, we'll plan our liaison with the buyers.

I HATE that Ruger wants to talk about dad and I hate that he cries like a baby. Dad's gone, he's right. But crying about it won't bring him back.

And it's none of Ruger's business how much I miss my father. *He was the head of our household and we all loved the hell out of that man. How can Ruger doubt that?*

I'd rather talk about him with mom than my brother, if at all. He had a funny way of looking at the world that fit so perfectly with my mother's. They were made for each other – highschool sweethearts that never had eyes for anyone else. My mother loves telling the story of how they met, especially now that dad's dead.

He rode with my cousin Harley and I was only thirteen years old when I saw him. I said to myself, I'm going to be at homecoming with a senior. I don't care if I'm in eighth grade.

They got permission to be married when mom was fifteen. I'm glad she never had to see him dead.

MY MOTHER COULDN'T WAIT to be rid of me 'cause I drank so much and I was loose when I was drinking. Jesus Christ saved both me and your father. I had the twins when I was seventeen and they were a goddamn blessing.

SHE LOVES our family and now that dad's dead, I know she expects me to keep everything together.

Maybe I should oversee the gun deal myself instead of sending the twins out to handle it. Ruger's job sounds like it could have some potential, but I'd rather give the work to the twins and take 20% off the top. Southpaw wants me to stay in Tucumcari so... I'll get some extra money from the deal, wait for shit to settle down, and handle my shit here. I might like it out here.

I'm in no mood to go through all that trouble for some cash and I don't think dad's death has anything to do with it. If I didn't have club business to attend to... I'd do more.

. . .

I DON'T KNOW what the hell is going to happen to me out here. Most likely nothing. Since dad died, I've had to grow accustomed to this lack of purpose that pervades everything…

Chapter Four
Tamiya

I quit working for Rebecca Knight the day after I found Nathaniel Davis's name. She begs me to keep working for her and offers me half her bottle of Xanax to keep me on staff. I'm tempted to take the bottle and disappear on her because I can sell the pills for $15 a pop to some college kids, but I'm better off not pissing off a crazy drug addict with connections to cops. Even if she's a nice suburban white lady on the outside.

My first day of unemployment almost makes me wish I quit working earlier to pursue this investigation more completely. I only have enough money to survive the next three months, so this fantasy might fall apart pretty quickly, but for now, I'm in bliss.

Instead of getting out of bed at 5 in the morning to reply to my boss's deranged text messages, I wake up at 7:30 a.m. and make myself a cup of coffee. I open my PDF about Nathaniel Davis on my iPad and continue my research. My sister never used social media but when I look up Nathaniel, I find a Photobucket account and there are pictures of them together there. Just three pictures and I can't tell where they are - outside a camper van near a lake, but I don't know which one.

It doesn't look like it was that long ago. Nathaniel uploaded the picture a little over three years ago, so I'm right, but the caption is vague.

UTAH OR BUST.

I SCOFF. Utah? I know Damara had no interest in being out in Utah. Maybe this was Nathaniel's dream. I don't know anything about Utah except it's far away.

NO MATTER how much I try to detach myself, I'm still looking at a picture of my dead sister and it's hard to tear myself away. People always said we looked alike, but in this picture with her boyfriend, I completely disagree. She looks like an Instagram model. *Seriously.*

Damara was shaped like a girl who had surgery several times over and she barely hit the gym. Her skin was smooth and she knew exactly how to wear her hair and dress to have guys falling all over her. Even white guys like Nathaniel – tall, blond, church-going and by all accounts, perfect.

What happened to them?

EVEN IF IT isn't much, the only clue I have from the picture is Utah, so that's where I guide my research next. Nathaniel Davis. Utah. Damara Simmons. I type as many combinations of the names into Google as I can. But I swear search engines keep getting worse. I don't turn up anything interesting.

What if...

INSTEAD OF UTAH, I guess madly and type in Salt Lake City. **Bingo.** The page instantly populates with search results and the first one definitely intrigues me. So much information pops up about Nathaniel Davis that I make a crazy decision.

I'M GOING to Salt Lake City.

I STAND out way too much in Salt Lake City. I admit, I should have looked up the racial demographics before jumping on a plane and flying out here. People stare at me like they've never seen a black person before. I've never been somewhere with this many blonds before. I also should have checked the weather before hopping on the plane. When I thought of Utah, I assumed it would be hot as hell. It's a desert, right?

Everyone giving me funny looks on the plane should have been a clue that I was in over my head. I thought they were just white people doing what white people do – minding my business. I looked stupid as hell when I collected my baggage in shorts and a hoodie.

My ass was *not* prepared for Salt Lake City in February and I have to go straight to Walmart to get a jacket once I get off the plane. My Uber driver struggles to hold in his laughter, but he's the friendliest person I've ever met, so I get a good feeling about my investigation.

Nobody else in my family cares about what happened. They all think I'm stirring up trouble by tracking down what happened to her. There wasn't any point in telling anyone I know that I moved to Salt Lake City. I have an affordable AirBnB lined up since I only plan on being here for two months and once I get a job, I'll work part-time and research for the rest of the time.

The studio apartment is tiny for the price. I knew what I was getting into giving up Midwestern housing prices, but I didn't expect the studio to have this funky smell or barely have room for a queen-sized bed. It was the cheapest that I could find, but I am paying for my decisions in every way possible.

Alone again. It used to bother me, but a couple years of working with Rebecca Knight and I came to appreciate it. Rebecca was never alone. I have never witnessed a woman go on so many dates before. The impressive part wasn't just the sheer number of men but the fact that all of them were incredibly handsome, over six feet tall, wealthy... and none of them stayed.

All of them hurt Rebecca worse than her pill addiction. Learning that Damara might be dead because of her boyfriend only solidifies my commitment to staying single. Men are nothing but trouble. If they don't break your heart, they'll drag you off to the middle of nowhere and get you killed.

Loneliness settles into my bones so deeply during my second week in Salt Lake City that I almost take up my neighbors' invitation to go to church with them. My job working for a local gym is nice, but the owner Jeanette is a neat freak and even if it's technically not in my job description, I spend my entire shift cleaning every single machine down like she's planning to eat off it.

My Google alert for all keywords connected to Nathaniel Davis's name buzzes aggressively on my phone a few hours before my 10 a.m. shift at the gym. *Interesting.* I sit down with my breakfast taco and glance at the alert, ignoring the pit in my stomach that the only text I received was from an indie thriller author I follow online.

The alert isn't even about a Nathaniel Davis, but a Samuel Davis from the same area and with a similar background – same high school, same elementary school... That's about all I can find that connects them. My gut instincts tell me to pursue the lead despite a lack of additional evidence.

I can't tell if there's any relation, but it's the closest I've come to a lead all week. The names are all common, Southern names which might be a hint that they're related to each other since Utah folks all have last names that are a mixture of all the different settlers that came out to Salt Lake and first names that are a bit more contemporary rather than traditional.

I open up the news article on my phone over breakfast. The newspapers here publish weekly reports on the DUIs and DWIs with full names, most likely to deter people from drinking and driving. Samuel

Davis was caught pulled over with his hazard lights flashing on South Highland Drive at 1 a.m.

There isn't a picture attached to the article, but I have this man's full name and age. We don't have privacy anymore in America, so I have no doubt I'll be able to pull up more, even without access to Rebecca's fancy private investigator software. Investigating can be boring as hell and it quickly gets boring for me to click around hunting down pictures of Nathaniel and attempting to see if he looks related to Samuel Davis, another man I don't know very well.

I don't think I'll get anywhere without seeing this man in person and talking to him, but the address I turn up is far away from where I live on the southern side of Salt Lake City. He doesn't look like the type of person who would want to talk to me. His rap sheet is pretty long and I think he might have been either a former cop or an ex-accountant. Like I said, the names aren't exactly uncommon.

My new car in Salt Lake City was the cheapest I could get my hands on. The champagne Ford sedan blends in everywhere, so I don't mind driving down to unknown parts of town. Aside from my skin tone, I won't stand out. Considering I don't know a damn thing about this man, I decide to stalk him before I approach his address. What? It's not like he knows I'm stalking him, right?

After work, I drive my car down to his address and stalk the house. I learned plenty working for Rebecca and did my fair share of surveillance with her. This time, watching Samuel is a lot more peaceful than other times I've done surveillance because I don't have to check Rebecca's breath every few hours.

Samuel is definitely the man I'm looking for but after a week of watching him, I realize I can't approach him and have a face to face conversation. He's involved in some type of criminal activity and I doubt he was either a cop or an accountant, unless he was a crooked one of both. First, he's in a biker gang. There are constantly motorcycles parked out front and noisy engines disturb the neighborhood at all hours of the night, all of them coming back and forth to Samuel Davis' place.

Tough guys wearing leather cuts, covered in tattoos and carrying mysterious, large wrapped packages come and go from his house from dusk till dawn. If I had Rebecca's camera, I could take pictures and identify some of the other men who stop by Samuel's place. It might be even more important to identify the women.

He must be running some type of prostitution ring out of there based on the types of women that come filtering in and out of the place. Never the same ones. I take whatever notes I can about their physical appearance and what they're wearing in case I notice the faces on missing posters. The women only stay in the house for an hour or so. Sometimes only one man walks in for twenty minutes to an hour. Sometimes several men walk in. Those men are different from the bikers. The men look normal, but it doesn't take much observation for me to figure out some vile shit is happening behind those doors.

Whenever the women leave, they're covered in bruises. Or worse.

One of the girls I saw could hardly walk when a man carried her unconscious body out of the house fireman style before sliding her limply onto the back of his bike and driving away. I don't know if I should do more than take notes here.

One week of intense observation gives me detailed, meticulous notes about Samuel's habits and I even learn his club name, which might come in handy later... *Legion.*

IT'S NOT MUCH, but it's more helpful than I think. Traditional searches don't turn anything up, which forces me to do something that I didn't think I would have to do since moving out to Utah.

My old boss Rebecca picks up after the first ring. I guess she's taken on the role of secretary since I left.

"Tamiya?" she says. "Oh my goodness. I cannot *believe* you're calling."

She sounds sober. I don't comment on it, but her current sobriety gives me hope.

"Can I ask you a favor? I'm looking into someone and–

"I KNEW IT!" she yells, nearly blowing out my eardrum. I hold my phone away from my face.

"Knew what?"

"I knew you were investigating something. I knew the only way you would leave me is to start an investigation of your own…" she says, rambling on about how her mentorship helped me grow from an 'underdeveloped youth' into the woman I am today. I don't bother pointing out to her that I'm hardly underprivileged. Sure, I dropped out of college, but I got in and would have done well enough if my older sister hadn't disappeared, turning my world upside down.

Even if we weren't close, it feels wrong that no one seems to care about her. I'm not going to let her go out like that. I confess everything to Rebecca except the part where I was lowkey using her software free for years. She doesn't seem bothered in the slightest.

"I'll look him up for you. Sure. Legion… That's a demon name. Have you been watching that series *Who the fuck did I marry?*"

I have no idea what she's talking about.

"Uh huh. Listen, can you call me when you get any info, Rebecca? I'm in a situation."

I CONSIDER DRIVING my car into northern Salt Lake City as impatience and suspense torment me for the next month in Utah. My job at the gym is boring and monotonous. My nose hairs are permanently singed from cleaning chemicals, but I have two new friends, which makes coming to work a lot easier.

It's not like I spilled all the details of my traumatic past to people I just met, so I can't share the suspense and worry with them. My mind comes up with the craziest stories about Legion and his connection to my sister. I mean, technically he's only connected to my sister's boyfriend. They might not have ever met. I only knew about her boyfriend from pictures on social media.

…And they seemed happy. Normal.

I FEEL like something was ripped away from me that I can never get back and I just want somewhere to place the blame. If she's dead, someone killed her. Maybe it was this Legion guy or maybe it was someone else, but whoever killed her will pay for what they did.

We should have had more time together. Being grown, I could have followed her all over America. Now, I'm chasing a ghost. Or maybe the grim reaper. I don't know which. For the first three weeks of waiting for Rebecca's call, I stop tailing Legion. I don't see the point in continuing to lose sleep just to grow my catalog of his gang activities.

ODDS ARE PRETTY good his brother was involved in the same business. They were brothers. *Close.*

JUST WHEN I'M about to lose hope in Salt Lake, I stalk Legion's house a few hours a night just to keep myself focused. It doesn't matter how bored I am in Utah. I'm not here to make lifelong friends or find love or any of the traditional reasons a woman my age moves to a big city. I don't see the point in any of that stuff.

I just want to find out what happened to Damara. That's it.

THE THIRD NIGHT after my refreshed interest in surveilling Legion's house, Rebecca calls. My vibrating phone scares the crap out of me. After two Monster Energy drinks, I am less sleepy than jittery and out of whack.

"How the fuck did you find this guy?" Rebecca says.

"It's 10:45 p.m., Rebecca. How was your night?"

"Not great?" she says. It sounds like she's chewing something. "I've gone four days without... you know what. It's impossible. How do normal people function?"

I bite my tongue before I blurt out something inappropriate. It's a rhetorical question, no need for me to drag Rebecca further off topic with my sass. Rebecca sighs loudly and continues without my response, which I expected.

"Okay. Legion. He's a bad dude. It took some work finding this but honestly, Tamiya… You put up with me for *so* many years."

Her voice warbles like she's about to cry, but my girl pulls herself together and just sniffles three times before continuing. "He used to be a cop but he resigned."

"Lots of cops resign. Anything else?"

"I was getting to the good part, Tamiya."

"Sorry."

I bite my tongue to stop myself from interrupting. Rebecca doesn't get how lonely it's been out here without anyone to talk to about this stuff.

"He resigned because he was caught in three separate scandals. The first one in 2016 got covered up because he was just a junior detective, but there was an alleged police brutality case involving Samuel Davis and a nineteen-year-old who he knew previously."

"Interesting," I mutter. I wait for her to tell me the rest of her findings, but I already know enough to worry about my sister and the types of people she was involved with. It doesn't seem to add up with what I knew about her. She just seemed… normal. Not just normal. She seemed larger than life. She wasn't a part of our boring, monotonous small town world. Her life always seemed like it was so full of adventure that it was bursting at the seams.

But what adventure could bring her so close to a person like Legion?

"The second case involved sexual assault of a junior female officer," Rebecca rattles off, like she's mentioning a trivial detail and not a felony. "The female officer transferred to another department and he attended counseling."

Rebecca sounds like the person I used to know before the pill problem. I didn't know her very well back then, but she enjoyed reading mystery novels and everyone knew she wanted to be a cop, but thought she wouldn't fit in with cop types.

Private investigation suits her, but the Xanax addiction was causing her to spiral. The more distance we have between us, the more I appreciate my old boss. She wasn't that bad, was she? Or maybe I'm really that lonely out in Salt Lake City.

"This guy sounds like a menace," I answer Rebecca. I don't know if I'm ready to hear the rest of the charges. This man sounds dangerous and I've been lurking around him like I'm tracking a cheating suburban housewife and not a crazy person. I should get a gun. You can do that in Salt Lake City, right?

"The third one is bad. Really bad," Rebecca says, taking a loud sip of her soda that nearly blows my eardrums out over the phone.

I struggle to imagine a scandal worse than the first two, but Rebecca pulls through and I have chills by the time she reads off the ultimate reason Officer Samuel Davis resigned. It's one of the many stories that doesn't go viral. A simple traffic stop turned into a violent situation. Officer Samuel Davis didn't even care that his body cam was on when he assaulted a fifteen-year-old Native American kid within an inch of his life.

Rebecca doesn't sound disturbed, just curious and awake. I haven't heard her sound this wide awake in a long time.

"Who the fuck is this guy?" I ask her once she reads the list of charges off. The officer was acquitted — despite the evidence. They blamed his mental health and PTSD for the situation, and he voluntarily resigned.

Rebecca takes another sip of something fizzy in the background.

"I don't know. But some woman decided to breed with him," Rebecca says gleefully. The spirit of the investigation has a gorilla grip on her.

"Yeah..." I mutter. "Did you learn anything about his brother?"

I don't want to sound ungrateful but I've been so desperate for information that I can't help but push Rebecca for more. I start pacing, despite myself.

IT'S BEEN A MONTH. Surely that was enough time for Rebecca to discover the entire body of human knowledge. But she just says...

"Sorry. Just got into the stuff on the brother. Be careful if you get anywhere near this guy, Tamiya. He's part of this group called the Blue Blood Knights and most of those guys seem just as fucked up as he is."

We end our call with some pleasantries and I have a jumping off point for more research. Legion's history and this motorcycle club called the Blue Blood Knights. I don't know much about motorcycle clubs, but I've heard of the television show *Sons of Anarchy*. The skinny white boy was cute and all but he never looked like a tough as shit biker to me.

Once I research the Blue Blood Knights, I start seeing men who look like bikers.

AND THEY ALL scare the shit out of me.

COULD my sister have really been involved with someone who was a part of this world? It doesn't make any sense.

CHAPTER FIVE
REAPER

OKLAHOMA

THE NIGHT OF THE INCIDENT

The ground shakes beneath our bikes. *What the fuck was that?* My crucifix vibrates against my chest. I've barely been outside for half an hour and the blazing Oklahoma sun already burned my face purple. I love riding but goddamn, I prefer riding at night. This is urgent though, and I have to admit curiosity pulls me along the highway.

There's been a thought nagging at my mind since Hawk's old lady got taken.

I'M NOT A PERFECT MAN.

LIKE THE OTHER men in the club, I've participated in vices. I sat in church on Sunday morning after killing a man on Saturday night. But I have always meant it when I asked for forgiveness... I want to be a good man. The circumstances of my life have just led to me making difficult choices. Choices that would change anyone. Choices that any man in my position would understand I've made.

MY BROTHERS HAVE KEPT my secrets for the past five years, but you can't bury the truth forever. Dad would have been the first to warn me of that. Goddamn, I wish I could get this nagging thought out of my mind. That all this shit was all my fucking fault...

SOUTHPAW PULLS our bikes over after the loud explosion. We're three miles away from the Blue Blood Knights clubhouse and it sounds like someone set off a goddamn grenade. Hawk stops behind Southpaw first and I pull over behind Cash Hollingsworth, the only one of our group twice as red as I am.

What the hell is happening over there?

"That sounded bad," Southpaw says. "You two hang back."

"Are you sure?"

He nods. "We don't have time for backup and it doesn't make sense for all of us to get killed."

"Nobody's getting killed," Hawk says. "Except Juliette when I finally get her ass on the back of my bike. If Juliette is anywhere near that explosion, I can be damn near sure she's the one who caused it."

I wouldn't be so sure if I were him. God has a strange sense of humor. A dark sense of humor, I think. Cash and I hang back as Southpaw and Hawk wrestle their bikes back onto the highway and speed in the direction of what has now turned into a thick plume of black smoke.

"Matter of time before this place is crawling with cops," Cash says, wiping sweat off the back of his reddened neck.

"Sure hope not."

"You okay, Gideon?" Cash asks, giving me a glance I would describe as pitying – something I hate.

"I'm fine," I grumble. Cash is pushy. He doesn't know how to relax and he thinks everyone else lives on the edge. We just need to stop scuttling about like roaches and think a little.

"None of us are fine," he says, nodding at me approvingly. "But I appreciate the stiff upper lip."

We're a military family. None of us cried. Not even mom. Cash hands me some tobacco, which I stuff into my lip. I feel better, but not a hundred percent. I don't know how long those fools expect us to wait.

"Any guesses why the pigs won't leave us alone? I never heard of any Blue Blood Knights before they took Southpaw's girl."

Cash missed most of the events that happened back out in Missouri. I assumed the Blue Blood Knights were after Southpaw due to some gambling debt or trouble related to that. I've seen that man gamble the shirt off his back when any other rational man would have pulled himself away from the card game.

This strikes me as something deeper. Maybe Cash Hollingsworth with his big Texan family, interwoven into all of ours, sees something that I don't. Judging by the blank, confused look on the big redhead's face, maybe I judged him wrong.

Cash shrugs. "We make our fair share of enemies with the types of business we conduct."

Vague. All we have is vague, vague, vague. I fucking hate it. We need something specific. Something we can sink our teeth into.

"Do you mean anything by that in particular?"

"Nope," Cash says calmly. "I mean it doesn't matter how we made our enemies. What matters now is handling our problems."

I suppose he's right, but him being right does nothing to ease the nagging thought in the back of my head. Shit, the thought just nags me worse that all of this has something to do with the past that the club tried to bury.

My fuck up.

. . .

I NEVER ASKED Harley Shaw to handle shit the way he did, but back then we just listened to him whether we agreed or not. Steel took the fall for the machine gun charge. Cash Hollingsworth's cousin – not a club member – got him off easy with a $7,500 fine and five years in federal prison. I got to walk free, even if I was the one who pulled the trigger.

AND NOBODY ever found out about the *real* crime. Steel had to take the fall to stop the investigation and he did that, but what if the truth comes out?

I GOT OFF FREE, even if the whole thing was all my damn fault. God will come collect his due. I just know it.

I FEEL NERVOUS, even if I have enough tobacco in me to calm me down. "You ever wonder if it's what happened in Utah?"

Cash responds with immediate tension. "Steel is in prison." *Drop the goddamn subject.* I just can't afford to let this go. Not with the Blue Blood Knights closing in around us and my instincts telling me that this is much deeper than we realize.

Out in Utah, we were far away from Rebel Barbarian territory... This shouldn't have followed us all the way here. There shouldn't have been any way for what happened to follow us home. To have caused so much destruction.

"I know but–"

"We don't talk about that," Cash says, stopping me dead.

"I know. I know. But if it is that. We ought to talk about it."

Cash turns to me with a cold look. "Nobody gave a shit about that girl when you shot her. Why the hell should anyone care now? Now drop it, Gideon. Southpaw will lose his shit if you bring it up."

. . .

HE HANDS me more tobacco to make up for digging into me like that. I want Cash to be right, but I can't get it out of my mind that this has something to do with what I did. Maybe it's the guilt eating away at me.

I TOLD my mama what happened. I wanted her to tell me it was all going to be okay, but all she said was that I couldn't hide from the truth and that God would punish me for taking a life. She had no sympathy for me. She still wouldn't.

RIGHT WHEN I start getting nervous, Cash and I prickle up at the sound of motorcycles. We keep our hands on our weapons until we can clearly identify the riders. I spot Juliette first, even if she's behind Hawk. It's hard to miss the extra person and her exposed, tawny skin makes her easy to spot.

They slow down and stop in front of us, out of breath.

"WE NEED to get out of here," Southpaw says. "We'll meet back up in Santa Fe. We called Ghost already. Ride as long as it takes and don't stop for anything except gas and taking a piss. I'll text you the address when I can."

"Yes, sir," Cash says, already on his bike with his helmet on. I nod. We can ask any questions once we get to Santa Fe.

MY ASS HURTS when I pull up outside the tiny home I'm staying at in Santa Fe. We're all staying in different spots tonight and laying low until tomorrow. I'm burnt as fuck from riding around all day and I hate Santa Fe, so I refuse to meet up with anyone until tomorrow evening.

I've had enough of this goddamn sun.

Can't imagine Southpaw will leave me alone until then. Given the subject matter I brought up in my conversation with Cash Hollingsworth, he'll be here bright and early tomorrow morning. Hopefully he'll come alone and not bring Hawk. I don't mind him, but I don't need the two of them to be moralizing to me. It's bad enough when it's Southpaw.

THE SMALL, wooden house looks run down and it's deep in the Mexican side of town, giving me some concern about leaving my bike out on the street where anyone could get their hands on it. I text Ghost a concerned message and he sends one back telling me to stop being a goddamned pussy and shoot anyone who puts their hands on my bike if I'm so concerned.

Once I plug in the keycode to enter the small wooden house and get my ass in the door, I feel a lot better. Haven't had much of an appetite all day. Can't say exactly what happened, but it doesn't seem like any of those Blue Blood Knights made it out alive. If they did, I guess we're on the run from them, which means... I doubt I'll get much sleep.

HAVEN'T SLEPT MUCH ANYWAY since the murder.

THE ONLY PERSON who understands is Hawk's twin brother.

MAYBE THAT'S why it's so goddamn hard to face him now. It's the guilt.

I THOUGHT CONFESSING to my mama would make it go away. Or prayer.

.   .   .

BUT I BELIEVE there's some shit you do on this earth that's so damn evil, it gives the devil a doorway into your life that you can't shut.

THAT'S what I did when I shot that woman in cold blood five years ago.

THE HAUNTING IS WORSE when I'm alone. Worse on nights like tonight.

LUCKY FOR ME, I have some of dad's old pills from his war injury. They're my last ones, so I'll have to do something about my sleep tomorrow night. I can't think about tomorrow when the clawing, painful anxiety already threatens to choke me out of existence. I reach for the pills and crush them between my morals, fading to black before I even get my sore ass in the bed.

LOUD POUNDING on the front door wakes me up. He could just enter the code, but it's Southpaw, so he has to make a terrible, miserable loud as fuck scene instead of letting himself in here like we're brothers instead of strangers.

"REAPER! REAPER IT'S ELEVEN IN THE MORNING, I LET YOU SLEEP IN PLENTY."

Hawk would have at least had the decency to bring me some liquor and I regret wishing he stayed away.

"I brought you coffee," Southpaw adds after I ignore his initial unhinged greeting.

.   .   .

I GROAN and try to sit up. I don't know how many pills I took, but I must have taken enough to lose my head. I can't sit up.

"DAMN IT, GIDEON!" Southpaw says, losing his patience too damn quickly.

"I'M UP! I'M UP."

WILLPOWER GETS my ass up off the couch and I stumble to the front door despite my headache, opening it up to find Southpaw holding Starbucks.

"Are you serious?"

"It was the only place I could find."

"Starbucks?"

"It's coffee, Reaper. It can't turn you gay."

"This had better be coffee and not some pumpkin spice bullshit."

Southpaw turns red. "Anna ordered it for me and it tastes delicious. Quit your bitching."

"You can't be serious."

"Drink," he snaps, handing me a suspicious looking drink. Coffee shouldn't be that color. I glare at him and sniff it. Pumpkin spice, just like I suspected.

"Drink the fucking coffee," Southpaw snaps. "Then tell me why the hell you brought up Utah to Cash Hollingsworth. Because I don't want to kill you, Gideon... But I will if I have to."

Chapter Six
Tamiya

SALT LAKE CITY

Before The Blue Blood Knights Clubhouse Incident...

I track down all the information I can about the known members of the Blue Blood Knights. It's not easy and involves a lot of creepy ass behavior like digging through their trash and taking my surveillance to the next level. Thankfully, my job at the gym isn't taxing at all, except for the occasional hardcore janitorial work I have to do in the locker rooms. I'm tired as fuck at work and my friend situation has grown worse, not better.

It's my fault for being entirely wrapped up in my investigation, but it's not like I'm settling in Salt Lake City, anyway. What's the point? To cope with the loneliness, I consider doing drugs, but I don't even know where to buy them so I stick to a legal drug. Ice-cream. After work, I walk to this fro-yo place every day and order whatever the hell I want. I can feel the pounds cushioning me after just two weeks of this habit.

Maybe I should actually work out at the gym after my shift...

As the thought enters my mind, Rebecca calls and distracts me from my own life with news about the investigation.

. . .

"I AM GRINDING my teeth so fucking hard right now," Rebecca says. "Are you somewhere quiet?"

"I'm eating something that is currently giving me diabetes. So no."

"It doesn't matter," she says. "This is too big for me to wait. I tracked down everything about his brother Nathaniel, but there's not that much and what I found required tapping my connections."

"Thank you, Rebecca. You didn't have to go out of your way for me."

I only half mean that. I've done my fair share of crazy shit to help Rebecca out, especially when her pill addiction was at its worst. I don't have to ask if she's clean. She sounds clean.

"I did," she says. "I really did. I owe you, Tamiya. I should have appreciated you while you were here."

I could honestly say the same. Maybe we're better off now that we're not working together. Maybe we are better off as friends than having a professional relationship.

"There's an FBI investigation into this guy and it's all related to child trafficking. Nearly every official document I read was redacted to hell and no arrests were ever made. I don't even know if they're still looking for him because no one reported him missing."

"His dad didn't report him missing?"

"Nobody did. *Nobody.* And he has connections. There's something weird going on here, Tamiya. I don't have proof but if I had to speculate based on everything I found, I would guess that the Blue Blood Knights are somehow involved in trafficking kids. Or Nathaniel was and the Blue Blood Knights were involved with him or covering it up."

"Without information, speculation could lead us anywhere. I have to talk to one of these people."

"Are you crazy, Tamiya? You shouldn't go anywhere near these assholes. They're dangerous. This is deeper than some small town asshole cheating on his wife."

"I know that. But my sister went missing and I think someone killed her."

. . .

REBECCA IS QUIET. I don't like that. Normally, the rattling of pill bottles and the nasty gulping sound she made while dry swallowing would follow a bout of silence this long. But she's contemplative and I wonder if she's thinking something she doesn't want to say.

"WHAT IS IT, REBECCA?"

"HAVE you considered that your sister wasn't the person you thought she was?"

MY DEFENSES IMMEDIATELY SHOOT UP. I didn't know her well because she was technically my half-sister and when she wasn't hanging out with her friends, she was staying at her dad's house. I don't think she liked living with us. It wasn't because she was a bad person. Sure, she might have spent some time in jail and done drugs in her early teens... but she inspired me to leave my small town.

She was the first person I knew who really went somewhere and did something. She just seemed larger than life.

"SHE WASN'T A CRIMINAL, Rebecca. I'm not saying she had great taste in men, but she wasn't a criminal."

REBECCA SIGHS. "I'm not saying she was. But I've heard you tell stories about her and some of those stories were just... larger than life. Maybe she wanted you to think her life was glamorous because she was going through something that wasn't."

"Don't you think she would have told me that?"

The second I say it, I know it's ridiculous. Who would confide in someone who was almost half their age? I'm glad that I have those good memories of my sister, but she wasn't the type to tell me her problems. Rebecca has good insights, which is why she would be a great private investigator if she didn't have the pill problem. I'm still rooting for my old boss, especially now that I've been in Salt Lake City away from everyone I know.

"You were her little sister," Rebecca says with a soothing voice like she thinks she's going to upset me. "Maybe she wanted to protect you."

Given everything I've heard so far about the Blue Blood Knights and everyone involved with them, I can't exactly blame Rebecca for her speculation. But it goes against everything I knew about Damara. I remember her smiling. Her laughter. Stories about her friends.

I can't imagine that person getting involved in an FBI investigation. If she was, something must have gone wrong.

"She wasn't a bad person, Rebecca," I said.

"Was?" Rebecca asks. "Are you sure she's not hiding out somewhere? If she wasn't involved with these people, maybe she hid from them."

"Don't get my hopes up. There's no chance she's alive, okay?"

It's a fantasy I indulged multiple times. In this day and age, it's impossible to stay off the map. She would have used her private social media page at least once. I know she would have answered my text messages no less than once to let me know she was laying low. I hate the way everyone always spoke about her in hushed tones just because she didn't want to live in our town anymore. I know Rebecca can't help her small town suspicions, but my sister was not a criminal. I can't believe it. Rebecca exhales slowly, like she's glad I didn't react more.

"Okay," Rebecca says. "Sorry, I didn't mean it like that. I'll keep researching this FBI situation and I'll type your sister's name into a few state databases to see what comes up."

"Thanks."

I can't lie, her words get to me. Rebecca keeps updating me. "Nathaniel has a criminal history in some states that I don't think you ever mentioned her visiting."

Hearing about Nathaniel's criminal history makes me feel numb. I didn't really see that coming, but maybe I should have. His dad is a criminal. But that doesn't make me feel better about Damara and who she might have been involved with.

"Which states?"

"Idaho. Arizona. Amarillo, Texas. There's some shit in here about Alberta, Canada but I couldn't tell you much about that. I'll have to call you again."

"Amarillo? Why is Texas the only place you have somewhere specific?"

"I have a couple addresses in the files I'm sending over," Rebecca says. "I don't know how they're connected because none of them look residential."

I already can't handle the restlessness of not knowing. I know Rebecca will stuff my inbox with files to sort through, but I want to go out there and investigate on foot. We're missing *something*. I don't see how my sister could be connected to a bunch of bikers in the middle of the desert and what child trafficking has to do with any of that.

I blurt out my plan to Rebecca. "I'm going to talk to the bikers. Maybe if I can tell this man something about Nathaniel that he wants to know, he'll help me. I can play it cool."

This immediately makes Rebecca nervous because she easily slips into her boss voice.

"You shouldn't talk to these people, Tamiya," Rebecca says. "These aren't normal criminals. The Blue Blood Knights have connections to white supremacist gangs and almost all the members have some dark shit in their past."

I hear her, but if my sister got close to them, I can get close too. I just want information. It's not like I want to join them or turn them into the cops.

"I know. But his brother is missing. He has to care about that."

Rebecca scoffs. "You have a lot of faith in people for a woman who worked for a private investigator."

"I have faith in people *because* I worked for you, Rebecca."

"I can't tell if that's a compliment or an insult," Rebecca says. "I'll hang up and figure it out. Don't do anything crazy. I'll be in touch next weekend."

My gut reaction is desperation for her not to hang up. It's lonely out here. My two friends here have their own lives and their own networks. I like them, but I still feel like a weirdo who moved to their town out of nowhere and doesn't really fit in. The guys who work out at the gym are all creeps. My only obsession is this investigation.

"You said that last time and I had to wait six weeks."

"I'm sorry, but I didn't expect the FBI situation to pop up. I'll do my best to work faster. It's not like we have many clients."

REBECCA SENDS over the files via email so I can search through them myself. I might notice something that she doesn't since I'm more attached to the situation. Even if I waited so long to get this information, I don't have the mental energy to go through it the same day I get it.

I know she was just being honest, but does Rebecca have to blurt out everything on her mind? I brushed her off as much as I could, but I can't help but think about what she said. I never considered my closeness to the search for my sister might complicate things. Maybe it's clouding my judgment. I don't want that to be the case, but it might be.

I SPEND three days reading Rebecca's files before I work up the courage to confront Samuel Davis. The day I head over to his place to talk to him, he's gone. At least someone answers the door. The woman who answers has a thick, Texan accent and she's about four-foot-eleven with a full-figure and red hair cut like Jane Fonda's hair in *Klute*. Her eyes are rimmed in thick black eyeliner and she has an unlit cigarette hanging out of her mouth when she answers the door.

"Shit," she says when she sees me, her sea-green eyes giving me a surprising once-over. "Are you a cop or something?"

"No, ma'am. I'm looking for Samuel Davis?"

She grins and shakes her head. "No you aren't. You might think you are, but you aren't."

She makes no move to light her cigarette, but I came prepared to interview a biker, so I offer her a light, which she accepts. When she cups her hand around the flame, I see a tattoo on her forearm — *Property of Legion*. There are bruises around her wrist, scars from razor blades all over her arms, and several more tattoos amongst the markings covering her body.

"I'm Devon, by the way," she says. "So if you aren't a cop, did you come looking to score? Legion doesn't sell anymore."

"No. I didn't come here looking for drugs. I came to ask him questions about his brother..."

She puffs on the cigarette and then smiles at me. "Nathaniel? Come on inside. I need to fix myself something and we can talk about Nathaniel."

My heart races. Maybe I'm lucky the terrifying ass biker isn't around right now. Considering everything I've heard about him, I don't think I would want to be alone in a house with him. This little home would be cozy if someone cleaned up. Devon doesn't appear bothered by the mess.

She kicks aside a few half-emptied cans of Diet Coke out of the way as she leads me towards the living room. An emaciated dog trots out of the kitchen holding a dead rat in its mouth. It drops the rat once it sees us and then barks loudly before pissing itself. I glance around, searching for somewhere I can sit without acting visibly disturbed by my surroundings. The smell of piss fills the room.

"Shit!" Devon says, chasing after the dog. "Carol, no! Don't piss on the floor, you fucking bitch!"

The dog yelps and runs into the back room. I try not to flinch. Devon puffs again and gestures towards an L-shaped couch that was once white. Every inch of the couch has a thick layer of black and brown dog hair on it. I can feel my air passages closing up just looking at it. But I don't want to be rude. I find the cleanest patch and suck it up, setting my ass down in a monumental amount of dog fur to get some information from this woman who smokes indoors and has a very disturbing tattoo on her forearm.

"I'll get you some Diet Coke," Devon says. "I'll clean up after Carol later. She does that because she's inbred."

Devon returns with some Diet Coke. There are too many smells for me to worry about any one smell in particular. A spider the size of an Oreo climbs up the wall behind Devon's head as she plops her ass on the couch, unbothered by the dog hair.

"Legion doesn't want me having people over, so it's a miracle you stopped by. He's gone for the next week."

"Oh…"

I don't want to come across as too pushy, but Devon keeps talking.

"He's off on club business in Amarillo. He doesn't tell me shit about the club though, fucking bastard. Mind if I smoke in here?"

She sets down the cigarette, which really confuses me. I can barely see her ass because of the smoke. Does she really need permission? Devon reaches for a little box on the coffee table, clarifying the situation in an instant. Pink velvet fabric lines the bottle of the box which contains all the instruments for smoking crack.

ONE OF THE cases I worked with Rebecca involved the discovery that a 74 year old woman at a country club was not in fact cheating with her pool boy. She was smoking crack with him.

I recognize the glass pipe and mouthpieces immediately. My heart thuds in my chest like a buck running away from a hunter in the deep woods. She means smoke crack, and she doesn't wait for an answer. Devon smiles, exposing all her uneven teeth as she prepares her bowl.

Part of me is nervous as fuck, but another part of me knows I'm walking out of this damn room with all the information I need. It's about damn time I had some luck around here. I wait for her to take her first hit before I switch from pleasantries to hard questioning.

But I have to steel my nerves for every minute of the conversation.

"I was honestly surprised when I saw you because Legion doesn't like niggers. That was the thing with Nathaniel. He likes all types. And I mean all types."

This white woman just dropped the n-word in front of me like it was nothing. In this day and age? I know *technically* people like this exist, but we're in Salt Lake City, not the middle of nowhere. I stay calm and remind myself not to underestimate this woman or to dismiss her as a simple crackhead.

Crackheads trick people all the time. Stay vigilant.

"What do you mean by all types?"

"He fucks kids," she blurts out. "Touched all his sisters and their cop father didn't do nothing about it. His brother isn't completely innocent. He tries but... he helped with the cover up."

She shakes her head as I desperately try to make sense of the story. There must be bits of truth in there, even if I don't trust her completely.

She continues seriously, "The whole family is fucked in the head. Are you sure you don't want some?"

EVEN IF HER bold statement hits me like a rock to the head, it's no reason to immediately jump to crack.

"HE HURT KIDS?" I ask her, trying not to sound too much like a cop. People like Devon react poorly to that, even when hyped up on their drug of choice. I still don't like the crass way she blurted it out.

She nods and keeps rolling around her glass pipe.

"Oh yeah. He did all types of fucked up shit. Tried to make his dad think he turned straight by joining the Mormon church up here. I think that's why Legion ended up moving here. Hoping he'd run into him...."

"Move up here from where?"

"Denver, maybe?" she says. "Salt Lake? I can't remember. All I know is that I *love* Amarillo. Best place in the world to score..."

· · ·

SHE STARTS SINGING and goes on a nonsense rant about Amarillo for a while. I have to talk about all types of things irrelevant to the investigation to get the information that ends up changing everything. She tells me where the clubhouse is. I don't know if I should believe her about Nathaniel, but just thinking about what she said scares me to my core.

What type of thing is that to just blurt out about someone? It's a crime, that's what it is. She must have told me for a reason – true or not. Does she just want me to stop looking for Nathaniel? Or my sister?

These bikers scare me and considering how comfortable Devon was dropping the n-word, I can't imagine what the rest of them are like. I don't understand any of this, but I have an address to a clubhouse in Amarillo and I was getting tired of having a base in Salt Lake City, anyway. It's sudden, but I figure a more permanent address here can't hurt until I have more answers.

This is the closest I've come to answers, so it feels wrong to back out. I can't let go of the only thing that gives me purpose.

I KNOW Rebecca wouldn't approve, but my thirst for answers hasn't. I pack my shit, send my landlord an email and book an AirBnB ten miles East of the clubhouse address, not quite in Amarillo, but close enough.

The fastest route from Salt Lake City to Amarillo isn't what you would expect. Instead of crossing Utah heading Southwest, you head northwest across Wyoming and then turn South into Denver. From there, you keep going South until you hit Texas.

Everything in Texas is so goddamn spread out. The state is so vast, it almost gives you this powerful sense of anxiety from how *visible* you are from above.

Maybe I just like trees instead of blazing hot sun and desert.

REBECCA CAN TAKE ALL the time she needs to dig up more dirt on Nathaniel. Legion is in Amarillo at the clubhouse and that's where I'll find my answers. These days, it doesn't take much for me to pick up and leave. It's hard to get attached to anyone or anything.

And it's not just because I know she's dead. Hell, this is the only thing keeping me going. It's the only thing that gives me purpose...

PART TWO

Chapter Seven
Tamiya

AMARILLO

Right before the Blue Blood Knights Incident…

I find Legion and the other bikers. I didn't know what they were planning to do the night I found them and now that it's all over, it's the only reason I think they left me alive.

I stalk Legion all the way to his clubhouse, but meeting him there would have only made him suspicious so instead, I set myself up at the nearby motel where all the racist bikers appeared to be staying. I was surprised the motel owner even let me get a room considering the rest of the clientele. Call me naive, but I had never seen so many Americans brazenly sporting racist tattoos.

Salt Lake City might not have had many people of my complexion, but you didn't see brazen white supremacists roaming the streets. My skin color alone might have stopped Legion from talking to me, but I had to take the chance. One morning, he came to the lobby for motel breakfast early and away from the rest of the bikers.

He was alone. I felt like it was just my luck, especially considering I didn't know how long I would have to stay at this stupid motel and I didn't bother with a job in Amarillo.

"Are you Nathaniel's brother?"

He didn't miss a beat when he looked up at me.

"Shit. You look just like Damara."

He said it with no emotion and then went back to eating his buttered bagel and stirring two packets of sugar into his motel coffee.

"How did you find me?" he asked.

Even if it might get his old lady in trouble, I had to tell him the truth. I was quick to tell him that I didn't care about his past or his politics, I just wanted information about my sister's disappearance.

"She's not missing," he said calmly. "She's dead. Along with my brother. Buried out in Utah in the middle of the desert."

I thought I knew how I would react upon hearing an update about Damara. I pictured both outcomes – the good news and the bad news. But absolutely nothing could have prepared me for reality. The truth.

She's dead. He says it with calm numbness and absolute certainty.

"Are you sure?"

I ask even if I know the answer. He doesn't speak like an uncertain man.

"Yes. I have pictures of the bodies. I've seen them. They're dead."

"I'm sorry to be rude but... you can obviously tell I've done my research."

He locks eyes with me and terror runs straight through me. This man scares the ever living crap out of me, but I have to sit across from him with a straight face and do what Rebecca would tell me to do. She has experience with cops, even scary ones like this one who obviously don't give a crap...

"Yes. You have," he says.

"You're an ex-cop. Why haven't you gone to the police?"

"I don't need to go to the police. I'll handle the people who did this to him."

"What do you mean? These people killed my sister. I want to do something about it as well."

. . .

"You don't mean that," he says. "You think you do. But you don't. I can tell just from looking at you that you're not the type."

"I think you're wrong about me. I want vengeance too."

He leans forward and smiles. "Listen, lady. You're pretty for a black girl, just like your sister. That's why I'll give it to you straight. The man who shot your sister is named Gideon Blackwood and he's the son of a retired Army Ranger named Lyle Blackwood."

"Great. Thanks for the information. I'll be happy to give his name to the police or kill him myself."

"You won't go to the police," Legion says calmly. "There wouldn't be any point to it. Now quiet and let me explain before this place comes crawling with gang members who want to know why I'm talking to a nigger."

Why are *you talking to me?* I wonder privately, but think it smart to keep the wondering to myself. It doesn't matter why Legion is talking to me as long as he doesn't stop. I bite my tongue and by now, I'm fully ignoring the racial slurs to get at my information. I have come this far to let my personal feelings get in the way of solving this.

"Okay. I'll shut up."

Legion grunts and takes a disgustingly loud slurp of coffee. I keep my disgust to myself and wait for him to continue.

"Seems like Gideon Blackwood found out about my brother's extracurricular activities and took it upon himself to get revenge to honor one of the victims. I understand why he did what he did but... a life for a life. And he didn't work alone."

"What happened? And how do you know any of this?"

"Doesn't matter how I found out. All that matters is that I know the truth. Gideon Blackwood killed my brother and I'm gonna make sure he pays for what he did..."

And it was after that conversation the Blue Blood Knights burned down the Rebel Barbarians clubhouse. Legion ended his conversation with me after making me promise that I would get Gideon Blackwood "after he buried his daddy".

I barely listened to him after I heard the name Gideon. I latched onto it and committed it to memory.

I HAVE to find this man.

My obsession with learning everything possible about Gideon Blackwood becomes all consuming. I know details about this man that I shouldn't and I can't even explain my obsession since most of the details I learn about him have absolutely nothing to do with the murder.

Legion gave me all the details he could, but there's only one way to find out the truth. When I have a gun or a knife pressed against Gideon Blackwood's flesh, I'll get my answers. Until then, I prepare myself. Didn't God say "Know Thy Enemy"?

After my meeting with Legion, I spend one more night in the motel. The bikers check out mid-morning and I think nothing of it until the news that night.

He didn't exactly keep his plans from me and this man clearly doesn't fear the police or he wouldn't have shot up a clubhouse filled with bikers.

When I leave the motel, I move from my current AirBnB to another one, paranoid that my meeting with Legion in the motel lobby will somehow reach the ears of the local police. I don't want that to happen. My new AirBnB is a few miles outside of the city and I settle down there to keep my focus on research.

Gideon Blackwood enlisted in the army at 18, just like his twin brothers Jairus and Jotham, and like his father, Lyle Blackwood. His military portrait makes him look like a baby, not a killer. He doesn't have any face tattoos -- those would apparently come later -- and his hair is such pale blond that it's almost translucent.

His smile is awkward, like he never sat in front of a camera before.

· · ·

BUT DAMN. The man is handsome for a killer. His eyes are a pretty shade of reddish brown. The bright, rich color shows in every picture of him. I shouldn't think about how handsome he is, but he has the type of physical appearance that stands out.

Too bad he gave up the clean cut army look. After becoming an army ranger at 23, he spent time in the Middle East and a little time in Hawaii before coming back. That was when the tattoo situation exploded. And the arrests.

I've never seen someone get arrested that many times for aggravated assault without anyone pressing charges. His mug shots directly contrast his army photos and give me more hints about the other gang members that might be around Gideon Blackwood when I get to him.

The news never reported the slain biker's identities and all my research leads me to believe that somehow, someone buried the story. That doesn't turn me off my investigation, but I notice the story's rapid absence and how this might make my research more difficult.

I consider sneaking off to the crime scene but decide against it. For now, it makes sense to research Gideon's associates and assume that the bikers closer to my age are the ones I need to worry about the most. They're like gang members right? Or maybe a better comparison would be some type of small town country boy mafia. The elders eventually pass on the responsibility of carrying on gang activities to the young...

Gideon Blackwood has twin brothers, but he also appears to have another cousin who served -- Ruger Blackwood. Interesting. The other names I turn up associated with Gideon are code names of some kind. Southpaw. Hawk.

The only other name I got from Legion is Ryder Sinclair, since he's the one who took the charges for Gideon. That man has a twin brother, but I get no further information out of that angle of research.

EVERYTHING SEEMS FUTILE. My research spans the course of another week before Rebecca reaches out to me again.

"How is Salt Lake treating you?" she asks once we both greet each other. My stomach forms a fisherman's knot. I left Utah over a month ago and even if I know it's my sister's final resting place, I haven't had the heart to go back. I kept Rebecca abreast of all my research, but I conveniently forgot to tell her that I moved in my emails.

"I'm in Texas."

She's quiet for a few seconds, so my confession is definitely hitting her.

"Dare I ask what part of Texas?" Rebecca asks.

"You don't want to know."

"You're in Amarillo, aren't you?"

I BITE MY LIP. What the hell is the point of trying to keep secrets from a private investigator? Rebecca can read right through me. Her investigative instincts keep getting sharper the longer she stays away from her pills.

"Yes."

"You are going to get yourself killed," Rebecca says. "Didn't I tell you to stay away from these people?"

"Yes. I know. But Rebecca... I did it. I know what happened."

I DON'T WANT to tell her everything mostly because I don't want Rebecca to become an accomplice in anything that happens next with me and Gideon. But I want her to know that I am so much closer than before to having a sense of peace.

"ARE YOU GOING TO THE POLICE?" Rebecca asks. I know she wouldn't judge me for what I'm doing, but I still need to keep her safe from any consequences of my actions. She's right to think this is dangerous, because it is.

I try to tell as much of the truth as I can, even if I want to protect her. Rebecca has gone from the boss I wanted to tie up in a basement to my closest friend while I carry out this investigation.

"There's no point. It's too late," I tell her. "She's dead."

Rebecca allows the statement appropriate weight. I can hear her breathing on the other end of the line. I'm sad, don't get me wrong, but I haven't been able to make myself cry.

"Shit. I'm so sorry."

"I knew this was what I would find," I tell her, trying to keep myself together as much as I'm trying to reassure her. "I just have to keep going."

"Keep going with what? You know you can always come back here, Tamiya, right?"

"I know, Rebecca. I appreciate it. I still have work out here."

"What work? I'm sorry, Tamiya but I'm worried about you. All those months all alone. No family. No boyfriend..."

"I don't need a boyfriend to be happy."

"I'm not saying you do but... aren't you lonely?"

"No. I'm not, Rebecca, okay? I just need answers. I'll send over more information about the bikers. Okay?"

"Wait," Rebecca says. "I didn't just call for your health. I found something interesting. The Rebel Barbarian bikers might have some... captives."

"What do you mean captives?"

"I don't know. I just have a blurry picture from a surveillance camera, but I saw one of them with a short black woman and a baby. I'll let you know if I learn more."

"Thanks. I appreciate it."

Rebecca's phone call this time leaves me off balance. I'm not lonely. I don't need anyone and she's crazy for even suggesting it. No offense to Rebecca, but she has no idea how disappointing my love life has been.

This investigation gives me purpose in a way romance never did. I don't have the personality guys like, anyway. They feel more than comfortable giving me the feedback. I'm too rough around the edges. Too argumentative.

No point to relationships. Look what happened to Damara. Her relationship didn't save her.

THAT CONVERSATION with Rebecca leads to more waiting. I extend my stay at my Amarillo AirBnB because I don't know what to do next and I have enough savings to last another month, so I might as well stay.

The only problem with my stay in Amarillo is that I make one critical mistake. I let my guard down. I assumed the police didn't know where I was and didn't know about my brief connection with Legion. Cops never showed up at my place and I never saw any other signs that I was being followed.

UNTIL ONE FRIDAY. I swore things looked different in my AirBnB. But when I got there, the door was locked and there were no real signs of entry -- just the sense that my items had been moved around my apartment.

By Saturday, I developed a strange sense that someone was watching the AirBnB. No matter how I scanned the streets, I could never make out anything unusual. Without any proof, I'm not sure I see the point in alerting Rebecca to the fact that there might be someone following me.

I just have to lay low. I spend all of Saturday night locked in my apartment doing research and pass out on the couch at two in the morning.

WHEN I WAKE UP, it's dark and there's a figure in my apartment. I sit up on the couch, my chest catching as I briefly think the figure is Gideon Blackwood, emerging from the stack of papers around me like a ghost to punish me for even looking into him.

The figure watches me sit up and waits for me to impulsively jump to my feet before shoving me back. Fuck, he's strong. The giant figure easily knocks the wind out of me. I fly back and grunt as I land on the couch.

Terror surges through me.

"WHY ARE you lurking around the club?" the figure asks. "What do you want with us?"

A CAR DRIVES past the AirBnB and the headlights illuminate the figure just enough for me to see the patch sewn onto his leather jacket.

SOUTHPAW.

Chapter Eight
Reaper

For the next few months, I'm staying out of the way in Tucumcari so I can keep an eye on Rebel Barbarians club business. Southpaw went up to Missouri for the birth of his son, who I am almost certain will get a traditional Shaw name, but he'll be back tonight for us to discuss what happened in Amarillo and then in with the cops' clubhouse.

We finally know what they want from us.

And I was right.

My criminal past has come back to haunt me worse than my nightmares could have ever imagined. Southpaw's urge to lay low doesn't sit right with me. We still don't know who else might be out there and want my blood. I didn't just shoot a woman that night... If I had only killed one person, maybe it would have been easier to work through the guilt.

I tell myself that I did what any sane person would have done, but the federal government can still consider the most lucid moment of ethical decision making in a man's life a crime...

And God still has to punish me for taking a life.

THE WOMAN I shot had a boyfriend and a family. That boyfriend had a family too. They shouldn't have been much trouble according to our research.

But our research was wrong. Because that motherfuker's "deadbeat" dad apparently wasn't too far off. A racist cop, member of the Blue Blood Knights, a connection to the night we left no goddamn witnesses.

I don't know how it all adds up, but it does. I haven't had a moment of peace since Southpaw spread those charred bits of identification and evidence over my dining room table.

I haven't cleaned up the evidence. All I've done is smoke enough American Spirits to clear out my personal cash supply, and make my nicotine addiction ten times worse. All I've had to eat is pizza and prayer. But God stopped answering my prayers the day I took a life. I stare at the nine pieces of identification laid out before me.

Alan Wilder and Nate Wilder's Oklahoma state license cards show a pair of identical twins. Southpaw found out the pair of ex-cops left the Stillwater police department after laundering $850,000 of public funds and getting caught. Their administrative leave turned to jail time when they refused to pay the money back and both spent a few years in FCI El Reno Federal Prison. They must have been released recently, he thinks.

Most of the cop bikers have similar pasts. Police brutality charges, repeated domestic violence charges, a couple illegal weapons charges, one human trafficking charge and a couple cases of fraud.

The main piece of identification connecting the Blue Blood Knights to our past is a police badge with a 387110 and the name... Darryl Doxon.

There are only 15 people with that last name in America. I shot one of them. *We left no witnesses, this is impossible.*

CASH THINKS IT'S A COINCIDENCE. Southpaw, Hawk and I know – ain't such a thing as coincidences. Not ones like this. Whatever I did has come back to haunt the club. It's the reason my father died. I don't know how I'm supposed to hold my head up after that.

Half of what my mama says about Christ sounds more like voodoo than something in the Bible, but maybe she was right when she said what I did would bring a curse on my head three times worse than what I did.

My place in Tucumcari ain't terrible, but the more I stay here staring at the burnt pieces of plastic, I feel more haunted than before. The smoke doesn't help. Drinking doesn't help. God is silent when I pray.

I hear a knock at the door, and I bury my head in my hands. Wouldn't be the first time I imagined knocking since Southpaw left. *Everybody knows Reaper lost his head when he shot that girl...*

Dad smacked the shit out of Ruger so hard when he said that. Broke his damn nose. Ruger followed him like a dog but he could never love that boy like a son. I miss my father...

KNOCK, knock, knock.

I DON'T KNOW anybody in this goddamn town and Southpaw wasn't supposed to be here for another day.

"Go away," I groan. "No solicitors."

We're in the middle of New Mexico. If it ain't Southpaw, it has to be those goddamn Mormons. Listen, everyone is entitled to practice in their own living room, as long as it ain't in my living room. I already have a relationship with Jesus and it's pretty strained at the moment. I prefer not to drag new prophets and rituals into the situation.

.   .   .

"I'M NOT A GODDAMN SOLICITOR," Southpaw growls. "I'm trying to be quiet..."

I BURY my head in my hands, again assuming the voice is something I made up. Southpaw doesn't approach quietly...

"OPEN THE FUCKING DOOR!" he snarls. "CHRIST!"

OKAY. That has to be him. Half-drunk, I stumble over to the door and swing it open.

"BITCH TIT."

SOUTHPAW SHOVES a woman into my house and follows, slamming the door behind him. It's a dead woman. No... that woman ain't dead but...

I STUMBLE BACKWARDS. No color in my face. No thoughts in my head. Just a churning stomach as a wrecking ball slams into my consciousness. I can't form a single word, just stare. The girl stares at me too, with pure hatred on her face. Southpaw watches both of us, like he's introducing two feral cats to each other.

Or like he's introducing two fighting dogs to a cage. She don't look like a pitbull...

.   .   .

"Look who I found snooping around," he says. "Cops working on the murder case didn't want to give up her address at first but... Cash handled it."

"You shouldn't have brought me here," she says, still staring at me with pure loathing. *I know who she is.* I might not know exactly who she is, but some families have such strong traits that when you meet one of them, you can recognize the rest across space and time. It's like the Hollingsworths all being tall as fuck with red hair. The fair-haired Blackwoods or the hairy, beady-eyed Sinclairs.

This girl looks exactly like...

"She's right," I whisper, staring straight at her, but talking to Southpaw. What does he want me to do with her?

"Where the fuck else was I supposed to bring her? She killed your father. I brought her to you."

"A life for a life," she says. "It was only fair."

Blood pools in the back of my mouth. This can't be possible.

"How did she–

"Does it matter how I found out?" she says. "You killed my sister."

Southpaw scoffs. "Your sister was involved in some horrific shit, princess."

She whips around and clearly, she doesn't have a lick of sense, because she snaps at Wyatt, "Don't you *dare* speak ill of my sister."

She raises her hand to slap him and cries out when Southpaw grabs her wrist and twists her arm all the way around, wrenching her into submission. She yelps loudly, but tries to fight him off. Southpaw slams her into the wall, knocking the wind and the fight out of her before he throws her onto the couch with relative ease.

. . .

Goddamn.

How the hell did this woman find us? How the hell did she know? It's impossible.

"Reaper? Let's talk outside. She won't run. She knows I'll kill her if she does."

I give Southpaw a serious look. Should we really leave this woman in there with my guns and knives? She wants to kill me and she has every right to.

"If she leaves or fucks up in any way, she's going straight to prison in Texas for over eight counts of murder. We have nothing to worry about."

"Would it surprise you to learn that doesn't comfort me?"

She just glares at us from the couch. Southpaw grunts and puts his hand on my back, dragging me out to the porch where we can talk without her listening. The second I get outside, I feel some of my lightness returning. I don't like being in the same room as that woman.

"We have a big problem on our hands," Southpaw says. I know him well enough to know that he's just using that gentle introduction so he can ask me to do something I don't want to do.

"That's clear."

"I need you to keep her here," he says. "I know it's a lot to ask but… we're building the clubhouse here, I'm working with the cops in Amarillo, and Cash is still tracking down information on the Blue Blood Knights so we can see which of them are left."

I shake my head. "She'll kill me in my sleep. No goddamn way."

"She won't."

"I'm not like you, Southpaw. I don't trust folks like her."

I narrow my eyes so he doesn't make me say the quiet part out loud, but he acts confused, like he wants me to be explicit. Goddamn.

"You can't trust black folks," I explain. "Especially not the women. They're crazy. Talk back too much. And she's only here because she wants to blow our fucking brains out."

That part seems especially important.

"She's a fucked up girl on a suicide mission. If she knew what we knew…"

Southpaw locks eyes with me. We don't need words to communicate this part. This part, we understand. I committed a crime, but given the circumstances, anyone would have done what I did… *anyone.*

"Please, Southpaw…"

"Do whatever you must to keep her. I don't care if you use violence. She's better off in our hands than running around plotting our demise."

"Easy for you to say."

"Find a way to keep her compliant," he says. "Hawk found a way. So did I. You can handle it."

"Skinny little things like that ain't my type," I answer quickly. "I like a woman with tits and ass."

Southpaw laughs. "Right. I think you should be happy to let just about any woman touch your crazy dick."

"Shut the hell up."

"Let's go in there and talk to her. Once she gets tired of answering our questions, I'll leave you to it."

CHAPTER NINE
REAPER

I don't know what Southpaw was thinking, bringing this girl to me. The minute I lay eyes on her, I know she's going to be worse than trouble, that she really means it about putting a knife against my throat. I deserve every ounce of her hate. I killed her kin, I accept that. But just like I knew back then, I know now that I wouldn't have done anything differently.

I had every intention of killing Nathaniel. When I leveled my pistol at his face and looked him in the eye, I knew exactly what I was doing. *God, forgive me for my sins and if I rot in hell, at least I saved some babies on the way out.*

Questioning her leads to nothing useful. Southpaw grabs her identification off her and gives Tamiya Simmons's information to Cash for him to do some research. Whenever she can get away with it, she answers with one word. She gets sassy once and Southpaw smacks her hard against the face. I point out that we'll get a lot further if we don't treat her like dirt.

"I'll talk to her before our club meeting," I tell him. "I got Anna to talk to me."

"Let's hope all you did was talk," Southpaw grumbles jealously.

I convince him to leave the condo and then I return inside where

Tamiya sits on the couch, her skinny legs curled up against her body. She's glaring at me with nothing but pure hatred.

"You belong in prison," she says.

"So do the people I killed."

"Fuck you," she says.

I turn on her sharply. "I just stopped that man from hitting you across the face with a pistol and this is the thanks I get?"

"Thank you, oh Jesus Christ for saving my life and *murdering my sister.*"

"I didn't do shit."

"I am sick of this."

SHE GETS UP and walks towards the door. I let her walk past me in disbelief. She doesn't have her hand on the door handle yet, so I don't have to worry.

"Just where do you think you're going?" I ask her. Tamiya stops walking and puts a hand on her hip. She's skinny. Real skinny. I don't *really* mind it, I've just never seen a black woman that skinny before.

"I'm going outside to scream for help," she says. "I don't think you have what it takes to kill me or tie me up. If you weren't soft, you would have let your friend keep cutting my ass up."

My eyes must be as wide as a salmon right now. I've never heard a woman run her mouth like this and I've sure as shit never witnessed it happen without seeing said woman get slapped. Me? Soft? Has this woman lost her fucking mind? She knows I killed her sister. What's to stop me from putting her in the ground?

"If you take one more step towards that door, you're gonna find out that just because I'm quiet doesn't mean I'm soft."

TAMIYA DOESN'T TAKE her eyes off me. She has large, pretty fox eyes that are an incredibly dark shade of brown and framed by sexy long eyelashes like a girl from a music video. (The type of music videos my parents whooped us for watching.)

"I think you're soft," she says. "Only a weak man shoots a woman."

She takes an unfortunate step towards the door. I react immediately and instinctively to her disobedience. Tamiya's wrist feels so fucking small in my hand that I don't realize how easily it would be to hurt her. I twist her around a little bit and she yelps bloody murder. I throw her up against the wall and she cries out even more loudly.

Her screams are so exaggerated that even if I think she's faking her emotional reactions, I let go of her. Tamiya falls on the ground, grabbing her wrist while she yells in pain.

"I didn't hurt you that bad."

"You broke my wrist!" she shrieks.

"GET UP," I yell at her. "Get your ass up."

TAMIYA HOLDS up her wrist as she glares at me. "Look at it! Look at it, you misogynistic monster!"

When I look at her wrist, she kicks at my knees. I don't see her attack coming as she leans back on her forearms which are clearly goddamn fine. I cry out from surprise more than the pain but she gets me good and I fall to my knees on the rug. Tamiya leaps to her feet and jumps over me.

I'm an ex-Army Ranger. She never stood a chance. I grab her and pull her down to the ground, easily wrestling her skinny ass body into submission and rolling over so I pin her to the ground. We're face to face and she's still fighting me. This time, her screaming is covering my face in spit.

"STOP!" I scream at her. Tamiya scratches my face. I feel her nails sink into my cheek like hooks and she yanks her hand across my skin forcefully with every intention to hurt me. Blood spills out and the second her nails come declawed from my face, I grab her arms again and pin them over her head.

"GET OFF ME! RAPE! HELP! HELP!"

She notices we're in a small house, which is smart and observant, but nobody else lives here yet. Ruger won't move in until the fall and Lafayette Shaw turns nineteen this summer, so he's putting in his bid for recruitment into the club while he does summer courses at Mesalands Community College.

"Quit your yelling," I grunt, tightening my grasp on her wrists. "There's no one around to hear you and the louder you get, the more I want to break your damn arm…"

This only makes the situation worse. She shrieks so loudly I swear my eardrums pop, but she can't kick me in the position I have her in, so I suppose I have to let her fight me with all her might until she tires herself out.

"I am not going to give up," she says through grunts as she tries to wriggle out from under me as I press her into the floor. I hold her tighter, covering her body entirely with mine. I grew up fighting enough siblings and cousins not to give her the chance to spit in my damn face.

Tamiya's convulsing doesn't work to loosen my grip on her, but the movement has an unfortunate effect on me. I'm a normal man after all, and the little thing keeps moving her body around on my crotch in her efforts to escape me. I can feel my dick rising the more she moves and I keep trying to adjust my dick away from her so she doesn't freak out.

Her fighting gets weaker after just a few minutes and she stops fighting entirely after ten minutes. It's like calming down a toddler. Who wants to slit my throat.

"Are you done fucking fighting me?" I grunt. The words struggle to leave my mouth because my current priority is calming the raging erection Tamiya stimulated with her movement beneath me. I straddle her beneath me in an attempt to move my body away from hers, but still contain her and remain face to face with our club's new captive.

"No," she yells. "I'll never stop."

"Well you'd better," I growl. "Because even if I don't want to hurt you, I'll do what I must to tame you."

"Go fuck yourself."

"Doesn't sound like a bad idea," I tell her. "But I'd much rather stick my dick in you than jack myself off."

This drives her fucking crazy.

BUT THEN, her energy evaporates and she lets out an anguished sob. Her body shudders and it's like I feel her give up. Not just fighting me. I feel Tamiya give up on everything.

AND SOMETHING strange happens within me. Something I want to stop. But I just can't. My body doesn't know the difference between instinct and impulse. I follow both. My hand snakes around Tamiya's brown neck. I hold her still beneath my grasp, maintaining complete control over her. It feels so fucking sweet. My dick strains through my pants, preparing me with desire I'm sure she doesn't return.

My heart pounds. This shouldn't be happening. I just met her. I can't find logic behind the sensations I feel, nor do I normally have desires like this for women like her. She's a skinny, helpless, pain in my ass. I could just as easily throw her off the back of my back as I could take her to my bedroom. She shivers as I touch her. I don't want to stop.

I KISS HER NECK. She moans in obvious pain. Like she can't believe this is happening to her. Like she thinks I'm a monster.

"I know you think I'm a monster."

"You're a murderer," she spits violently. "A goddamn murderer…"

"I know," I whisper, kissing her neck again. Her skin is soft. Succulent. She tastes good and not just that, she feels fragile. This woman might have fought me off with the strength of a lion but underneath it all, I know there's someone soft. "I know what I've done."

"You deserve to rot in prison."

It's like a punch to the gut. But for some fucking reason, I'm in love with the pain. I slide my hand up under her shirt. She yelps and makes her disapproval known by her facial expression, but she doesn't stop my hand from touching her soft brown stomach and she makes no effort to fight me off as I touch her nipples through her bra.

She already thinks I'm the goddamn devil. I might as well prove her right. It's a sick, twisted thought, but it makes me push her shirt all the way up. She sucks in air with tight anxiety as I pin her arms across her chest and kiss my way over her clothes until I hit the bare flesh of her stomach.

"No..." she whispers.

This woman is in pain. I can feel it. Deep, emotional pain. That gets my dick hard almost as much as her soft skin and how fucking sexy she is – even if she's skinnier than the women I usually end up in bed with.

"I never meant to hurt anyone else," I whisper.

She whimpers and then finally breathes. "Stop talking. Just stop fucking talking..."

I kiss her stomach and stop Tamiya from talking instead. I've held on to a lot of guilt about the situation with her sister, and right now with Tamiya lying beneath me and breathing, I can't help myself. I couldn't stop myself if I wanted to. For some twisted, fucked up reason, I feel like what I'm doing could help both of us.

But maybe I'm just horny and selfish.

"I swear it," I tell her. "I only wanted to protect the innocent. I never meant to hurt anyone else. Shit. I didn't even know you existed."

She whimpers and I kiss her stomach again. Then I hike her thighs up so I can roll the tight black leggings off her thighs. She smells like dirt from the highway and sweat, but the natural scent of her gets me instantly hard in a way that confuses the hell out of me because Tamiya's body is so damn different from any other woman I've been with.

Her underwear is wet, but I can tell it's from sweat and most likely not from arousal. Her legs shake from fear. I don't bother comforting her. I spread her thighs apart and put my face between them. I kiss the outside of her underwear and she yelps.

"How long has it been?" I whisper, touching her mound through the outside of her underwear. The only way I can describe the noise she makes is *disbelief.*

But she doesn't answer my question. I kiss the top of her mound again, provoking her to make another noise.

"I asked you how long?"

"Stop..."

"Answer the question," I say to her firmly. She's so soft. I want to get between her legs but I have to know the truth.

"A long time."

"How long?"

My heart is pounding. The last time I even came close to feeling temptation from a woman, I knew Southpaw would kill me for even trying. And even then... that was just to satisfy an urge. This is something deeper. This woman is so scared. She's in so much goddamn pain.

I can feel it. She shudders beneath my grasp and still doesn't answer me. I kiss her mound again. Silence won't stop me from taking her, but I genuinely want to hear what she says.

"Come on now... How long..."

"Over five years..."

I stop kissing her mound. "Fuck."

"Shut up," she says. "If I knew this would be... Oh God... Just get it over with..."

YOU WON'T BE SAYING that when I'm done. I think to myself.

I CUT through the fabric of her underwear, getting more excited as my knife rips her clothing away from Tamiya's pretty dark skin. The reaction this woman stimulates in me spreads gooseflesh all over my skin. She doesn't share my immediate pleasure as I rip the final shreds of fabric away from her. Tamiya whimpers again. My dick stiffens in my pants. There is something seriously wrong with me, but I can't stop myself. I have to taste her. I kiss the tops of her thighs as I peel her panties off.

She smells damn good too.

I want to make her feel good. I want to take all the pain away...

"Why ten years?" I ask her, stroking the outside of her mound. Tamiya reacts by pushing against me with her feet. She uses her toes for all the grip they have to push against my arms, but I just spread her legs wider apart.

She stops squirming.

"Answer me," I whisper as my fingers slowly touch her bare lips. I don't spread them or push inside her even slightly. I just keep touching her. Holding myself back like this causes a deep ache between my legs that I won't get rid of until I bury myself inside her. Tamiya's lips spread apart despite her protests and she gets so frustrated with my gentle touch that I force an answer out of her.

"Haven't met the right guy..." she says as her legs continue their futile fight against my control. I keep touching her outer pussy lips, teasing and taunting Tamiya as her body reluctantly yields to physical sensation.

"That's it?" I ask her. "You're waiting for the right guy?"

Ten years. After ten years, this woman must belong so fiercely to herself that she won't let me in. That makes me want her even more.

"I'm better off alone," Tamiya gasps, her pussy gushing against her will and coating her inner thighs with a thin dribbling of her juices.

I spread her lower lips purposefully and touch her engorged nub. Tamiya emits a loud cry of relief that she immediately attempts to stifle by biting down hard on her lower lip. Hot damn, this woman has mind control over me.

"That's not true about anyone, Tamiya. Most people are better off with someone else. Don't let the modern world fool you."

I pinch her full lower lips just to enjoy the sensation of their fullness and how fat her sweet pussy lips are around her entrance. She looks juicy and delicious even before I bend my head to taste her. Tamiya whimpers again and I press my tongue between the top part of her lips so I can access her juicy clit.

She can't help herself. It's been too long for her to fight physical sensation, even if her head is most likely screaming at her to run far away from a psychotic outlaw killer. Tamiya's moan forces more juices out of her pussy and I take advantage by running my tongue all over her thighs and indulging in her taste.

The next moan she makes causes my dick to jump in my pants.

"You can't do this," she says. "You can't be the first one in this long..."

"I can feel your hurt," I whisper, kissing her thighs and slowly down. Her juices are all over the place and if I don't slow down, I know I won't be able to hold myself back. Tasting and smelling her juices all over me drives me crazy. It's been a long time for me too. "I can feel how much you hurt everywhere and I can make it go away..."

"You can't..." she says.

I stop her from saying anything else by pressing my tongue right up against Tamiya's clit and sucking on it. I might not stop her from getting revenge on me, but at least I can come up with a creative way to apologize to this woman. She cries out in pleasure as I suck on her clit. Wrapping my lips tighter around it, I run my tongue over the length of her slit.

She gets wetter as I suck on her clit and her moans of pain melt into moans of pleasure and get crazier as I take a finger and spread her entrance open. I groan along with Tamiya and nearly cum in my pants as I thrust a single index finger inside her. There is something special about this woman's pussy. It's like she was made for me. I can feel it just by having my finger inside her. I can't hold myself back and I spread her pussy wider with a second finger.

Tamiya moans again and I don't stop myself from sucking on her clit while I thrust two fingers inside her. I eat her sweet pussy on the floor of my house with slow, sensitive licks, tuning into her body's needs and pushing this strange, angry, lonely woman close to the edge of orgasm.

I grab onto Tamiya's thighs and draw her closer to me, burying my face deeper between her puffy lower lips as she gasps and gushes juices all over me. I can feel her getting closer and I want her to cum.

"It's okay to feel good," I whisper. "Just let go..."

"I can't..." she gasps, desperately arching her hips up to meet my lips. Her thighs and hips are covered in her sweat now and the taste of her covers every inch of my face. I want so much more from her than this but for now, I just need to feel Tamiya finish...

"Yes you can. Cum..." I whisper before licking her clit slowly. "Cum for me, little mama..."

She cums so hard the floor shakes. I grab her closer to me and keep licking on her clit as she finishes all over my face. I don't want her to stop, but everything has its time and Tamiya floats down from her high into a gasping mess on my floor. Her skinny thighs tremble with pleasure. Her pussy juices are everywhere and my dick wants freedom from my pants so fucking badly.

"I'm going to tie your ass up so you don't slit my throat while you sleep," I tell her. It's easy for me to rise to my feet and get the advantage before she even catches her breath. My dick strains through my pants desperately, practically screaming at me for denying him his pleasure.

All things in due time.

She yelps a little as I pick her up off the floor and throw her skinny ass over my shoulder. This woman is so fucking weightless. She lets out a little sob as I drag her to what was meant to be the guest bedroom. Tamiya's ass is so light that she bounces on the bed a little. I take my belt off and secure Tamiya's wrists to the bed.

Even if she breaks free... I have my training and every confidence that I can handle her. She cries as I tie her to the bed frame, which doesn't make me feel too good about myself. It's only for my safety, but it hurts to hear this woman cry and feel the anguish of what happened between us. I don't bother putting her pants and underwear back on. I think it might help her stay in the mentality of a captive. I don't want Tamiya getting the idea that she has any power here whatsoever.

A woman like that can't handle any power. I have to keep an eye on her.

"I'LL COME GET you in the morning with some breakfast," I tell her as she sobs. Her crying gets to me, but I can't let it show so I just shut the door and head outside to vape and clear my head.

WHAT THE HELL was I thinking tasting this woman's pussy? And why do I still want more?

SOMETHING IS WRONG WITH ME. Really fucking wrong with me. I killed her sister. The only thing I owe her is answers and maybe an opportunity for revenge. I should never have put my tongue between her legs. I should have never tasted her.

BECAUSE I DON'T KNOW how the hell I'm going to get this woman off my mind.

Chapter Ten
Tamiya

I can't believe that I let that monster touch me. He's a killer – not just any killer. I should have tried harder to escape. I should have done things differently.

But maybe some small part of me wanted to face him. Maybe I wanted to come up close to something that fucking dangerous and touch it for myself. I don't know why. To prove I can? To prove I can survive it?

The more I sob, the more hopeless I feel. I don't know when he's coming back or what Reaper will do when he finally returns. He can do anything he wants to me. Touch me. Torture me. Kill me. I am utterly at this man's mercy in a way I've never been before.

Even if I could get in touch with Rebecca, I wouldn't want her to go to the police and I wouldn't want her to do something even crazier and get involved with a bunch of deranged bikers.

Southpaw was no angel on the way over here. When he wasn't stopping to smoke, he was stopping to call his wife and lying through his teeth about where he was. I feel sorry for whatever poor Becky he's married to...

This bed feels rock hard beneath me and the wet spot between my legs sends guilt and shame through me. I haven't had an experience like that with a man in forever. I never saw myself as being attracted to the kind of man who looks like Reaper either.

His muscles and body are all long and lean. But his strength surprises me. I thought I could take his ass, but I was wrong to underestimate his strength. That man's lean muscles are perfectly capable of pinning me to the floor. Or pinning me to the bed. I can't get out of here without him, that much is clear.

AND WHEN I do get out of here... what am I going to do? Kill him and spend the rest of my life on the run...

I DON'T KNOW if I thought that far ahead. Finding the man who killed my sister already seems like such a goddamn pipe dream. And what the hell happens the second I face him.

HE GIVES ME AN ORGASM.

NOT JUST A REGULAR ORGASM, either. The best one I've ever had. The shame causes another gush between my legs, skyrocketing my guilt. His lips were so soft. He knew exactly what he was doing. How can a monster like that know every way to please a woman?

I didn't even have to teach him.

Nothing stopped this man from putting his tongue right up against my clit when I struggle to find men who go down on me without having an argument and a discussion about the advancement of women's rights. It feels like begging so much that I stopped asking men. What's the point of all that fuss for a few half-assed licks?

My whole body shudders with the recent memory. My physiological responses don't give a shit about Reaper's past. All my body knows is that man's tongue. Juices gush from between my legs. I fight uselessly against the binds keeping me tied to the bed. Nothing I do can get what just happened out of my head.

If I think of something else, it ends up scaring the shit out of me and it's much more pleasurable to think of what just happened between my legs – ironically.

Reaper ate my pussy like it was his last meal. There's definitely something fucked up about what he did but he didn't take his dick out. The lack of penetration has me shocked and confused.

Not like I want him but... what type of man ties a woman up just to eat her out?

I DON'T FEEL like I understand the maniac who has me tied to the bed and that bothers me almost as much as the fact that I felt so fucking good while this demon ran his tongue over every inch of my pussy.

How long is he going to keep me tied to the bed?

AND WHAT ELSE IS THIS man going to do to me...

HE'S TALL. Immensely powerful. Wheat colored hair. Copper eyes. Then there's his body. His monstrous, muscular, terrifying body.

IT DOESN'T MATTER how this man just made me feel. I have to get away from him. I can't lie here and let him worm his way into my mind by putting his tongue in my pussy. Eating me out won't take away the fact that he's cruel beyond belief.

MY MIND SKIPS BETWEEN THOUGHTS – his physical attractiveness and his psychopathic destructiveness.

. . .

I CAN'T SLEEP, especially when my arms grow numb from the binds.

NOTHING HERE IS HAPPENING the way I thought it would.

Chapter Eleven
Reaper

I 'm too scared to untie Tamiya from the bed for five days. Day one, I did what worked with Anna. I got a McDonalds breakfast with all the fixings – A bacon, egg and cheese McGriddle, a hash brown, black coffee, and a milkshake. The damn woman spits at me. She refuses to eat even if I call her a "skinny little tree branch". She won't eat any of the food until noon, but I leave her ass tied up.

I don't want any more trouble and tell Tamiya she'll need to be good if she wants to be free. She quiets down enough so I let her go to the bathroom after she eats and then I tie her right back up. Her fighting gets worse until the fifth day, when she seems completely despondent. Solitary confinement can have that effect on a woman.

"Are you ready to have a real conversation with me?" I ask her when I walk into the guest bedroom, which smells totally rank from Tamiya's five days without showering. I'll let her use the bathroom, but I don't want her getting too comfortable in that bed. The more it smells like her gross sweat, the more likely I am to convince her to behave herself.

She glares at me and rolls around like she does every morning. I haven't made any progress in making this woman gain weight.

"I'm going to piss myself," she says. "And I'm tired of eating

McDonald's every morning. Don't you cook? I'd rather starve than eat anymore."

"You look like you're in a weight loss contest with Anne Frank. Sit your ass up and eat some breakfast."

"That is *seriously* offensive," she says. "Although I suppose you are a murderer so you probably don't give a shit."

No mention of the fact that I ate her pussy to orgasm a while back.

"Eat."

"I'm tired of lying on this bed. It's not helping your cause, anyway. I only want to slit your throat the more you keep me here."

"That would be very foolish. Southpaw told me to keep your ass out of trouble and you would much rather be my responsibility than his."

"That violent monster belongs in prison," Tamiya grunts as she uses what little energy she has to fight her binds. She hasn't been able to get out yet, so she's only putting on this show of escape to let me know that she still has what it takes to slit my throat. Message received.

"Okay, we can agree there. You still need to eat. So can we make a deal?"

"I eat and then I get to slit your throat."

"That doesn't sound like a very good deal," I tell her. "How about fifteen minutes untied. That's about all I trust you with."

She glares at me and she is so fucking pretty. Damn. But then she gives me a look of hope.

"That's enough time to shower. Will you let me shower?"

"Sure."

Honestly, my mind instantly wanders to seeing her naked. Tamiya looks grateful.

"Okay. Fine. I'll eat if you untie me and then I get an additional fifteen minutes of free time starting once I finish eating."

"Whatever it takes to get your skinny ass fed," I reply to her, running my tongue over my lips and seriously wondering how a woman gets that skinny. I find her strangely sexy with small tits just as womanly as any other... just smaller. *Cute.* Her hips are narrow, with no ass to speak of, which I find entertaining.

I thought all black women had an ass like that one rapper I caught Ruger jacking off to a few years ago... Can't remember her name. Tamiya glares at me and then gives a pointed look towards her binds as if to hurry my ass up. I love the audacity this woman has to be impatient. With all those days tied to the bed, she won't have her full strength which is what I'm counting on to survive the next few minutes.

Reaching around for her wrists, I work Tamiya free and she doesn't fight me off at all as I get her free. She falls limply to the bed almost in disbelief that she can move freely.

"Sit up," I command her plainly. "Come on."

Tamiya sits up and glances at her wrists, groaning as she tries to move her arms to rub them. Her body is too stiff to cooperate with her yet, something I fully intend to take advantage of. I consider her patiently as she closes and opens her fists to send blood flowing to her fingers. *Why do I find her so pretty?* Tamiya has long, thin arms and her skin is so goddamn dark. My cock throbs.

I toss the food onto her lap before my thoughts wander too far out of my control.

"Start eating. I don't have all day."

"What exactly have you got going on?" She asks. "You don't seem like you have a job."

WELL. I might not have a job in the traditional 9-to-5 sense, but we all have ways and means of making money. Mostly above board and completely in line with the law. But those lines of business are less profitable. If you can handle big risks, you have the opportunity to reap big rewards and that's what I prefer, honestly.

Since dad died, I haven't had much energy for work and not much need for it either. I made $214,000 during our last weapons run and unless I go back to Vegas with Southpaw or make some other stupid fucking decision, it might last me a while. To be fair, I have cleaned some of my money and invested it in the stock market and rental properties… perks of my strong relationship with my mother.

I suppose Tamiya thinks since I spend most of my time enjoying the most real parts of America I must be a dirty broke ass redneck. Better for her not to get any ideas about my money considering she already wants to slit my throat.

"I don't need a job. Now eat."

"Aren't you going to eat?"

"I already ate."

"It's going to be weird if you just stand there watching me."

"Don't think about it then."

She glares at me as she reaches into the brown paper bag. She reacts worse than Anna does.

"Don't you ever eat salad?"

"Yes. When my mom makes it for me, now hush up and appreciate the food in front of you."

Tamiya throws me the dirtiest look possible. "Don't expect me to bow down for some ice cold McDonalds."

"It wouldn't be ice cold if you weren't constantly pitching bitch fits."

She unwraps the breakfast sandwich and sinks her teeth into it. The hash brown looks sad, but very tempting. If she weren't so damn skinny, I would have taken away her responsibility to eat it. I watch her nibble around the edges like a rabbit and try not to lose my mind.

Doesn't she want to get to that shower of hers?

"I can't eat with you watching me like a freak."

Trust me, I have far more freaky ideas for Tamiya than watching her eat. I scowl and try not to let her sour ass attitude get to me. She smells ripe and as much as she protests and whines, the woman must be hungry.

"I'll turn around and give you a minute. But I'm not leaving you alone for long when I don't trust you as far as I can throw you."

And considering this woman's size, that's pretty fucking far. I turn around, nervous the moment I take my eyes off her. Even with her lightweight, I'll at least be able to hear her move. I hear chewing sounds behind me and fight the temptation to turn around too soon. Once Tamiya swallows a couple bites, I turn around to observe her. *Damn.* She nearly finished the entire thing in two bites.

I knew her ass was hungry.

"Please let me eat a vegetable."

"We don't have time for vegetables. I have places to be woman, so let's get you in the shower."

"Right. Your 9-to-5."

"Club business. Which means it's none of yours."

"Going to get on your knees and suck Southpaw's dick?"

"Watch your mouth, woman. I'm not afraid to hit you."

"Or kill me, if it came to that," she says. Then her eyes snap fearfully to mine, like she's afraid she went too far.

"I'm not going to kill you."

Not unless she gives me a good reason to, but I don't need her to know all of that. She's almost done with that damn food and I consider that progress. Once she finishes off, I snatch the trash from Tamiya and hold her by the less bruised part of her forearm.

"Get your ass in the shower. I'll have a timer on."

"Okay," she says, glancing away from me meekly. "Will you give me new bedsheets? I don't want to get bed bugs."

She has to get closer to me to walk to the shower and I get a full whiff of her. With so many days unwashed, Tamiya's scent ought to disgust me. Except all I want to do is pin her ass against the wall of the shower and take her hard and deep. She has the strangest effect on me and I don't know how much longer I can handle this.

"I'll change the sheets. Just get in the shower."

She nods and heads into the guest bedroom bathroom. I hear her lock it, not like it would take much for me to break an old home's door down. The buildings out here haven't had many updates and not just to preserve the neon signs vintage Route 66 look tourists and bikers expect.

I hear the shower turn on and strip the sheets. They smell terrible.

If I could trust Tamiya to have her wrists untied, that would be something. Southpaw told me to make her loyal. Eating her pussy did absolutely nothing to help the situation.

DOES HE WANT ME TO...

I KNOW what happened with Hawk and Juliette. I didn't want to know the details, but every last one of the Sinclair boys has a problem with alcohol and they all talk in ways they shouldn't about their personal business when they've been drinking. Hawk didn't even confess the truth to me — it was his twin brother.

The idea sticks with me all the same.

IT COULD BOND Tamiya to me.

IT COULD WORK.

I HAVE NEVER BEEN the kind of man to take those interactions lightly. Part of it was a religious upbringing that told us sex was something sacred. I was never perfect and before going off to the army, I thought I would die so I lost it to Tylee Shaw. She still hates me for it, because I might have ghosted her when I left for basic training.

Didn't want her brothers to kick my ass over her and truthfully, I didn't see myself marrying Tylee Shaw. I never wanted to be with a woman born into this life like my mother. It makes you too harsh and rough around the edges.

DOESN'T EXPLAIN what I feel for Tamiya. Lust that's stronger than anything else. Very dark temptation.

The woman begins singing in the shower and something stirs in me. *I know that song.* Since dad's funeral, I haven't been able to bring myself to go to church, but all the hymns still move me the same way, especially this beautiful hymn coming from the condo guest bathroom.

Her voice... How can that wildcat have a voice like that? Distracted and with an irrational pounding heart, I approach the bathroom door, telling myself that I just want to listen to her more closely and there's nothing more to it.

Tamiya has a beautiful voice. Her singing voice is goddamn spectacular. My dick gets hard just from hearing her on the other side of the door. This isn't the point of listening to her. I'm trying to make sure she isn't going to slit my throat. Not getting hard to an angel's voice.

SHE ABRUPTLY STOPS singing and turns the water off quickly after. My dick stays hard as I stay pressed up against the door. The thoughts flooding into my head are demented and dirty. If I get my dick in her right now, I can change things. I can get her loyal to me. I wait a few minutes, but I hear nothing from the other side of the door. No movement.

My first thought is that Tamiya ran out the window, but I remember there isn't any window in that bathroom, so she's safe. But she *is* taking a long time to get ready considering she has to come out here for clothing. I knock on the door gently.

"Everything okay in there?"

Tamiya doesn't respond to me. I wait for a little while.

"Tamiya?"

Again, I hear nothing from the other side of the door. My gut tells me to be suspicious. Tamiya made her intentions to harm me clear and I just had her tied to the bed for the past few days, so I doubt I've made my way onto her good side.

"TAMIYA, if you don't open the door, I'll come in."

Again, nothing. Shit. I consider running to the kitchen so I can grab a pistol, but that's not necessary for me to subdue this little thing.

"Tamiya, open the damn door."

I hit the door a few times with my fist and it somehow gets even more quiet in there. Tamiya is really going to make me break down my own bathroom door. Thank goodness this place was affordable enough and the door is old, which means I can find a weak point and slam my fist through it. I've given her plenty of warning at this point.

It takes one hit for me to break the door down. I hear nothing when I step into the bathroom. What the hell? I whip my head around looking for Tamiya and she springs out from behind the shower curtain and throws some liquid at my face. *Shit.*

It's soapy water and hydrogen peroxide which hurts like a mother-fucker and foams. *Shit.* Tamiya mixed something else in her twisted fucked up potion. I choke and cough as the chemicals sear through me and pure agony follows when she tosses something else at me.

"Eat shit, asshole."

I feel something wrap around my neck and adrenaline surges through me. Thanks to my Ranger training, the adrenaline causes me to spring into action. I push the pain to the back of my mind and react. With Tamiya on my back, I slam my body against the wall. She cries out loudly and tightens whatever she has wrapped around her neck.

She lets go of me and drops to the ground. I turn around and chase her. She speeds out of the bedroom ass naked and grabs an article of clothing off the bed before zooming out of the room. Using absolutely every ounce of strength, I tear around the corner after her, reaching out to grab her. She's smarter than I thought and faster than I expected. It must help that she's the weight of a goddamn bird.

Tamiya moves towards the front door and I don't even know how she gets halfway dressed by the time she gets there. Unfortunately for her, she has to slow down to grab the door handle and it's just enough time that I get my hands on her again. She shrieks loudly, nearly blowing out my eardrums as I drag her away from the door.

. . .

"WHAT THE HELL do you think you're doing?"

"LET ME GO!" she yells, kicking me as hard as possible, nearly missing my junk by a hair. My heart pounds like crazy. How the hell am I going to calm this woman down?

YOU KNOW HOW, Reaper. You know what Southpaw would tell you.

"I SAID CALM DOWN, Tamiya. Your ass had better listen."
"NO!" She shrieks.

GODDAMN. I'm going to have to do it. I'm going to have to fuck some sense into this woman.

Chapter Twelve
Tamiya

That blond asshole is so much stronger than he looks. After everything I've been through, I know I have a death wish. I let the man who killed my sister eat my pussy until I came. I experienced more pleasure with him than I have with any other man. The worst part is I have been tied to the bed for the past five days with nothing to do but contemplate this.

Rebecca doesn't know where I am. I don't know where my phone is. I know I should be happy that I somehow ended up right where I needed to, but Gideon Blackwood has been nothing but unexpected. He looks even more scary and racist than any of his mugshots.

Right now, I appear to have underestimated his size again. He overpowers me easily and drags me away from the front door and the escape I dreamed of for the past five days. I knew he would have some chemicals beneath the bathroom sink and the cocktail I made should have disabled him. This man is a fucking beast.

If I had a knife on me, I would need to work hard to get it between his ribs. He yells at me again to stop fighting him, which only makes me fight back harder. I will never obey him and I will *never* forgive him. Especially not for what he did to me on the floor of his house before tying me up.

It's psychological torture. It has been so long since I've been with a man that eventually I just caved to the sensations. He cupped my ass so gently as he pushed his tongue into my depths. He used his fingers on me. The man ate my pussy like it was his last meal and then he just walked off. *I want you to feel good.*

He's sick in the head.

When he gets me back into that stupid ass bedroom, I fight him harder. I get turned around so I can kick him better and scratch at his face, but he keeps plowing ahead towards the bed. *He's going to tie me up and leave me there to die. I need to fight him off.*

Reaper tosses me on the bed and I immediately curl my body up and try to roll away so I can escape. He drags me back by the ankle like I'm a rag doll and not an adult woman. I screech bloody murder, but he doesn't care and there's no one around to hear me. I'm alone.

He holds me upside down until blood rushes to my head and it gets hard to breathe, let alone scream. Then he throws me on the bed again and fastens my ankle to the bed frame at the foot of the bed with a piece of rope he pulls out of his back pocket. I kick him as much as I can while he ties me there but I don't appear to hurt him at all. He glares as he ties me up, but he's quiet. I'm the only one making any sound and once I have my ankle tied all the way up... *that worries me.*

He takes one of my arms and ties me back up to my original spot at the head of the bed. I feel strangely vulnerable, but at least I have the large shirt I stole off the bed draped over me. I have some unusual skills from my brief thot phase, like dressing while running out of a man's apartment. A couple of those men lied about the presence of wives and I was not trying to go out like that.

"What are you doing?"

"Shut the fuck up," Reaper snaps, his voice vibrating with genuine anger.

"You should have known that I would try to escape again. Be lucky I didn't actually kill you."

"My eyes burn you fucking psychotic creature!"

"If I'm a psychotic creature, you're a sick rapist asshole."

He doesn't respond. He just steps back and glares at me. Reaper has a sharp nose, and hair the color of wheat that he has in a shoulder length mess like an animal. The scars all over his mole-rat pale body tell me he's gotten himself into plenty of trouble since his time serving in the US army. Plus, I know he's a killer.

My sister's killer. Our eyes meet and our hatred for each other pulses between us. He has no right to hate me. *But why isn't he saying anything?*

Reaper walks out of the room and I don't feel any better. I don't know what he could be doing out there, but it scares the crap out of me. He comes back into the bedroom and my heart sinks into my stomach. He slams a pistol on the dresser across the room from the bed and turns to look at me.

"You try any shit like that again, I'll shoot your foot. I'm keeping you here for the next couple months and we are going to sort our shit out. Because you aren't going to the cops to get justice for someone who touched kids. I won't fucking let you."

"Is that a threat?"

He approaches the bed and flicks open a switchblade knife he pulled out of his back pocket. I scream loudly, but the expression on his face doesn't shift. He looks like he could effortlessly gut me without feeling. The knowledge that this man has killed before flashes through my head and I absolutely lose control, screaming my head off as Reaper gets closer to me with the sharp, shimmering blade. He cuts my foot loose, which immediately makes me scream louder, and attempt to scramble back away from him. Because he doesn't put the blade away and I have a feeling he wants me to run and that he wants to use it on me. I can't stop the racing thoughts.

He's going to kill me. I scream louder, even if I thought I wasn't the type of chick to act like that. I laughed at the women who gave that *Final Girl* scream in horror movies. I didn't expect to be that girl. Reaper doesn't stop glaring at me with an increasingly dark expression on his face, his grasp on the knife tightening.

"Shut your ass up," he snarls.

My screaming doesn't affect him. It's like I pissed him off past the point of control. I try to escape off the bed, not to give him the chase he wants, but because it's my only damn chance at getting out of here.

Reaper reaches up and cuts my arm free before he grabs onto me, thwarting my escape, and flips me over effortlessly. No point tying me up anymore, he has all the power here and the pistol on the dresser which I know he can get to faster than I ever could just because his limbs are insanely and unfairly long. I can't stop myself from screaming and trying to kick, despite the knife hovering over my flesh.

"I ought to cut your damn skin until you bleed," he roars, pressing the knife flat against my thigh. I stop screaming. My body freezes, rushing into its other instinct for protection. Fight, flight, *or freeze.* They forget to mention that third one in science class, but it's more real than anyone realizes until they're right in the thick of fucking danger like this and their body refuses to move.

Reaper's eyes bulge out with red all around them from the chemical mix I tossed in his face. One layer of the skin around his eyes peels away from the burn and he's clutching that damn knife in a death grip. We both want to kill each other, but right now, I can't tell who wants to kill who more. I've never felt anything like this before – the simultaneous desire to have that man between my legs and to slide that knife right into his belly. He's looking at me like he's thinking the same thing, which can't be possible.

"I never asked for this shit to come back and haunt me," he says, his voice getting deep and his tone shifting into something serious and confessional. "I took care of it in the desert and I did the right thing. Doesn't matter what you think."

"You killed my sister," I hiss at him, yelping as Reaper responds by pressing the blade slightly closer to my skin, threatening to slice me open. For all I know, my shuddered breathing could be more than enough to cause him to accidentally cut me. His face changes for a moment, but only to get more angry. Then the voice that bursts out of him makes me yelp like a puppy.

"Were you there?" he yells. "Were you fucking there?!"

And then he slides the knife away. At first, I think he's moving it away from me, but then I feel hot liquid gush from my thigh and I know... *he cut me.* I scream bloody murder, scrambling up the sheets and then throwing myself off the bed by accident. He swears and Reaper drops the knife. The thud sounds like he dropped something bigger, or maybe it's just all my senses heightening from the adrenaline rush.

"You have no idea what you're talking about," Reaper continues screaming at me as blood gushes out of my leg and he makes no move to help me. "Do you think I would have shot her if I knew? I spent all that time in Iraq and never did something like that. Other men did, but not me. I had standards. I had goddamn principles."

Fuck his goddamn principles. Him releasing the knife gives me enough of a break to breathe and collect myself enough to actually *do something* that moves me towards escape. With pain searing through my leg, I get to my feet and lunge for the gun sitting on top of the dresser. Knowing escape is futile doesn't stop me from trying. If I don't get the gun, Reaper will, so my only way out of here involves wrapping my fingers around the handle.

Reaper goes crazy when he sees what I'm about to do. He throws himself in my way and it feels like I'm being tackled. His body might be cut with lean muscles rather than pure bulk, but it still feels like slamming into a wall. He knocks the wind out of me with contact and the force he hits me with even surprises him because he cries out too and we both fall to the floor.

His body covers mine with his full weight and I cry out with desperation for air as my arms shoot out from my sides. I turn my head and see the bloody knife on the ground, possibly within reach of my fingers. Reaper groans in pain from the surprise of landing on the ground almost face first. My hand shoots out in a desperate effort to grab the knife. The handle is so slippery that I touch it, but it slips out of reach.

Reaper groans again and gets a slightly better hold of himself, but I grunt too and stick my hand out further, wrapping my hand around the knife handle and grabbing hold of it. Once he realizes what I've done, I know I have milliseconds to act before Reaper uses the sheer physical difference between us to take control again. I try to stab him in the back, but it takes more effort than I think and I just cut his shirt. He cries out as the knife rips through and then he grabs onto me and rolls us both over so I'm on top of him.

I get giddy with the sense of control for a split second until Reaper uses his feet to shove me off him. I swing the knife madly and I think I cut him because he cries out, but then his feet send me flying and the knife escapes my grasp. I fall backwards, my head slamming into the dresser and causes fuzzy silver balls of static to splatter randomly in front of my head.

"I'm tired of this fucking shit..."

My leg throbs. I hear a familiar click. Rebecca taught me the basics about guns from her law enforcement days and there really isn't another sound like a bullet loading into a pistol chamber. *He's going to shoot me, just like he shot Damara.* I cry out from pain as the cut from my leg finally has the capacity to send signals to my brain. The hard knock to the head spreads pain everywhere. My hands shoot out madly searching for the knife, but I know it's futile.

"Stop fucking moving, or I'll paint the floor with your brains."

Reaper's voice drips with pure loathing. My vision returns to normal and I see that I cut his ass up pretty bad as I waved the knife. There's a large slice on his cheek and blood dripping from his forearm. His cuts are way worse than the cut on my leg, which continues to bleed everywhere. I shudder and try not to think of how gross it is, or how the cut might be deep enough for me to bleed out... shit, I'm not a doctor.

I might be brave, but I'm not stupid. I stop moving, but I take the one piece of power I can. I look Reaper dead in the eye. If he's going to shoot me, he's going to have to do it while looking me in the eye. He's not going to get out of this easily.

"You are fucking crazy," He says, his voice dropping to a whisper.

"So? Wouldn't you be in my situation?"

"I didn't mean to cut you," he says. "If you weren't such a damn... fuck..."

His body shudders with anger and Reaper's finger moves towards the trigger. I will myself not to flinch or betray any weakness. I don't understand him. I don't understand myself. I had all the power to kill him with that fucking knife and I let him get the upper hand again. I might lie to myself and say he was bigger and stronger than me, but I had a chance to kill this motherfucker and for some reason... I didn't.

"Get up," Reaper commands fiercely.

"Why? So you can make me turn around and execute me?"

His upper lip curls and twitches with disgust that he quickly tries to bury once he sees his response provoking a smirk on my face. All I have right now is the power to piss him off, and I'll take what little advantage I have right now.

"If I wanted to kill you, I would have done it already."

CHAPTER THIRTEEN
REAPER

I shouldn't let her get under my skin like this. I can tell she's enjoying it, but the way my face burns from her goddamn concoction and then her swinging the knife around like a maniac has me far outside of myself. I feel all the emotions that came the first time I shot somebody swelling in my head at once and then bursting out through every corner of my body. It's a part of what happens from what they call 'traumatic stress'. Your body puts you in the same place you were the first time, even if the situation is entirely different.

I was never able to say what would trigger me to lose my shit, but this damn woman cutting me in the face has turned me into a nuclear bomb. My finger hovers over the trigger and all emotion and sentiment leaves me. Adrenaline turns me into a monster, not a dove.

"Why the fuck would you prefer to fight me rather than learn the truth?" I snarl at her. "If I were a real monster, I wouldn't just threaten you. I would hurt you."

"I'm bleeding," she hisses through gritted teeth, never taking her cruel ass gaze off me. Her bitterness crosses the room and wraps its hands around my throat. Tamiya's dark brown eyes pulse with rage, loathing and every hateful emotion in between. It feels good to see her reflect exactly what I feel for myself in some strange fucked up way and as I point the gun at her, my dick goes hard.

"Good," I snap at her. "Something will eventually work to teach you how to behave."

Her nostrils flare up, making her dark brown face look even prettier. Why is it always attractive women that have to be crazy fucking animals? And why do I find her of all people to be one of the prettiest and the craziest.

"Shoot me and get it over with," she snarls, and despite her best efforts to hide her true feelings from me, I can tell deep down she doesn't mean it. Maybe it's obvious that she doesn't want to get shot in the head. But she does act like she has a death wish, so it's truly up in the air.

"No. That would be too fucking easy on you. Since you think you know me so goddamn well, I'll tell you exactly what happened the night I killed your sister... and why I wouldn't do a damn thing differently."

"What kind of monster would say that about killing someone?"

"The kind of monster that's tired of your shit. Now this is how it's going to go down. I tell you the truth and then you take all your clothes off and you make me happy to make up for the cuts and the bleach."

Horror doesn't take long to settle into her heart. I can see it written all over her face and a twisted part of me enjoys it. This damn woman got under my skin and the more she pisses me off, the harder it gets for me to control the erection desperate to burst out of my pants. She can't deny me forever and fuck, I don't want her to deny me much longer. I can't stand it. Not the adrenaline coursing through me or the blood rushing to my dick.

Part of me wants to put the pistol to my own fucking head just to stop all this shit from exploding inside me like a thousand fucking nuclear bombs.

"You're sick in the head," Tamiya says, testing me to see if I'll snap. She does have a death wish, doesn't she? This woman ain't all the way right in the head and it has nothing to do with the fact that I killed her sister. I know I'm fucking crazy, which is why I recognize crazy when I'm looking it right in the eye.

"Yes. I'm very sick in the head because life fucking made me that way. And your sister should have stayed away from the wrong types of men."

"I don't believe you," she says. "Damara would have never been with a guy who touched kids as you put it earlier."

"I know what I know."

"She wouldn't have!"

"You don't understand how those types of criminals operate."

"And you do?"

WE PUT that part of the family business to rest after what happened in the desert. A job gone wrong. The Blackwoods didn't just sell arms, we used our skills as Army Rangers to once in a while do *other work* for people who really needed it. Mostly, abusive husbands. Mom always knew a woman in trouble with some asshole beating the shit out of her. Sometimes the lady's father would pay the money.

Dad would plan everything, Ruger would carry out the plan with the rest of us running backup if necessary. Ruger was a natural killer. It sounds like a satanic thing to say about someone, but it's true. He killed nearly every living thing he got his hands on up until he was five years old and strangled a rat he found in the pantry. His mama whooped him so hard he couldn't sit for a week and then she took off on a fentanyl bender with dad's bike for the rest of the summer.

Rarely, we would get help from some of the other boys in the club but taking hitman work was always rare. It's too risky and most people are willing to empty their savings accounts for a hit, but American savings accounts have only been getting smaller and smaller. It ain't often worth $75,000 to risk life in prison or worse when you could just as easily run guns or drugs over the border to Mexico or Canada and make three times as much without risking execution.

"I understand both sides of the law quite well," I respond to her calmly. I can feel my rage and my nerves settling as I set my mind on telling her the whole truth. The only part of me I can't calm between my legs I won't have to worry about for long because I'll get Tamiya's pretty ass lips wrapped around my dick before the end of the night.

"My sister was not a pedophile."

"I never said she was. But if you conducted your investigation correctly, you will know that Davis motherfucker had a list of charges a mile fucking long and he messed with someone who paid my family to take him out."

"Who?"

Considering every fucking part of me still stings from her assault, I don't like the way she keeps breaking up the damn story.

"I would tell you the damn story if you keep quiet," I snap at her. I see a look of fear cross her face which tells me she won't be entirely impossible to control once this is over. My eyes dart down to her lips for a second and my dick jumps in my pants again.

It's not that her fear turns me on, it's that everything about Tamiya has an intense effect on me. I have to keep my mind straight on the story not to get too distracted by her lips and my desires for them. At least she keeps quiet, giving me space to continue.

"He went up to live with the Mormons and acted like he was going to convert or he did convert, something like that. But he messed with a powerful Mormon man's daughter, and he paid my father to end Nathaniel's life. Maybe that's how he convinced your sister he was a good man. Religion."

"How could my sister have something to do with the Mormons?" she replies. "Don't they only recruit blond people?"

I just told her ass to be quiet, but she doesn't seem like she's asking for the sake of making trouble.

"How can you live out West and not know about Mormons? Anyone can be a Mormon, that's the point."

"Well I only saw blond Mormons in Salt Lake City."

"Maybe you weren't looking very hard…"

"Why are you defending Mormons?" she asks sharply. "Focus on the story."

I lower the pistol, despite her sass. It's not entirely out of the goodness of my heart. My arm hurts and talking to this crazy ass woman appears to have calmed her down enough that she isn't lunging for any weapon. I keep my hand ready just in case she does anything foolish. But I'll only shoot her in the foot. Nothing that will kill her.

"They accept all types," I answer sternly, giving her a warning not to cross me with my vocal tone instead of screaming at her. It's just as effective because Tamiya rolls her eyes, like she's sure I'm wrong. "There are folks out here who dabble in dirty business to make money. Worse than drugs and weapons. We have our limits in my club, but that ain't the case with everybody."

"Right."

She might not believe me, but Southpaw's cousin Oske is living proof of what goes on out here in the desert. You can see the signs from looking at her if you know what to look for. There is truth to the rumors that these abandoned highways out West are the ones used to traffic human beings across the country.

It's the type of thing you don't believe could truly happen until you meet someone who can tell you what to look for. After what happened in Utah, I could see the signs plainly on Oske. I don't know if the Shaws were on the right side or the wrong side of whatever happened to the Indian girl, but she carries herself like everyone else I met who fell into the hands of human traffickers.

Paranoid. Shit, I can't blame her. I'm paranoid too. I still have my finger on the goddamn trigger, even if I could subdue Tamiya's skinny ass with my bare hands.

"I don't know why Davis got swept up in that shit, all I know is that he convinced some big time Mormon's daughter to follow him wherever he went. She was fourteen. Her daddy sent folks down to get her back, but they weren't the kind willing to get their hands dirty."

"But you were fine getting your hands dirty," Tamiya says, an embarrassed expression crossing her face as she grapples with her inability to stay quiet and let me tell the story.

"The government made me kill people. I got paid half as much. And I can't say for sure any of the Arabs I killed were evil. Maybe they thought of themselves as just like me... men fighting for their country."

Fuck. She moves her thighs a little, pushing her body away from me, giving herself the distance most civilians do when we talk about what happened. How complicated it feels. Listen, I know any of the men I killed would have killed me and they probably wouldn't have felt sorry about it. But I grew up riding bikes and spending my summers under the open sky.

I never thought I was the type to take a life until I had to do it. Once you do it the first couple times, you get used to the numbness that follows. If I don't keep forcing myself to relive and repeat what the hell happened over there, I'll lose myself. Those words are too much for her already, so I stay quiet. *Crazier than a kookaburra to think those death to America motherfuckers wouldn't have laughed as they pissed on my body, but that doesn't make it feel right that I shot 'em. One of the soldiers I killed was eighteen years old. He looked like he was barely sixteen, he was so fucking skinny. Way skinnier than skinny ass Tamiya.*

"Hey," she says gently, and she stammers. I lost myself in my thoughts and probably scared her, staring off into space like a crazy person. She has a strange way of looking at me that makes me feel warm all over. I don't know if it's guilt. I always told myself I did what I had to do.

"I already got my hands dirty once. No point pretending I'm a saint," I respond.

I hate the way she's looking at me right now. Her eyes make me feel guilty and it's not an emotion I particularly enjoy...

"Damara's name wasn't on your hitlist, was it?" She asks.

I shake my head. That woman was in the wrong place at the wrong time, but what the hell was I supposed to do? I tried to back out of the job at the last minute, and the Mormon convinced me. He had pictures. If he gave a shit he was showing me his own daughter, he didn't show it.

Do you understand why I want that man six feet under?

Yes, sir. You get used to following orders and shit, I couldn't blame the man once I saw what Davis had done to her. Branded her. Shaved the pretty blonde hair off her head. And much worse. That man has to contend with the fact that those pictures are out there forever.

. . .

SOME SHIT you can't unsee, but you really wish you could.

"SHE DIDN'T WANT me to kill him. She wanted me to get the police and send him to jail. But that wasn't what I was paid for. Pedophiles get a fucking smack on the wrist. He has cop family members. You can't leave shit like that up to chance."

"So you killed both of them."

IT DOESN'T MAKE a difference now that Tamiya's sister jumped in front of a bullet meant for her boyfriend and I panicked, pulling the trigger three more times because I wanted to make sure the job was done. I lost my shit. Lost my control. I could have gotten away from just injuring her.

But I stood over them both and emptied the clip. *I was so goddamn angry.*

"Yes. I killed both of them," I answer. "But nobody knew except... club members. So I don't know how the fuck you found out."

My eyes flicker angrily to hers again, and Tamiya scoots her butt another foot back, attempting to put even more distance between us.

"I'm a private investigator," she says. "I put my ear to the ground and followed the leads."

SHE SOUNDS all smart but there's just one problem... I don't like that answer very much. I don't think it's quite that simple. Secrets don't slip out just like that. *Loose lips sink ships.*

CHAPTER FOURTEEN
TAMIYA

It's not hard to piece together Reaper's implications. His secret escaped from someone's lips, which means someone betrayed him. Judging by his unstable attitude and easily read emotions, it must be someone close.

Reaper sets the gun back on the dresser and gives me a stern look. "You aren't going anywhere until you tell me who it was that gave you your information."

"I didn't mean I literally put my ear to the ground. I tracked down Legion, one of the bikers your club killed, and he led me straight to you. In fact, he was coming to find you himself. I'm pretty sure he *did* get to your people."

Reaper doesn't betray any emotion, but he seems to be openly calculating the possibilities.

"There are only a handful of people who know what happened, and I would trust all of them with my life. They're family and none of them would have sold out to any motherfucker outside the club."

"Don't get all emotional. I'm just deducing the truth like you are."

"What you're doing is accusing decent men of disloyalty when there must be another explanation. *Where did you get your information?*"

He exerts all his effort in creating these threatening undertones, which don't make me want to spill the information faster. Does it matter at this point? Because right now, all I can think about is that I have my answers and if I don't kill Reaper... *What the hell am I supposed to do?*

I didn't plan my life out past this point. I thought I would find the man who killed my sister and it would be easy to get that shit out of the way and then...

I NEVER THOUGHT about what the hell would happen after that.

"OKAY," he says. "If you don't want to answer my question, I can think of another way you can make me happy."

Oh hell no. I don't like the sound of Reaper's voice and right now, considering we're both cut up and bleeding, getting the fuck away from each other seems like it might be the best choice, not like either of us are reaching for that choice immediately. Well, I'll be the first. Reaper doesn't have his hand on the gun... I have to be able to convince him that I'm more trouble than I'm worth and that I have no interest in taking this shit to the cops.

What the hell would the cops do? Nothing. Reaper and I can at least agree about that when it comes to his version of events. I have to take his word for it that his reasons for killing my sister weren't sadistic. That seems like a big risk, but I don't see that I have much of a choice but to give him the benefit of the doubt.

He has all the power here and no reason to lie. If he thought the truth would be a problem, he would just as soon kill me as he would hide from it. I can sense that on him. Unfortunately, I also sense his uncertainty and something dark looming around that uncertainty.

Why the hell is he looking at me like that? I pretend I don't notice the strange look on Reaper's face and try to sound like I'm just offering a very normal rational and reasonable suggestion.

"Right. I can promise to let this go if you let me go. I'll walk away from this and leave you alone."

Reaper grins. "Are you fucking crazy?"

"Not any crazier than you."

I refrain from calling him a 'bitch' or a 'motherfucker', although the temptation is there. I need his ass to let me go, so pushing his buttons doesn't seem like a good idea right now.

"As much as you piss me off, letting you go is not going to make me happy right now. Not with blood all over my fucking face."

"And whose fault is that?"

"Yours," Reaper says. "And you're going to make it right. So get over here."

He points at his feet. I give him the worst look I can because he must be out of his fucking mind.

"What are you doing? Why are you pointing at your feet."

"You're a private investigator. Figure it out."

Reaper and I are both covered in blood, both gasping for breath as we try to stifle the pain that follows the dissipation of adrenaline in our bodies. We could always lash out at each other again. Go for another round of fighting and forget that I have a huge gash on my leg and he has several gashes on his body.

He keeps his finger pointed at the spot on the floor in front of him. The room suddenly feels hot as it occurs to me what he wants me to do there. *He wants you to kneel, Tamiya. Your mind wants to block out that possibility, but you know that it's more than an option to him. It's what he wants. Why do you think he put his tongue down there earlier?*

I refuse to break eye contact with Reaper or give any acknowledgment of his command. But the more I stare at his face, the more I wonder if I'm going to get out of this alive. Or if I ever even planned on it. Because I don't know what comes after this. I don't want to run back to Rebecca, and I definitely don't want to run back to Salt Lake City.

Reaper's red eyes pulse with hatred and he continues pointing at the ground between his feet. My gut twists in an uncomfortable knot. I guess throwing chemicals into his face didn't help improve his appearance, so maybe I should have chilled out a little bit. I did what anyone sane in my position would have done. *Right, because sane people poke sleeping bears all the time.*

"I want you to kneel, Tamiya," Reaper says, his sorrel-brown eyes so fiercely fixed on mine that they send a shudder straight through me. "And I don't want you complaining about it. Because if you don't do what I say, I'll make you. And that way will be a lot less fun."

"Coercing me to do it is just as bad as forcing me to."

"I don't know what that word means," Reaper says with the genuine frustration of a man who has heard a word he deems too big to understand. "All I know is, you're going to kneel right there and do what I say until I'm finished."

"And why would I do that when you're going to kill me anyway?"

"Because I won't kill you," he says. "I have no interest in killing you. I just don't like the way you piss me off."

He smiles again, but then his face goes through about three unhinged emotions like he's cycling through them with uncertainty. There's something that seems fucking crazy about his facial expressions and how quickly his emotions cycle from outrage to that eerie, semi-controlled calm. I don't know who the fuck is in control here, I'm just sure it's not me.

"Right. So I do what you want and you let me go?"

"I never said that."

Okay. Let the negotiation begin. He might not let me go (right away), but it's better than killing me. Reaper's face cycles through a few emotions again and the one he settles on sends a chill straight down my spine.

"Shit, if you do a good job, I might just keep you."

"A good job of kneeling?"

"Get your ass over here," he says. "Because you know damn well that's not what I mean."

Sure, I might know what he means, but that doesn't mean I can't pretend he means something else. Because it would be very convenient to me if this violent stranger wasn't implying that he wants me on my knees to suck his dick. My hesitation clearly frustrates him in a way he can't hide because his cheeks turn very red.

The flushed cheeks being entirely outside of Reaper's control causes my gaze to dart between his legs for the first time. I wasn't going to stare at that man's crotch or even look at it for fear of giving him any wrong ideas but that first glance between his legs tells me that I don't have to worry about giving Reaper any wrong ideas.

I've never seen a man's erection so blatantly obvious through his clothes. It's not just that his arousal is obvious that's the problem. It's the size of the fucking thing. If he wanted to keep it a secret from me, he couldn't. My stomach turns. There's no way that bulge is all him. He must have wrapped it up in two socks and maybe even a Christmas stocking. The bulge is big enough that it moved his zipper down a bit, like his dick is literally about to jump out.

His eyes don't budge and it's almost like he's embarrassed about his urgent need for relief. The mixture of his desperation and forceful command gives me the strangest push. I can hear myself justifying it in my head. *He won't last long and then he'll be nice and relaxed, making it ten times easier to get an advantage over him and kill his ass for good.*

Despite the current calm between us, I can't fully let go of my murder plot.

"Don't make me ask you again, Tamiya," he says, tugging on the 'y' in my name just enough with his accent that it feels like he's drawing me to him with physical force instead of mental force. That's how powerful he sounds when he says my name and I hate it.

My eyes flicker with rage as I glare at him, but I know that I'll obey him and I'm not entirely sure it's just because he isn't giving me another choice. I tell myself that obeying him will stop the pain, and that's why I'm doing it. Keeping my eyes glued to Reaper's cut up and tattooed face, I begin to move towards the spot on the floor.

He keeps his finger pointing to *my spot*, relentless and unforgiving in his desire or maybe even his hatred for me. It hurts my thigh to move it, but the bleeding finally stopped and I realize the cut wasn't deep enough to need stitches. It's hard not to be grateful for a temporary reduction in pain.

I can't kneel on the floor without sending agonizing bursts of pain up through my knees and cut up thigh, so I crawl to the spot between Reaper's legs, making a display of pain despite my obedience so he doesn't get too pissed off and overreact. The closer I get to the spot between his legs, the more I swear I can feel the heat coming off his dick it's so big and hard.

When I get to the spot, I'm half-sitting instead of kneeling and not tall enough to reach Reaper's crotch with my mouth, but I'm definitely tall enough to see it. *Holy fuck, he has a big one. I guess it would still be a Christmas stocking although that doesn't seem realistic, does it...?*

"I can't kneel," I tell him.

"Put a pillow under your knees."

He reaches for his gun again and once he has it, he gets a pillow for me and sets it at his feet. I kneel and while the pillow helps, it doesn't take all the pain away. I try not to make my discomfort too obvious. I have bigger problems than achy knees. Reaper makes a low groan and shifts his hips forward.

"You put me in this situation," he says earnestly, like he genuinely blames me for his *erection*. I understand blaming me for the chemical concoction I threw into his face, but I am not responsible for his body doing all of that. I definitely am not doing anything that would provoke a normal man to get hard like that.

I give Reaper a sharp look, which is the closest I dare get to defying him at this point. He pats his belt buckle.

"You're grown enough to know what to do. Shit, you might even be older than I am."

"Watch your mouth, white boy."

"How old are you?" he asks. "I suppose I'd better check."

"Twenty-five."

He laughs. "You're crazy."

"What's so crazy about that? Am I older than you?"

I know some white people age like milk, so maybe he's nineteen or something crazy. I hesitate in my position on my knees, waiting for Reaper's answer.

"No," he says. "But you're crazy to waste your life chasing ghosts when you still have time on your side…"

I glance up from his crotch, but he stops my head from moving with a forceful palm. His fingers slip through the strands of my hair as he grips my head and holds me in place.

"Don't get any crazy ideas," he says. "What's going to happen now is we're going to get very close to each other, okay? Because I'm not going to kill you and I'm not going to let you go. I need you, Tamiya."

"Need me?"

"Yes," he says. His facial expression changes again. His grip on my hair tightens and he moves my head so I'm looking him in the eye this time. "I choose to trust your skinny ass that you don't know who betrayed the club, but I need you to find out who did."

"What does that have to do with me sucking your dick?"

Someone should be able to just come right out and say it. Reaper's dick jumps in his pants and if I thought he was blushing before, he sure is blushing now. His grip on my hair tightens and his red face twists up like a pissed off fox.

"What I learned in the army is that rituals have a way of bonding people together."

"So you sucked dick in the army?"

This is the wrong thing to poke him about. Reaper rains down immediate punishment. He smacks me across the face and my immediate response is to yelp in disbelief before I outright physically attack him.

This man has lost his entire mind if he thinks I'm going to let him *slap me across the damn face.* I get up off my knees without thinking about how he will respond, especially since he has his other hand on my head. Reaper immediately smacks me down. I slam down on my knees again and look up at him with outrage.

.   .   .

HE'S A MONSTER.

"WHAT THE HELL IS YOUR PROBLEM?" I bark at him. He looks at me bewildered.

"What the hell do you expect me to do when you say crazy shit."

"Not slap me across the damn face."

HIS NOSTRILS FLARE OUT and his red face makes me want to bite him. Hard.

"I NEVER HEARD any woman complain about a little slap."

"Well you're hearing it now."

He grunts. "Then I guess I'm sorry."

"You guess?"

"I'm sorry," he says. Then just as quickly as he apologizes, his expression hardens. I want to fight him now more than before. How dare he act like I'm the one offending him?

Chapter Fifteen
Reaper

Blind rage overwhelms me as I slam Tamiya's knees back into the pillow. I'm tired of waiting and it's not just that, her reaction to me pisses me off and pushes me over the edge of rage I have just barely been holding back. I have to blame her for this because there's no way it's my fault. I've never done anything like this before. Ask Southpaw's old lady. I spent all that time locked up with her in a motel and never once did I face temptation like this.

Angrily, I squeeze Tamiya's cheeks and force her to look up at me. She looks so goddamn beautiful on her knees. The only thing I don't like about her in this position is the loathing on her face. She rolls her tongue around in her mouth and I warn her sternly, "You had better not spit on me, crazy woman..."

I crouch down and kiss her. If she's going to spit, I'd prefer her doing it right in my mouth. She tastes so fucking good. I don't know how I thought kissing her would help my situation. It doesn't. I feel goddamn desperate for Tamiya the moment my lips touch hers. I already don't have any control over myself. Kissing her was too risky.

But I don't care. I thrust my tongue into Tamiya's mouth. She tries to bite me, making another effort to draw blood. Her fighting turns me on and I just kiss her harder before I pull away and keep one hand on her head while I use the other to get my dick out of my pants. I want to feel her lips around my cock so fucking bad.

Tamiya squeezes her lips shut once my dick gets free, but I tilt her head back to force them open before commanding her sternly.

"This is for the best for both of us."

"Take a hint, asshole."

"You owe me," I respond sharply. "I don't need a hint."

I convince myself that she parts her lips to accept my cock before I slide the full length into Tamiya's mouth… piercings and all. I only have two of them – one weighted barbell at the base of the head, and a Prince Albert piercing that I got on a dare after losing a bet against Condom.

Her lips spread enough and her mouth makes a tight sleeve around my cock that makes it almost impossible not to burst right away. It's not fair how fucking good she feels. *Damn.* I groan loudly as I hold Tamiya's head still and thrust the rest of my length in her mouth. Tears pierce the corners of her eyes and I feel her throat constricting around my dick as she struggles not to gag.

I pull out. Slowly. Fuck. I know I just pushed her too far. Once I take my dick out, she gags, but refuses to show more weakness than necessary. After dry swallowing and gasping for breath again, she sits back on her heels and gazes up at me defiantly. I loosen my grip on her hair and gaze down at my dick and the string of spit connecting it to Tamiya's perfect lips.

"I'm sorry. I'm trying to control myself."

Her glaring intensifies.

"I need to cum," I whisper. "I promise I'll be quick. I don't want to hurt you. I just need to cum in that pretty ass mouth."

I slowly run my tongue over my lips, wishing I could soak in the gorgeous scene of Tamiya on her knees forever. She looks fucking beautiful down there. Even with tears in her eyes. My heart pounds nervously as this connection between us feels better than I expected.

I push my hips forward again, jutting towards those sexy ass lips. Tamiya reaches for my dick and takes hold of it. I don't bother making eye contact with her once she does it out of fear that she'll stop touching me without me forcing her to do it. Her hand feels so goddamn good. I could cum instantly just from how good her hands feel.

But my dick wants to feel those lips and it won't tolerate anything else. I can't control myself. I groan and push my hips forward again, practically begging her to give me more. Tamiya's lips spread just enough that I can thrust my dick inside and then she takes me all the way in. *Holy shit, she feels good.* Her lips feel even softer this time and I'm far less worried about her chomping down on my dick, although maybe I shouldn't feel that safe...

I can feel myself getting harder as she takes me deeper. All logical thoughts evaporate and I just want to exist here in this moment. With her. Tamiya's throat expands to accept my cock. I work up a steady rhythm as I let her tease me with her lips. She can't help herself. She runs her tongue over the length of my shaft. She pleasures me with her lips and tongue despite hating me.

Her hand pumps my shaft into her mouth like she's begging for my cum. I don't know how the fuck I'm supposed to resist this shit. I don't even know if I want to. I pump my hips faster, working up a steady rhythm as I make love to Tamiya's mouth. Her lips feel better than any woman I've been with. I let out a low, animal groan as she teases my barbell piercing with her tongue.

She knows exactly what the fuck she's doing.

Tamiya tightens her lips around my dick. Those soft lips make me want to cum immediately. I make another low groan as she gives me even more suction around my cock. I can't handle it. She feels too fucking good. I take control of her head and try to push my dick even deeper into this woman's mouth. She can take it and I can feel it.

There's something fucking terrifying and special about getting the best head of your life from a woman who hates your guts. As I slide deeper past those soft ass lips, the fear that she'll change her mind and fuck me up instead just gets me harder. I want to cum. I need to cum. I don't care if it's goddamn dangerous to take this woman's lips like they belong to me.

I tell myself that she's the one who pushed me to the point of being this sick in the head as I use Tamiya like every inch of her belongs to me. The sound of my tip sliding past her lip's tight suction and the tight, pleasurable sensation of her sweet ass lips around my dick only makes me feel even better than before.

I know there's something sick about the way I'm using her mouth. I just can't stop myself. Tamiya's lips are addictive and my dick is just about ready to burst. I can't think of a man on earth in this situation who could resist the temptation. Grabbing her hair, I slide all the way down her throat again and groan as the tip of my dick grazes the back of Tamiya's throat. The pleasure is too much for me to handle.

My dick stiffens and then bursts before I can warn her. Shit, I don't have any warning before I cum straight down the back of Tamiya's throat. I tilt her head back to make it easier for the cum to spill down her throat but then I just stay there and wait for my dick to empty every last drop.

The euphoria is almost too much for me to bear. Goddamn, her mouth is perfect. Even if it pains me, I have to leave her mouth. Keeping a firm grip on her head, I withdraw my dick from Tamiya's full lips, enjoying the way the skin on my shaft feels from her as I pull my dick all the way out.

She makes another gagging noise and bends forward once I release her hair to gasp for breath. I barely have any control over myself and find myself desperately gasping for breath too. Holy shit. I don't even know what I'm supposed to say to this woman, if there's anything right to say to her. I crouch down and kiss her again before I stuff my dick back in my pants.

The second I put my dick away, everything immediately feels wrong. *I'm not done with her.*

Still, Tamiya gives me a look I can only describe as hopeful from her knees. I knocked at least some of the fight out of her.

I SHOULD HAVE KNOWN the effect on her would only be temporary. Once she catches me looking at her with admiration, she wipes her mouth with the back of her hand and twists up her pretty face in an absolutely disgusted expression.

"Are you proud of yourself?" She asks bitterly, her voice dripping with pure hatred. My heart skips a beat.

"No. But I did cum in your mouth. That felt pretty good."

She responds with a disgusted and disapproving look before she says definitively, "I think I hate you more."

Heat spreads all over my cheeks and fuck, I wish this woman hadn't said that. How exactly does she expect me to respond when she already knows that I'm the furthest fucking thing from a saint.

"Is that so?" I respond, my dick getting hard for another round of action in my pants at just the slightest suggestion that Tamiya needs more than my dick in her mouth for her to feel a connection to me. She wants a connection? I'll give it to her.

She glances nervously at my crotch like she can read my mind. After the way she just sucked the life out of my dick, I shouldn't be surprised. What I don't expect is for her to start behaving like a maniac when she notices my dick moving in my pants again. It's an unconscious biological response. It's not something I can help.

"There is no way you can go again," she says in a mixture of disbelief and genuine offense.

"I'm not getting my dick near those teeth again," I say to her. The first time she sucked me off, I got lucky. Maybe she did it because of my size. Maybe I just shocked her into sucking my dick without biting me. My instincts tell me not to put my dick in her mouth when she's this feisty.

And not when I have other holes available to me.

"Good," she says. "That's a very smart idea."

"Get up. I want you on the bed."

"Excuse me?"

She doesn't budge.

.   .   .

"I made myself clear, I think."

"You slapped me and then shoved your dick in my mouth. I'm not doing a goddamn thing that you ask me to do."

"I only slapped you because you weren't listening. What else do you expect me to do?"

"When were you born? 1876? You could try talking to me."

"You're my woman. I don't need to talk to you when my hand is a hell of a lot faster."

I don't know how the fuck I always manage to say the wrong thing to this woman. She gets up off her feet and smacks me across the face. I have never witnessed anything so fucking crazy in my life. I grab her by the wrists and hold them together while Tamiya screams and then uses my restraints as an opportunity to kick me.

She doesn't even care that she's losing her balance.

"You will *not* hit me!" She screeches.

"I certainly will if you don't quiet the hell down!" I yell at her, trying to get control of this increasingly difficult woman. If I hadn't just expended all my energy spilling my seed down her throat, ensuring her obedience would be *much* simpler.

I try throwing her back against the wall and pinning her there with my hips which works to get her still, but doesn't stop her from fighting me like she's training for a match with Floyd Mayweather. I shove my hips forward to press her more tightly against the wall and those skinny little legs slam aggressively into the backs of my thighs.

Tamiya does the goddamn unthinkable. I watch her roll the ball of spit around her mouth and yell at her "don't you dare" right before she fucking dares to spit at me. Lucky for her, I dodge her nasty spit bomb and it lands on my shoulder.

She immediately knows she fucked up. Our eyes lock and her punishment becomes certain.

"Slapping your pretty fucking face was me going easy on you," I whisper, using my complete force to hold her against the wall as I slide my tongue possessively from her shoulder all the way up to her earlobe. "What put the crazy fucking idea in your head that you could spit on me?"

I run my tongue back down the way it came, stopping at her neck in a spot where I know I can hurt her. Easily. I run my tongue over the exact spot a few times until she makes a strangled sound. "Shhhh," I whisper as I stroke her hair. "Screaming won't help you. I'm still going to fuck the fight out of you. This will be much easier if you're quiet, baby. Much much easier." Then I bite her. Hard. Tamiya screams, but I follow up my bite by pressing a hand to her mouth to silence it.

She squirms beneath me as I slowly release the flesh on her neck from my desperate lips and teeth. I slide my hand up her chest and all the way up her neck, fighting the temptation to wrap my hands around Tamiya's sexy black throat and really lose myself with her. I keep my hands balanced precariously around her neck, using just the threat of squeezing her to keep her still.

For once, something works with her the first time I try it. Once I get her still enough to manage. I kiss her on the cheek, which provokes an irritated, strangled noise from her throat. This woman. I expect to hear nothing but soft, pleasurable moans from her. I tighten my grasp just enough to scare her more and force Tamiya's eyes to gaze directly into mine.

"Why do you have such a problem with me fucking you?" I whisper. "Do you hate me that fucking badly?"

"Yes," she says. "I don't care if you had a good reason. You're still a goddamn killer."

Her hatred gets me so fucking hard for her. I hate it.

"I might be a killer, but I bet I get your pussy wet."

Chapter Sixteen
Tamiya

This man has to be the most disrespectful man I have ever met. I don't see the point in continuing to waste my energy fighting his gigantic, upsettingly muscular body when it doesn't work. He's a brute and using physical force to stop him from pinning me against the wall and taking my dignity has done absolutely nothing to discourage him so far. My face still stings too and I don't want him to smack it again. It's bad enough that the enormous sociopath hit me so hard it *burns* for the crime of disobeying him, and he doesn't appear to think it's a big problem.

Like I said, there is something deeply wrong with him. Spitting on him again will only make him more upset and I can tell from the look on his face that he could snap my neck in an instant and without any remorse. As much as I want to be a fearless badass, I'm not stupid. You don't poke a sleeping bear. You try to get out of its clutches and then you *run like hell.*

Except this bear is very much awake and I'm doing a shitty job of staying out of his clutches. Reaper has me exactly where he wants me. I hope he doesn't become upset when I refuse to answer that completely inappropriate comment he just made. I squirm because of

Reaper's spit drying on my neck, but his spit on my neck is the *only* wet part of me.

There is nothing arousing about having a crude giant spread your legs and press you up against a wall with his dick moving around in his pants against your crotch like a loose anaconda. My angry glare should tell him exactly how I feel about his comment, but Reaper pretends not to understand what I mean, which just pisses me off even more.

"Come on," he whispers, refusing to let me go. "You're telling me that if I feel your pretty pussy lips, they won't be wet as fuck?"

"Don't touch me," I hiss with all the hatred I can muster. Maybe I can scare him into thinking I'll fight too much. At this point, I'll try anything. He's so close to me, I can smell him and I wish Reaper's smell made me nauseous instead of confusing the fuck out of my senses. He has no right to smell like freshly cut grass and a Midwestern summer. *He's disgusting.*

And his hands don't stop roaming all over me as he pins me to the wall. Reaper has big hands, the perfect mixture of strong and dangerous. I can't break free from his grasp or stop myself from reacting as his hands roam all over my hips and Reaper presses his crotch into me, revealing that he is very much *hard* and aroused by me. I don't know how he can get aroused again considering he just came in my mouth.

I can still taste him, a sugary sweet flavor at the back of my throat. I can't produce enough spit to wash him away yet and then Reaper makes it worse by kissing me and touching my pussy, ignoring my commands for him not to touch me. The way he smacked me across the face told me everything I needed to know about how this dangerous man thinks. I grunt with frustration as he invades my privacy, his rough hands eagerly reaching past my underwear as I continue to fight him.

"Goddamn," he whispers. "You're even more wet than I thought."

I WANT TO DESTROY HIM, but I am entirely beneath his control and judging by the look on his face and the way his hardness grows in his crotch, he enjoys this. His fingers spread my lower lips apart and he stops being so goddamn rough for a minute as he rubs the length of my slit slowly and then lands on my hardened nub with excitement. His dick throbs in his pants as Reaper rubs my clit in a slow, smooth circle.

I bite my lower lip to stop him from drawing a moan out of me. I refuse to give in. But Reaper keeps moving his finger over my clit and he touches me with such a smooth, perfect touch that my eyes flutter closed. I don't notice what happens at first as my eyes shut and I give in to those big country boy hands pleasuring me between my legs. *Oh God...* I lose control of myself, if I ever even had it.

Once I moan loudly, my back arches inadvertently to meet Reaper's hands. My lack of control stuns me into awareness and I gasp as my eyes snap open only for Reaper to plant his lips to my neck and kiss me hard as he continues massaging my pussy with his hands.

"You keep getting wetter, baby. Just let it happen."

My stomach throbs. I tell myself he isn't turning me on and what I'm really feeling for him is nothing but outright disgust. His hands invade me in a much worse way as he finds my entrance and slides a finger inside me. I don't know why my disgusted scream sounds like a moan of pleasure, but it makes the situation so much worse as Reaper sucks on my neck and thrusts his fingers all the way inside me. The way I moan when Reaper's fingers plunge between my folds feels humiliating, but I can't stop myself.

He grunts and works them inside me deeper as his thumb massages my clit. Pressure builds between my legs, approaching an unfair climax. I try to beg him to stop but all that comes out of my mouth is one pathetic word... "Please..."

Reaper interprets it the way he wants to and slides both fingers inside me deeper. The way I cry out only encourages him to groan, "Fuck..." with absolute lust in his voice. I hate feeling him this close to me and I especially hate the effect his fingers have between my legs. Pressure builds around his fingers as my entrance tightens and plea-sure pulses through my core. I try to push Reaper off me but all I end up doing is bucking my hips and taking his fingers deeper as he massages my clit.

Damn. He feels so fucking good. I suppress the thought and kick

Reaper again in an effort to get him to peel himself away from me. It doesn't work. He kisses my neck harder, sucking on my flesh so hard, I can tell from the intense throbbing that he kissed me hard enough to leave a mark even on skin as dark as mine...

"Monster..." I gasp, which is the closest thing to a protest that has come out of my mouth despite my powerful inner desire to get Reaper away from me.

"You're wet," he whispers. "If giving you what you want makes me a monster, that's what I'll be..."

I fight him with unmistakable fury as he removes my clothes. He has to pin me to the wall to stop me from kicking and scratching at him, so he shouldn't be surprised when I try to bite him as he kisses my neck. My back aches from the cold as he presses me against the wall, forcing me to push myself forward and use his body for warmth just to escape the cold.

Naturally, he interprets this as genuine interest in the way he's touching me and he strokes the length of my body with gentleness that I would describe as loving in any other circumstance. He doesn't care that I'm wriggling away from him, he continues exploring my body with deep, slow fascination. His fingers stop at my nipples and I glare at him as he pinches them and then rolls them slowly, keeping steady eye contact with me as he tortures me. I couldn't make my displeasure more apparent on my face, but Reaper refuses to turn his gaze away.

His dick jerks again in his pants and it occurs to me that the more I hate him, the more aroused he gets from having me naked, pressed up against the wall beneath his grasp and completely underneath his control. He is fucking crazy. Reaper maintains his twisted eye contact with me as he moves from teasing one nipple to the other with his fingers. Then he uses his tongue on me. I try to move away from him, but Reaper grabs my tits possessively and sucks on my nipples until the noise that comes out of my mouth sounds downright approving of his aggressive tongue.

I gasp for breath as I desperately try to shove his head away. The last thing I want is to cum from the way his tongue teases my nipples. Reaper enjoys my movements far too much and I almost regret stopping him when he frees his dick again and immediately presses the pierced, bare head of his dick against my entrance.

To my complete humiliation, I am already soaked from his aggressive fingers but that doesn't mean I want to feel a giant pierced dick sliding all the way inside me. Taking Reaper's dick in my mouth was bad enough. My heart races like a hare hiding from a fox with every knowledge that hiding from that type of predator is entirely futile.

"What's wrong?" he whispers when he tries to kiss me on the lips and I turn my face away from him. He knows exactly what's wrong. He presses his bare dick against my lower lips and runs it slowly along the length of my slit, both teasing and threatening me with the sudden invasion. I grunt and press my back against the wall as if I could sink through it to get away from him.

He becomes immediately aggressive again, glaring at me and pressing the cold gold piercing against my entrance. He could take me in one swift motion and he wants me to know it. A cruel smirk sneaks across his face when he sees how much his torture scares me. My heart pumps more adrenaline through me, but it doesn't help. I'm still frozen against the wall with Reaper's dick ready to impale me in place.

"It's just a little dick, sweetheart. Nothing for you to be afraid of."

There is nothing little about Reaper's dick. My jaw still hurts from trying to take him down my throat. His smirk turns into a blatant grin as he slides the head past my lips just enough to stretch me out and prepare me for the inevitable invasion. The first push freezes me in place and Reaper becomes downright giddy with excitement. There is something wrong with this man.

He holds me in place, keeping his dick balanced in position as he lavishes kisses on my neck. I turn my head to avoid him every time he tries to kiss me on the lips. That man is fucking crazy if he thinks I'm letting him kiss my lips. The more I fight off Reaper's efforts to kiss my lips after he kisses my neck and collar bone, the more frustrated he becomes. He shoves another inch inside me just when I think I turned him off trying to kiss me.

I freeze again just long enough for him to plant a gentle kiss on my lips. I hate how gently he kisses me as I remain frozen beneath him and still vulnerable to his touch and torture, whichever he chooses.

"Let me kiss you or I'll make my piercing touch the back of your pussy before you can even scream..."

He doesn't wait for a response. Reaper roughly grabs my cheeks and forces a less than gentle kiss on me. I try to bite his lower lip, but this only turns him on and makes him kiss me harder. I whimper as he parts my lips with his tongue and then I don't know what happens next to change things between us. Our fighting with our lips turns into real kissing and I stop trying to bite him. I don't even scratch at him when he releases my hands from his grasp.

What the hell is happening? He doesn't give me time to think because he changes the pace of our kiss from aggressive and violent to slow and passionate. My eyes are closed, so I can lose myself in the physical sensations and pretend the man kissing me like this isn't a cold blooded murderer.

He's not just any murderer. He killed Damara. He admitted it. He isn't sorry. Clearly whatever went down left him with a clear conscience. So either he has no conscience or he's lying about everything. He doesn't kiss me like a liar. Reaper's kisses feel inappropriately honest. Like the feelings he has confuse him as much as they confuse me.

At exactly the wrong time, he slides inside me another inch, forcing my pussy to spread around all of his head and the large barbell piercing just beneath it. The loud moan that spills out of my mouth fills me with embarrassment. I can't hide from him like this. Not naked. Not with his dick inside me. He doesn't have to get it all the way in for him to see all my vulnerabilities.

"You get me so fucking hard, baby," he whispers. "You don't know what you do to me. You turn me into a goddamn animal."

He slides into me another inch, forcing the large balls of the barbell to massage my inner walls, sending forbidden shudders of pleasure emanating through my body. I try not to sound completely weak for him, but I can't stop myself from moaning anymore. The build-up of pleasure is far too intense. The sound I make encourages him to thrust into me deeper.

I can't control myself with that much dick inside me. Reaper is huge and the balls at the end of the barbells only add to the intense feeling of having a dick that big inside me. The sound that I make is desperate, and hearing myself out loud makes my heart jump because I sound so goddamn needy for him.

Maybe it will feel better if I close my eyes again.

Chapter Seventeen
Reaper

Sliding into Tamiya's pretty pussy is the most perfect feeling in the world. I feel like I've never fucked before. Holy shit. I push my dick all the way inside her and cup her perfect ass in one hand as I feel her soft, tight pussy engulfing my dick. I groan like a fucking animal as I bury my dick inside her.

There can't be any better feeling than getting inside some deliciously soft, sopping wet pussy that's spread open just for you. Just because you touched her the right way. If I wasn't so goddamn impatient to feel Tamiya wrapped around my dick, I would have put my tongue so deep in her pussy I'd taste her back walls. We'll have plenty of time for that.

"You feel so fucking good," I whisper, teasing her neck with my hot breath as I pump into her slowly. "I just want to feel that tight pussy so bad..."

Her pussy gushes when I say that, but she tightens her lips up and gives me the most cruel look, as if she can truly fight her body's reaction to me. It's not something she can control. Her sweet ass pussy likes feeling my dick all the way inside her. I withdraw slowly and pick up a steady rhythm fucking Tamiya against the wall.

I lose myself in her tightness and I know it won't take me long to cum, so I focus on drawing an orgasm out of her. *Bonding her to me.* She gets so fucking wet as I pound her against the wall that I know it won't take long. I push her hair out of the way and kiss her neck as I pump into her slowly. When Tamiya stops trying to hide her moans of pleasure, I know I'm close to getting her over the edge.

Fucking her slowly against the wall and massaging her clit brings her even closer. I bite down on her neck, losing myself in how fucking good she smells and tastes. That brings her to a finish. Tamiya lets out an uncontrolled moan and I feel her pussy clenching around my dick and nearly drawing me to my own finish.

In case cumming brings her to her senses, I wait for Tamiya's pussy to stop squeezing my dick as it pulses in pleasure and then I pin her hands over her head and hold her still so I can take the rest of my pleasure from her tight ass pussy. *Damn, she must be the best I've ever had.*

My dick stiffens inside her and I want to look into her pretty eyes as I finish, so I push myself all the way inside Tamiya and draw her gaze to mine. She looks at me and seems to realize what's about to happen. Her face contorts in horror as I withdraw slowly and then thrust inside her one last time, burying my dick in her pussy all the way to the hilt as I finish inside her.

She cries out in pleasure as I surprise her with the biggest eruption I think I've ever felt.

"Your pussy feels so good," I whisper as I bite her neck and push myself in all the way, making sure my sperm sinks into every inch of her folded inner walls. My heart pounds a million miles a minute and I don't know if I will ever feel control of myself around this woman.

I already want to cum inside her again.

"Fuck, you feel so good," I groan.

Tamiya replies in a horrified voice. "You came inside me…"

"Yes, baby…"

I slowly release her hands and move them to her hips. I don't want to let her go. She grunts and shoves hard against my chest. There is something seriously wrong with this woman. This was beautiful. And done for what God intended. Procreation.

"Are you crazy?!" she shrieks, kicking at me again and giving me more of the attitude I thought I just fucked out of her. I pin her hands above her head again and shove my dick inside her while it goes soft in an effort to remind her of the fun we just had. It doesn't work.

I kiss her and instead of responding like a normal human woman, she bites my fucking lip.

"Fuck," I cuss unwillingly and pull away from her as blood pools in my lower lip. What the fuck was that for? Of all the times to bite the fuck out of me, she chooses this moment right after our mutual satisfaction.

When I give her an angry look, she scowls right back. I keep her pinned to the wall with my hips as I use my hands to touch my bloody lip and assess the damage. I'm in too much immediate pain to think of the risk I'm taking letting this harpy have her hands free.

"Fuck you," Tamiya says pointedly. She will say *anything* to hurt me.

"I'm still inside you..."

I don't mean for my voice to sound like a growl, but this goddamn woman is testing me. My lip keeps getting fatter and there is enough blood on my fingers for me to question if I need stitches. What the fuck is wrong with this woman?

"I don't care," she snarls. "You had no right to do that. I could get pregnant."

The look of hatred plastered on her face prompts my next answer. "Good. I hope I get your skinny ass pregnant. Maybe then you'll put on some weight and give me something to grab onto."

She makes a sound halfway between a sigh and a gasp before slapping me hard across the face. I see it coming just in time so she hits me, but I don't flinch. She watches my expression change and yelps before I even get to punishing her ass properly. I grab her scrawny ass hands and pin them over her head with one hand again before withdrawing my dick from Tamiya's dripping pussy and grabbing onto her legs with my other hand. I keep having to pin this woman down...

She starts screeching like she didn't bring this on herself.

"Reaper! Let me go!" she screams. "Let me go!"

"My name is Gideon," I tell her. "You will call me Gideon from now on."

"FUCK YOU! I DON'T CARE ABOUT YOUR FUCKING NAME."

All the screaming in the world won't stop me from taking swift and easy control over this crazy woman's body. I drag her to the bedroom and toss her ass onto the bed.

I have finally lost my goddamn patience with Tamiya's defiance. Enough fucking fighting. When I toss her onto the bed, she attempts to crawl away from me dramatically. With her skinny ass in the air, all I can see are her dark brown thighs spreading lewdly as she makes an effort to crawl away and my cum spilling out of her pussy. I need to take her again.

I grab Tamiya's legs and drag her to the edge of the bed on all fours. She clutches the bedsheets to stop me from dragging her all the way off, but I had no intentions of getting her all the way in the air again. I don't need to do all of that for my intentions.

I'm so hard that I nearly burst at the sight of her ass in the air, glimpses of her pussy flashing as she struggles against me pulling her towards me. I hold my dick in one hand while I hold Tamiya's waist in the other and draw her crotch nearer to mine. She understands my intentions and fights them fiercely in the most foolish way possible.

My hand tightens forcefully around her waist as she arches her hips and slams back into me. My tongue hangs dry in my mouth as perspiration builds at the corners of my forehead. Goddamn. I have never had to work this hard for a woman in my life and no matter what happens, I only want her more and more.

Tamiya makes an ungodly noise as I press the tip of my dick against her entrance again. She was so fucking wet already but now she has my cum dribbling out of her tight ass pussy again and some-thing about those skinny legs framing those dark brown lips makes me lose my mind. I know I should be careful with her. She's so damn small. So damn tight.

But there's something dark and dangerous that takes over me, espe-cially when sweat builds up on her slim waist as I hold onto it and her pussy gushes another explosion of my cum as she screams in protest. I shove the first two inches inside her, feeling how tight she is around my dick and the intense pleasure of having her sweet ass pussy massaging my barbell piercing.

Tamiya can't help herself. Her protest turns into a moan. Her body wriggles in my grasp like she's trying to get away and I use both hands to grab onto her hips now that I have enough of my dick inside her to keep her still so I can use her sweet ass pussy for my pleasure.

She tries to kick me, but it does nothing to deter me from my mission. Holding on to her even tighter, I slide my dick halfway inside and wait for Tamiya's predictable response. The sexiest moan escapes her lips followed by her pussy clamping down on my dick like a vice, massaging my growing staff with tight, textured inner walls that feel like fucking heaven.

I want to cum inside her again. I can already tell I won't last long. Gripping her like she belongs to me, like she's already my old lady, I take her hard from behind without any concern for her pleasure. I feel her reach release once or maybe twice but I wouldn't care either way if she came or not. My only purpose for fucking Tamiya on the bed like this is my pleasure. This crazed creature's pleasure is not my concern.

I hear her whimper for mercy just once before I finish inside her. There's nothing that could stop me from taking what I want. From having her. When I finish inside her, she cries out and tries to wriggle away, which I can't allow to happen. I wrap my arms around her, pressing my forearm to her tits as I hold her skinny ass body against mine. She trembles like a deer with buckshot in its lungs. I kiss her neck and she moans. Or cries out. I can't tell which.

"Your pussy feels so fucking good," I whisper. She wriggles again. More defiance. I thrust into her one more time, pushing my hips all the way forward until she can feel the full length of my dick buried inside her.

"This is what's going to happen to you every night you're with me, baby. So get used to it and stop fucking fighting. The two of us are better off with a lot less fighting and a lot more of this."

She tries to bite my forearm, but I just laugh as I draw her closer to me and pull my dick out of her. Her little teeth sink into my forearm and I just let her have her way with me if that's what she wants. *Bite me all you want, baby. I'm not letting you go...*

CHAPTER EIGHTEEN
TAMIYA

I don't know why I let Reaper drag me under the covers, or why I let him cuddle with me the entire night. Technically, I could wait for him to fall asleep and then rip his balls off. I could search for a gun, find some ammo and put us both out of our misery. But I don't. I still hate him. I still want him dead… But I just can't do it.

It's not the sex. It's just… the wrong time.

FOR THE NEXT TWO WEEKS, I can't seem to stumble on the right time to end Reaper's life. Two full weeks. I tell myself that the time isn't right, but you don't have to be Lee Harvey Oswald to kill a man, despite what people think. Murderers are more often than not blunt instruments, not super geniuses.

Maybe I'm just not a killer. *But Gideon is a killer.* And that scares the fuck out of me.

For the entire two weeks, Reaper seems oblivious to my conflicting feelings. I shouldn't be surprised that he doesn't care. As long as he gets his dick wet and gets time to work on that stupid bike outside, nothing appears to concern him. I tell myself that what I'm doing is observation, like I would do for Rebecca's P.I. company. So obviously, I can't kill Reaper right away.

Observing him is more boring than you would expect for an outlaw murderer. I fantasized so many times about what it would be like to meet Damara's killer. I could have never anticipated Reaper. Or I guess I'm calling him Gideon now. He gets offended when I call him Reaper out loud because we're "too close for that now".

I beg to differ. I feel no closer to this violent brute than I did when Southpaw first dragged me in here. Not murdering someone is different from feeling close to them.

Reaper doesn't exactly expect breakfast on the table every morning but after five days of observation, I learned that he will only eat McDonald's if I don't cook for him. It's sickening to watch, honestly. He picks around the edges of four to five different sandwiches, calls them disgusting and then goes outside to hit his vape and work on his bike. The first time I make him eggs and French Toast, he acts like I built the Taj Mahal out of napkins.

"It's just breakfast. Get better ingredients and I'll cook."

I'm not dumb enough to ask for permission to go to the grocery store. And anyway, I'm trying to kill this man. I don't want him suddenly taking off on his bike to the Midwest or something. Luckily, Gideon agrees and he does a good job of shopping when I send him off with my list of ingredients.

Again, if I don't cook lunch, he doesn't eat until dinner, so I end up cooking that too. The housekeeping I don't worry about, or rather, I'm the problem. Gideon has an Army Ranger's unrealistic standards for cleanliness and hygiene. What the fuck are hospital corners, white boy? I'm sleeping on the bed, not dying in it.

I might not get much longer past two weeks without learning his way of making the bed because Gideon still hasn't learned how to handle his temper and perfectionism without physical discipline. He never smacks me across the face like he did before, but in the bedroom he feels completely justified in taking out his anger on my ass cheeks.

Bastard.

The evenings are the worst times between us because we engage in the dance of will we sleep together or not. And we always end up sleeping together. The worst part of it is after the first week... he wasn't always the one who started it.

I always like him to think he's the one who starts it. But the past three times, I have lost myself in some unhinged mixture of desperation and desire for him. It's not like I don't have a brain. It's just... He makes me cum. And I spend all day cooking for him, hanging out around the house, and doing absolutely nothing other than watching TV.

The body has a natural craving for excitement and when Reaper comes back home from working on the bike or wherever the hell he goes that makes him come back all red and sunburned, I can't help but feel a physical flutter between my legs.

He's still a monster. I understand that. But just because he's a monster doesn't mean he doesn't feel like a goddamn blessing when he slides next to me in bed. He wraps his muscular arms around me and pulls me close to him, holding me forcefully against him as he strips me with often violent urgency.

He doesn't care if I'm ready by the time he enters me. He knows I'll get ready for him. That my body wants him before my mind does. I can't ever predict if he's going to be rough or gentle and my body enjoys the uncertainty as he kisses me and touches me before he fucks me slowly into the bed or pounds me like its our last time together.

I turn off the logical part of my brain and just feel him. His body is so goddamn perfect. Every inch of him is covered in well-formed, lean muscles. He smells delicious, especially when he comes home covered in a thin layer of sweat. The way his body feels when his sweaty clothes stick to his abs turns me into a dripping mess.

I'm glad that it's just the two of us. And I don't have to hide the tortured, fucked up way he can bring all this pleasure out of me... while being a killer. The worst kind of killer, too. A man who killed someone in my own family.

. . .

I'm already in deep spiritual trouble for fucking this man, but I'm definitely going to hell for enjoying it.

Every day I tell myself I'm going to stop and shove him off of me, really fight him for my life, but I end up taking his dick all the way inside me and feeling that hoop piercing scrape my back walls.

This is how I know he's a demon. Because only a demon could kill someone I love and still get me in his bed to give me the best dick I have ever had in my life.

The only benefit my observation yields is that I notice Gideon coming home *extremely* early after he leaves for his usual mysterious 2 p.m. bike ride. He normally doesn't come back until 5:30 p.m., when I start cooking dinner. Today, he's back at 2:30 p.m. and he's out of breath when the door swings open.

"I need your ass to pack a bag," he says, barely looking at me as he drops some giant duffel bag on his living room couch. "We gotta head to Illinois."

I never gave much thought to what the hell was going to happen next, honestly. I keep telling myself that I'm going to kill Gideon eventually, but I can just keep going on this strange routine we have without giving it a second thought. Packing a bag and leaving forces me to consider something I intentionally pushed out of my mind.

The future.

"I'm not going anywhere," I say defiantly, staring at a news story about teenagers arrested for kidnapping a mute swan from a local pond on television, barely looking up now that Gideon revealed the reason for his craziness. How does he think we're going to get to Illinois?

He doesn't like my response because he stops moving and tries to act all serious.

"Yes, you are. I need you."

"For what?"

I assume he's going to say sex.

"Because. You're basically a fucking cop. Now get your ass off the couch."

"I don't like your tone. I spent all morning scrubbing your damn tub. I have every right to watch my stories."

"You are just like my m–

"What?"

"Nothing," he huffs. "Get off the couch and let's go. I'll explain when we stop for gas. We're already behind, but I can catch up if you hurry."

"I'm not doing shit unless you tell me why."

"You are the worst fucking thing to ever happen to me," Gideon snaps before stalking off to his bedroom.

"What the hell did you just say to me, white boy?"

I hop off the couch and storm after him. Gideon thinks because he throws hands that he can talk to me with his slick ass mouth and I won't get his Caucasian ass all the way together. Once I'm in his bedroom, he smirks victoriously. That motherfucker…

"Good. Get some clothes and let's get going."

"I'm the worst thing to ever happen to you?"

His brown eyes flicker angrily to mine. "Yes. Because I could go to prison if you run your goddamn mouth."

"Why would I send you to prison? I'm going to send you to your grave before you see the inside of a prison cell."

We don't break eye contact. My pussy throbs. I hate it here. You are not supposed to feel hatred for your worst enemy in your pussy. I have enough self-awareness to know that everything that happens between me and Gideon is completely wrong. I don't know why he has this effect on my body.

"Right," he says. "You can kill me after our job in Illinois."

"I'm not going to be a part of some criminal enterprise," I tell him. "Like you said, I'm basically a cop."

"Who said anything about a criminal enterprise?" Gideon says. "Having your ass in prison would be very inconvenient for me. Neither of us want my mom being the one to keep an eye on you."

"Your mom is in prison?"

I suspected Gideon had something deeply wrong with him, but now I'm painting the portrait of his past trauma with the narrative enthusiasm of a *True Crime* podcaster. He turned to murder and a life outside the law because he lacked a mother's touch. Makes sense.

"Yes," he says, getting nervous at the mention of her. "I talk to her every day."

"I've never heard you talk to her."

"Our conversations are private. Can you hurry your ass up?"

"You still haven't told me what we're doing."

"Southpaw got himself in some gambling trouble. If we don't get him out of it, his old lady might file for divorce."

"How the hell do you expect me to help?"

"Can you do what you're told before I stuff you in the trunk and drive you there?"

THE ONLY TRUNK around here is the trunk of the 1977 Cadillac he has parked out front. I don't think that vintage car even works, but Gideon doesn't have the mental stability not to follow through on a sadistic impulse once it enters his twisted mind.

"I'll do it if you promise me something."

"WHAT?" he says with frustration."

"A pregnancy test."

"You are so goddamned dramatic."

"Fine. I'll stay then."

"Get your ass ready," he says. "I'll get you the fucking test. But you're not pregnant. So get that notion out of your head."

Is this man stupid? We have been fucking raw for two weeks straight. He has to understand there's at least a chance he ruined both our lives with his insane sexual appetite. Maybe I should have asked for more, but this is the first thing I've tried asking for, so I didn't want to aim too high. I keep threatening to end this man's life so... I don't expect him to be generous.

Considering I haven't left the house since I got here, I don't have too much fight in me when it comes to Gideon's plans to drive out to Illinois. I'm not thrilled about getting on the back of his bike, but I would rather ride on the back of the bike than in the trunk.

I pack a duffel bag with what I imagine I might need for three days. Gideon hasn't shared even the slightest relevant detail with me, so I'll make it his problem if I end up needing extra conditioner for our road trip. He barges into my room before I'm done packing. I don't even know why I bother calling it 'my' room since I spend every night beneath Gideon.

"Ready?"

"Have you ever met a woman who could get ready that fast?" I grumble. "But yes. I'm used to life on the road."

"Excited for the bike?"

He grins with genuine enthusiasm which makes me feel a little for how little I look forward to straddling his death trap.

"No. Everyone who rides has lost about half their friends to those things. I have never had the slightest bit of interest."

"Coward."

"Excuse me?"

"You heard me," he says. "Don't tell me an adrenaline junkie like you is afraid of dying?"

"Who said I was afraid of dying?"

"Exactly," he says. "Just put your helmet on and learn to like it."

"I will never learn to like it."

. . .

HE MAKES A FRUSTRATED SOUND, the perfect mixture of disbelief and outrage, like no sane person could dare question the majesty of his dangerous hobby. I follow Gideon outside. He doesn't let me carry my bag. Once we're outside, I see his gleaming motorcycle, ready to kill us both.

Gideon packs away our duffel bags and my heart rate gets faster the closer I get to actually having to sit on the back of that thing. My body keeps telling me to run in the opposite direction, a fairly typical response to most activities involving Gideon.

CHAPTER NINETEEN
REAPER

Half the reason I don't give Tamiya any details about why the fuck the boss has me flying like a bat out of hell towards Illinois is because I don't have all the details. All I know is that Hawk is in Santa Fe with Juliette involved in a 'major situation', Steel is headed back out west from some deal he was handling out in Boston with some Irish Catholic asshole who owns a strip club, and I'm the closest and fastest rider to Southpaw's family home.

Southpaw fucked up gambling. That's the other side of the story, but there ain't anything new under the sun about that. The man has never met a game or situation he couldn't place a bet on. He was that way since he was young. Wired wrong.

Since he met Anna, he hasn't had one screw up or if he has, none of them have been as big as this one. It's just a damn miracle I get Tamiya on the back of the bike with as little fussing as she puts forward. I expected a hell of a lot worse from her since she conducted an entire investigation before packing her damn duffel bag.

I think it's her pride more than anything that stops her from making a scene when I get on the bike and gesture for her to hop on the back so she can hold onto me. I can feel her shaking a little bit as she hangs on. Nothing I feed her and none of her cooking makes her gain any weight.

Maybe I'm keeping her far too busy in the bedroom or something, because I'm half-worried she's so thin that a strong wind will send her ass flying off the bike. The Harley roars to life and her thighs rub against mine as she shifts her crotch forward and clings to me tightly. We haven't even started moving yet but judging by the force of her arms wrapping around me, Tamiya is already scared as shit.

I'll try to go easy on her. But considering the way this woman tortures me and her constant threats to kill me... I also want to remind her that her life is entirely in my hands until we get to Illinois. Possibly for the rest of her life if I find a way to get her to stop threatening to end my life.

Since the move to the new clubhouse, I haven't had much occasion to drive out East. It's been an especially long time since I have seen Southpaw's Old Lady. Anna was a nurse before she met her husband. Tamiya appears to have crawled directly out of the pits of hell. I don't know why Southpaw thinks her talents could help him out East.

It doesn't take a private investigator to solve a gambling problem. Just stop fucking gambling.

TAMIYA SETTLES into her position behind me after the first ninety minutes, which is far less time than I imagined it would take her considering her hesitation on the bike. Once we get a few hours away from Tucumcari, we end up low on fuel and need to stop. It'll be the perfect chance to check in with Southpaw, see if I need backup, and check on how Tamiya has been handling the ride.

Far in the distance on the old Route 66 highway headed back easy, I spot the large familiar red sign of the Flying J. Nobody who works there asks any questions. When I veer off the highway, Tamiya clutches me even more desperately. I slow down as we take a right turn and stop right in front of the first empty pump I see. She barely waits for me to stop the bike before jumping off.

Tamiya takes her helmet off and shakes her hair out, doing her very best not to seem terrified out of her fucking mind. I don't mind her all scared and jumpy. I grin as I take my own helmet off and dismount.

"We need gas. Go get yourself something to eat."

I reach into my pocket for some cash and hand Tamiya a couple fifty dollar bills. She looks at them with disgust without taking them and then shifts her persistently unhappy glare back to me.

"I hate you, Gideon. I seriously hate you."

"What the fuck is the problem now?"

"Didn't you hear me screaming at you to stop? I've had to pee for the past hour."

"Then get the fuck inside and take a piss. Stop screaming at me."

Her nostrils flare and she snatches the money, shoving her helmet into my chest before turning around and storming off. This woman...

I consider running off behind Tamiya right away, but I really need to get some gas in this bike. I check my phone, but don't have any messages from Southpaw. Just one message from Ruger's stupid ass.

RUGER: U in Mexico?

WHY THE FUCK would I be in Mexico? I ignore his text message and send one to Southpaw instead.

ME: What do we need the PI for? Tamiya asking questions.

I TRUST she's not stupid enough to run away in the middle of nowhere, although she might be enough of a daredevil to attempt hitchhiking. It wouldn't be hard to set up a biker blockade anywhere along this highway and stop her or anyone who had the misfortune of picking her ass up. I can't leave Tamiya alone this long without freaking out. Luckily, the bike doesn't take long to fill up.

.   .   .

I RUSH after her into the Flying J and I don't know why I'm surprised that Tamiya has snacks and some random items at the register instead of a shotgun aimed directly at my head. She doesn't look towards the door as I enter and she barely acknowledges me until I stand right behind her at the register.

I recognize the girl behind the register and it's possible she recognizes me, but she doesn't make eye contact with me, just Tamiya.

"That'll be $28.15."

She breaks a fifty. I put my arm around Tamiya's shoulders when I notice what she has sprinkled amongst her snacks and random items.

"Is that a pregnancy test?" I ask her.

"No. It's an AR-15."

The woman behind the counter doesn't break her stern expression. Doesn't surprise me. Certain men are strict about how their Old Lady interacts with other men and I have every ounce of respect for how a man chooses to run his household. My palm squeezes around Tamiya's shoulder, but she doesn't budge.

"Is that really necessary right now?"

"I told you, I have to pee."

"You still haven't done that?"

Tamiya's nostrils flare out and her voice gets aggressive and tight again. "I was hungry too, Reaper. You dragged my ass out of the house without enough time for me to make a sandwich."

I don't bother pointing out that she would have had time to make a sandwich if she wasn't pestering my ass with unnecessary questions. Once she checks out, Tamiya walks towards the bathroom in the back. I follow her, like any sane man would. She glances over her shoulder and glares at me.

"What the hell do you think you're doing?"

"You're taking a pregnancy test. I want to know the answer."

"I'm not pissing in front of you," Tamiya says, stopping in front of the door. I block her body with mine.

"Either you piss yourself out here right now or you push that door open and let me come in with you."

If Tamiya's looks could kill, I would have been dead a long time ago so her sassy fucking expressions don't bother me. She looks like she wants to bite me but she has to piss so damn badly that she gives in, opens the door and I follow this crazy fucking woman into the Flying J bathroom.

I close the door behind me, allowing the scent of purple Fabuloso and bleach to hit me like a Harley that veered off the highway. Tamiya turns around to shove me the second I shut the door.

"That woman is going to knock on the door and you are going to go to jail."

"For what? Fucking my woman in a gas station bathroom?"

"Turn around," she snaps, ignoring my comment about fucking her in the bathroom, which isn't a half bad idea, even if we don't have much space. Fuck, not having much space is half the fun.

"I don't think so."

"Fine," she says. "If you want to be a nasty ass freak, I can't stop you."

Damn straight. Tamiya turns around and ignores me as she gets the pregnancy test open. She elbows me hard as fuck when I edge closer to her in an effort to read the instructions.

"What the fuck is your problem?" I grunt, rubbing the part of my ribs she tried to beat up.

"If I'm pregnant, it would not be a moment for celebration. It would be the worst day of both our lives."

"Why? 'Cause we're not married? I know a preacher who could handle that part for us quickly."

I wrap my arms around Tamiya's waist since she's all distracted with the pregnancy test, but that proves to be another mistake. She elbows me even harder.

"Back off."

She tosses the instructions into the bathroom sink and then takes a couple steps over to the surprisingly clean toilet. They run a tight ship. Tamiya glares at me as she strips off her black leggings. I get an instant hard on when she exposes her skinny brown thighs. My dick jumps in my pants when I look at her in just her underwear.

"Stop staring," she says. "What normal person can take a piss with someone staring at them?"

"Calm down. It's just taking a piss."

Tamiya holds the pregnancy test with one hand and uses her other to scoot out of her underwear while doing her very best not to reveal the pussy I spend every night tasting. The woman is crazy as fuck. She squats over the toilet and I hear her stream hit the bowl.

I don't know why but I can't stop watching her and seeing her piss gets me so fucking hard it hurts. Tamiya stops looking at me when she sticks the pregnancy test between her legs, stopping her stream for a few seconds to get it soaked. She finishes up with a disgusted look on her face. I snatch the pregnancy test from her before she knows what hit her and cap it.

Tamiya's disgusted grunts don't bother me. She pulls her panties and leggings up and then stands to her very puny height.

"Your hands are covered in my pee, weirdo. Put that on the counter and wash them. We have to wait three minutes."

"You gotta wash your hands too, dirty girl. You first."

She wrinkles her nose disapprovingly because I called her 'dirty girl', but there is no fucking way she doesn't like it. Tamiya scoots her ass in front of me to get to the sink. She has to brush past my dick to get in front of me and stick her hands under the stream of water. My instinct is to press her into the sink and force her to feel just how fucking hard she gets me.

Three minutes. That is not enough time to play with my dirty girl's pussy.

Chapter Twenty
Tamiya

Gideon's scent didn't take long to overpower the scent of cleaner and bleach that fills the Flying J bathroom. I don't know what makes me more nervous now -- the pregnancy test or his dick poking into my ass. Gideon leans forward as he washes our hands together in the sink and he kisses my neck. Fuck, he is definitely more dangerous right now.

"Three minutes is not enough time," I say to Gideon. My traitorous voice comes out as a whisper. This is not the time for my sultry Meg Thee Stallion persona to come out. I need to sound unsexy.

"I could be about to ruin your life with the financial responsibility of a baby."

Gideon chuckles and kisses my neck harder. "What kind of dumb motherfucker is afraid of paying for his own kid? I don't mind. I'll give you four babies."

No. That is not the response I wanted him to have. I'm trying to inspire Gideon to think of the consequences, which should slow him down, not encourage him to have four babies.

"There's a woman working out there."

"She's Barbarian property."

I freeze, even if I know that I only make it worse when I stay still and let that crazy blond man have his way with me. I tell myself that he trained my body to respond to every inch of him, especially the dangerous inches between his legs.

"What the fuck is that supposed to mean?" I ask him. I hate everything about how he perceives and discusses women. Like this ass-backwards country boy thinks it's normal everywhere else. I might be able to accept it if he at least knew he was a freak.

"It means somebody tattooed her and she has to do whatever it is he wants. The man who owns her could sell her pussy if he wanted to. Don't worry. You don't have to worry about that. It goes against God."

I wriggle against him and try to form an intellectual rebuttal against Gideon's shocking revelation, but he sticks his tongue out and licks me possessively all over my neck and up to my earlobes so I just respond with a useless moan instead.

He chuckles and presses his dick into my ass again.

"I knew I could get you wet quickly," Gideon chuckles, reaching for the waist of my leggings and eagerly pulling them down without hesitating for permission of any kind. My underwear follows the path of my leggings and he unceremoniously shoves two fingers all the way inside me.

I cry out from pure surprise and Gideon just laughs before shushing me.

"I want to see if that gets her attention."

I turn around to glare at him and he just laughs harder as he thrusts those two fingers deeper inside me. I hate him. I hate him so fucking much. Juices gush around his fingers and he keeps moving behind me so I can feel his hard dick trailing along my bare ass through his pants.

"How long do you expect me to wait like this?" I whisper, trying not to moan again as Gideon keeps those fingers still inside me for a painfully long time.

"Why?" he asks. "You want me to start fucking you already?"

I want to deny it, but he rubs his thumb along my clit as he pushes those two fingers deep inside me and my moaning betrays me. My pussy is a goddamn traitor for this white boy.

"Dirty girl," Gideon whispers. "Getting finger-fucked in a gas station bathroom and loving every minute of it... That's how I know I'm gonna marry your sexy ass..."

"No," I moan, although I don't know if I'm talking about marriage or the way Gideon's fingers are manhandling me and bringing me very close to an orgasm without him even moving them. The more I move my hips and make some effort to get him to move them, he holds still and tortures me with the feeling of fullness in my pussy and the increasing desperation for some goddamn friction.

I clutch the sides of the sink and refuse to look at myself in the mirror as he finally moves those fingers and nearly pushes me to an immediate orgasm. Gideon withdraws them all the way after only a couple thrusts and I look up at him in the mirror just to see what he's doing.

I didn't have to look because I would have heard him slurping as he wraps his tongue around his fingers and sucks my pussy juice off like he's eating Ben and Jerry's ice cream off a cone. He makes eye contact with me in the mirror and then smacks my ass hard so he can watch my face twist in pain.

I donkey kick him in the shin for that, but he only chuckles and reaches for his belt buckle.

"No looking at this test until I fuck you good," he says. "That way if you're not pregnant, we have another chance."

"You seem to be missing the point," I mutter, but I have to keep clutching the sink since Gideon takes juices off my thighs with one finger and then shoves that finger deep inside me until I moan. He doesn't care about 'the point'. He just cares about his dick.

With his free hand, Gideon easily unleashes his dick and he presses the gold piercing to my entrance, holding onto the thick shaft and rolling the head of his dick around my entrance to get it soaked with my juices. He gets me so wet that there has never been any need for lubrication between the two of us. My pussy drips effortlessly in a way it never has for any other man.

"I love feeling how wet my dirty girl gets for my dick," Gideon says, rubbing the head along my slit in slow movements as he prepares me for entry.

I turn my head away from the pregnancy test and wait for him to thrust into me. I don't know if he'll be quick and impatient or slow. I don't know if the woman out front will come back here and kick us out while Gideon has his dick inside me to the hilt.

I don't know if he'll care enough to make me cum. The head of Gideon's fat dick presses into me with ominous pressure. It feels like my pussy is going to pop as the piercing enters me, followed by the rest of his thick head. My breathing shakes as I use every ounce of personal power not to cry out.

Gideon holds onto me with firm control as he drives his dick into me without giving a crap about the fact that we're in a gas station. He leans his body over mine and nibbles on my earlobe as he presses his dick even deeper inside me, forcing his barbell to massage my inner walls and making it even harder for me not to cry out as he fucks me in the bathroom.

"You like my big pierced dick in your pussy, don't you dirty girl," Gideon murmurs. I shiver and shove my hips back against him, hoping to buck him off me, but just taking him deeper.

"Fuck…" I gasp desperately instead of saying anything resistant to Gideon. This response pleases him greatly. He bites down on my ear lobe and I have to force myself not to cry out even louder. Grabbing me with both hands, he fucks me hard against the sink.

This time, he doesn't care if I cum. I can feel it. He just wants to take his pleasure from my pussy with that fierce masculine intensity. My body trembles as he fucks me hard and even if Gideon doesn't give a crap, I can feel an orgasm building in my core. I don't know why he has this much power over me.

The way his body feels taking over mine overwhelms my every sense. He smells so damn good. His dick is so big and the barbell that pierces Gideon's dick pushes my pussy to the edge of orgasm. This time when I thrust my hips back against Gideon's crotch, I want to feel him hitting my walls even deeper.

I cum even harder when I throw my hips back to meet him. My pussy juices squirt out from my entrance and dribble down both our thighs as Gideon slows down his pace. I can feel his dick growing in my pussy as his climax draws close to me. He reaches around the front of my pussy and rubs my clit as he fucks me nice and slow from behind. Torturing me with this slow fucking in the gas station bathroom after he just destroyed my pussy feels so damn unfair.

"How good does my dick make you feel, dirty girl?" Gideon whispers as he massages my clit and slides his dick into me nice and slow. I hate him so much. My pussy clenches around his cock, increasing the pressure as he fucks me slowly. I can feel every inch of him, both his piercings and the big veins wrapped around his dick.

I'm gonna cum. I'm gonna cum so hard on a killer's dick. I grip the sides of the sink and gasp for breath, trying not to scream. Gideon rubs my clit slowly and purposefully so that he forces me to cum. He knows I'm trying to hold back and that's the last thing he wants.

"Come on, dirty girl. Cum for me twice..."

I lose control of myself. It's not because of Gideon's words, but because of the hot breath on my neck tickling me and sending just the right sensations shooting straight through me. The sweat on both our skin makes him sliding into me feel even better. I stop giving a fuck and let loose, moaning loudly as I cum.

Gideon loves that. He thrusts into me one last time nice and deep and I feel his hot cum pulsing into me. I don't stop him. I can't let him make a mess. And I haven't looked at that test yet, but I'm clearly cursed. I might as well let him finish inside me.

He wraps his arms around me and holds my body tightly against his as he cums. I can feel the full force of Gideon's strength as he holds me. My body shudders as his dick jerks and releases another large spurt of cum between my legs. He kisses my neck before letting go of me. I don't really want to let him go, but the pregnancy test set on the side of the sink demands my attention.

This has definitely been longer than three minutes. We're lucky some trucker hasn't come pounding down the door desperate to take a shit. I wriggle my ass in an effort to get away from Gideon who finally allows me to get free. My pussy trembles as he removes himself and some of Gideon's cum drips down my thigh.

Gideon smacks my pussy gently like he's telling it goodbye.

"I don't know how you got me so addicted," he says. "Look at your skinny legs and that pussy all bare like that with my cum dripping out…"

"Gideon," I say sternly, shoving his thirsty ass off me before he drags this out even longer. "We have to look at that test."

He grabs my hips and flips me around, forcing me to look him in the eye. He looks so fucking happy. The man looks like a Labrador retriever who just heard the word 'walk'.

"Why do you look so happy?" I ask Gideon, suspicious that he has more pain that he plans to unleash on me. He doesn't stop smiling. Fuck, he has a sexy ass jawline. I know I shouldn't let his appearance affect me but my pussy throbs traitorously.

Gideon's words just make it worse. "Because I just got to cum in your pretty pussy. Puts me in a good mood."

"I could have used this time to pack more clothes."

Gideon chuckles and reaches over me to grab the pregnancy test, shoving his gross, hairy armpit in my face.

"Give me that!"

He holds it out of reach.

"I want to see," he says. "It's my baby."

My pussy throbs again. I reach for my underwear and leggings so I don't allow Gideon's cum to drip everywhere. Ew. Gideon looks at the test while I pull my pants up. I don't really care if he sees it first, I guess. When I stand up, I can't tell what the test says based on the expression on Gideon's face. He is… expressionless.

"What? Let me see that thing."

His expression doesn't change. I look at the pregnancy test.

"Seriously?"

I feel like I have a hive of wasps buzzing around my chest. I look up at Gideon again and his face darkens.

"This time should have done the trick."

"You should be celebrating."

I'm not pregnant. And Gideon is acting like somebody pissed in his cornflakes. He is downright crazy for that reaction.

"What? You got something better going on?"

He grabs my cheeks, forcing his thumb to tighten his grasp. I can feel his anger coursing through him as he forces me to keep my gaze on him.

"I'm getting you pregnant, Tamiya. I don't know why your skinny ass ended up in my apartment, but... I want you."

He's squeezing me too tightly for me to respond. My eyebrows scrunch together because I can't speak, so Gideon releases his grasp just a little. I guess he expects an answer.

"You already had me, Gideon. You don't really want me. You're a white redneck from the country and I'm some girl who wants to kill you."

The wasps in my chest go crazy when he smiles.

"Exactly why I have to put a baby in you," he says. "It's the only way I can keep your crazy ass from sticking a knife in me."

"Are you sure that's going to work?"

"It's worked so far," he whispers, reaching into my pants and underwear and just touching my pussy like it belongs to him. He strokes it a little bit with a smile on his face.

"Don't leave me, Tamiya," he whispers. "I don't care if you kill me, just don't go."

"You are out of your goddamn mind."

He already knows that.

"If you had anywhere better to be, you would have left already. So think about it. When we get back to Texas, find a big old house you want to start a family in and I'll buy it for you," Gideon says. I don't know what the hell he wants me to say to that.

A part of me doesn't believe him. Men say all types of crazy shit when they want something from you. But what the hell does Gideon want from me? I fell into his lap. I'm the one who chased him down.

"You don't have money for a house."

He laughs. "You don't know shit. I'm not one of those men who keeps women in my business."

He moves his fingers around my underwear. "Now come on... Let's go see how Southpaw fucked his life up."

Chapter Twenty-One
Reaper

It has been a long time since I've come out here. Anna has certainly put her feminine touches on the outdoor landscaping. I don't think Wyatt was the one who chose blue and purple hydrangea bushes in the front or those tall conifers that now line the driveway.

When I park the bike, I immediately notice very specific things are wrong. Wyatt has his bike tipped over and there are no other vehicles out front. Not Anna's. Not Tylee's. He also has the front door wide open, not like Wyatt has anything to fear from someone walking into his house, except for the safety of his old lady and his baby.

How badly did this motherfucker screw up to even scare Anna off? She doesn't seem like the type to scare easily, not to mention she already knew the depths of Wyatt's problem. That's how her ass ended up with me...

Tamiya hops off my bike and glances around, taking in the scene around her for the first time.

"A biker lives out here?"

"Yes. And his old lady. And their son."

"It looks nice. What does he do, sell drugs?"

I grunt and walk towards the front door. Tamiya can use her private investigation skills to look around at the signs of the orchards -- the main way Wyatt Shaw earns his money. At least she follows me instead of scouting around the house.

"He leaves his front door open like that?"

"Hang back, Tamiya," I grunt, just in case there really is danger lurking behind the door and not just Wyatt's reckless ass doing something stupid. Tamiya steps right up to my shoulders and gives me a disapproving look.

"I don't need you protecting me," she says stubbornly. My ass. Of course she needs me to protect her.

"Your skinny ass needs me so hang back before I smack the shit out of you."

"I thought you weren't doing that anymore," she says, getting stern and serious, but hanging back just like I told her to.

When we get to the threshold of the front door, a loud ominous groan greets us. It sounds like it's coming from the living room, a little bit past the entryway and off to the right.

"Is that him?" Tamiya whispers. Her body draws closer to mine. For all her tough talk, Wyatt must have found a way to scare Tamiya's ass into obedience because she seems legitimately frightened of what lies behind the threshold.

There aren't any lights on and in broad daylight, parts of the brick house are shrouded in suspicious and uncomfortable darkness.

"Southpaw?" I call loudly into the house, hoping something other than a tortured groan meets us. But nothing, just another groan. Then silence.

"HELLO?!" Tamiya calls out loudly.

"Christ, Tamiya. It's not a rap video."

"What the fuck kind of racist comment is that?" she snaps at me, elbowing me hard in the stomach. "Watch your damn mouth."

"Sorry..." I mutter, although I don't get what her problem is. If she were Swiss, I would have accused her ass of yodeling.

Fortunately for the both of us and the argument brewing between us, Tamiya's yelling provokes Wyatt to respond. And it's definitely Wyatt.

"Reaper. Get your ass in here. I'm fucking... I'm so goddamn fucking drunk..."

THAT'S NOT like Wyatt Shaw. He drinks, mind you, but he's not the type to lose himself. That's more Hunter Sinclair's business than his. Shit.

"Hang back," I snap at Tamiya, anticipating her disobedience as I walk into the house and follow Wyatt's voice. Once we enter the threshold properly, the smell hits my nostrils immediately. Liquor. Cigarettes.

Tamiya does not hang back. She immediately peels off into the kitchen. When I hiss her name and tell her to follow me, she presses her finger to her lips and disappears, leaving me to find Wyatt. I don't have time to whoop her ass right now.

I walk into his living room and the stench of an unwashed man follows the liquor and cigarette smell. I'm just surprised he isn't dead on the floor. It stinks so goddamn bad in there. Two half-gallon jugs that used to contain milk are filled to the brim with what looks and smells like piss.

Wyatt sits sprawled on the couch shirtless with sweatpants on at least. He looks greasy, with all his body hair glued to his sweaty and unclean body. How fucking long has he been like this? A pair of dice work their way anxiously across his fingers as he stares blankly at FOX News.

"I don't believe a word of this bullshit," Wyatt says, revealing what he has in the other hand - a gigantic can of Coors Light. There are several more cans at his feet and two bottles of Jack Daniels.

"Where the fuck is Tylee?"

"I'm not gonna let you fuck Tylee," Wyatt slurs. "Put your hands on my sister again and I'll cut your dick off."

My cheeks darken with embarrassment and the desire to punch the shit out of Wyatt Shaw. Putting my hands on his sister is a funny way of describing Tylee insisting I take her virginity and then ratting me out to her entire family when we got caught. Somehow, she has never forgiven me for our very brief but ill-fated 'relationship'.

"Where the hell is Anna? How did she let you get like this?"

"She's gone. And she left divorce papers."

"Divorce papers?"

"They're on the kitchen counter."

I walk towards the living room door to get to the kitchen, but Tamiya appears before I get out of the room, holding a stack of papers and looking pissed off, like I smacked her in the face or something. I take the papers from her and question before looking down, "Are these the divorce papers?"

Tamiya shrugs. Wyatt tips the beer down his throat and spills about half of what he intended to drink all over his beard. Tamiya looks at him with disgust. I glance down at the divorce papers.

"This is a handwritten letter asking you to get your shit together and threatening divorce. These aren't divorce papers, Wyatt."

"She's going to do it," he groans. "I fucked up too bad this time."

"Worse than before?"

"Worse than when you won her pussy in a bet," Wyatt says.

Tamiya makes a weird noise and then stomps off towards the kitchen. What the hell is her problem? Wyatt leans forward and then throws up. Fuck. Like this problem couldn't get any worse.

"TAMIYA!" I call out. Her ass doesn't show up. What the fuck is she doing back there?

I get supplies from Wyatt's guest bathroom and clean up the sick. When I go to the kitchen to get him water, Tamiya isn't there. I hear footsteps upstairs and figure she must be investigating up there. Wyatt can barely hold the damn glass of water, but I snap at him to drink and tidy up the living room as best I can.

My mama would have whipped my ass seven shades of pink growing up if she ever saw me in an environment like this. Wyatt should have spent some time in a Blackwood household or joined the military. This place is disgusting.

"TAMIYA! I need your help!"

"Who the fuck is Tamiya?" Wyatt asks, groaning and leaning back.

"I'm the one asking the questions," I snap at him aggressively. "What the fuck did you do to Anna?"

"It's a long story."

"We got nothing but time. You have to tell Tamiya the truth if you want her to help."

"Ohhhh," Wyatt says. "The private investigator."

I'm glad he's catching up.

"Yes."

"Anna is accusing me of starting an illegal gambling ring surrounding Williamsville Little League games just because some asshole who lost big on the McGlovin vs. Captain Duck game showed up to the last game and shot our bookie."

THE PROBLEM with gamblers is they're too fucking inventive. Wyatt has a special talent for creating problems that never existed in the first place.

"WHAT THE FUCK possessed you to bet on Little League games?"

"Open market."

"Think maybe there's a reason elite gamblers haven't taken their talents to toddler baseball?"

"I WENT COLD TURKEY FOR THREE MONTHS," Wyatt roars, throwing the glass of water against the wall on the other side of the room and shattering it. Does this motherfucker not see me cleaning up after his mentally unstable ass? He's lucky Anna didn't put a bullet in his goddamn head.

"DO SOME SHIT LIKE THAT AGAIN AND I'LL KILL YOUR SELF-DESTRUCTIVE ASS MYSELF."

Wyatt closes his eyes and leans back on the couch. "Sorry."

I hear footsteps pattering down the stairs and Tamiya appears in the doorway. She won't look at me.

"Just making sure you haven't killed each other," she says. "Although I guess that would solve one of my problems."

"You need to find her!" Wyatt blurts out. "Please... help me."

Tamiya gives him a look like he's the most pathetic man she's ever seen.

"Which room is hers? I'll look for clues."

"We share a goddamn bedroom," Wyatt growls. "She's my wife..."

Tamiya, never one to read the situation and back down responds sharply, "I understand that, but considering she left your ass, I wouldn't be surprised if she had a separate bedroom."

"Control your woman," Wyatt snarls.

I look at Tamiya who just takes a few more steps into the room without looking at me. Control her? I don't know how the fuck he expects me to do that. I keep trying, but I sense that if I ever get close to getting this woman under my control, I have somehow found a way to lose her.

SOMETHING IS the matter with Tamiya... I just don't know what. Hopefully her ass tells me first before she sets her mind to killing me.

"Control?" Tamiya says. "Have you lost your fucking mind talking to me about control? You look like a hot mess and you stink."

This woman is going to make me fight Wyatt on her behalf if she keeps running her fucking mouth like this. I give Tamiya a mean look to hush her up, but it doesn't work at all. She just keeps glaring at Wyatt, who barely has the energy to talk back to her.

"Anna's gone. Who gives a fuck..."

"She didn't go far," Tamiya says. "She has a toddler with her and judging by what I saw upstairs in your bedroom and the baby's room, she only went with about two week's worth of stuff. She could stock up, but I sense she wants you to get your act right and come find her, not wallow on the couch."

"How could you possibly know that?" Wyatt groans.

"First of all, she basically said that in the letter that you stupidly called 'divorce papers' and second, I found her journal under the mattress upstairs and read it. What kind of dumbass starts a gambling ring around Little League games?"

"Who murders someone over Little League gambling?" Wyatt says. "How could I have expected that?"

"Maybe because you're a criminal," Tamiya says. "And you know how they think."

Wyatt tips the Coor's back again, pissing Tamiya off enough that she struts straight past me - still avoiding eye contact with me - and grabs the can out of Wyatt's hands.

"That's enough drinking."

He grabs her wrist with his other hand.

"Let go of her!" I yell.

Tamiya yanks her hand away and slaps Wyatt hard across the face. He groans.

"I can fight my own fucking battles, Gideon."

She storms past me to throw the can out in the kitchen. What the fuck did I do to this woman? This is the most I've seen her pissed off in a long time and I thought we were past this shit. I'm not good enough with women to be able to read their minds.

When I call my mother tonight in prison maybe I'll ask her. Although, I can't say I mentioned too much about Tamiya. Just that I have "some girl" staying at the condo on Southpaw's behalf. I obviously haven't told her that Tamiya is black.

"You fucked up," Wyatt grunts.

"You're one to talk. Where could Anna be if she's not far?"

"I don't fucking know," he says. "I rode around and looked everywhere. I even went to Tylee's house."

That instantly makes me suspicious.

"What if someone took her while she was on the run? We should get back up."

Tamiya returns from the kitchen stomping past me and standing across from Wyatt so she can give him the full force of her disapproving gaze.

"You're right," Tamiya says. "Call your hooligan friends. But if I'm honest with you, I would check with her female friends and family. This doesn't require advanced investigation. In my time as a PI, most people don't go that far."

"You don't know Anna."

"She has your baby. If she saw that you had all of this going on and chose to marry you, she must be committed to you. She just wants you to get your life together."

"It's not just that I caused a shooting," Wyatt groans. "I had $50,000 on the game, betting against the home team. I lost."

I can't help but smile but Tamiya does not look amused in the slightest. That explains why he looks so goddamn downtrodden.

"What kind of idiot bets $50,000 on a Little League game?"

"I didn't expect there to be a shooting," Wyatt says gruffly. "And that Captain Duck pitcher had an early growth spurt. You wouldn't understand."

"You're right," Tamiya says. "Because I'm not stupid."

"When you find Anna, she's going to want answers. And I guess $50,000. And probably evidence that you're not going to fuck her life up like this again."

The dice keep moving across Wyatt's fingers.

"I just got in over my head," he says, leaning his head back and fluttering his eyes closed.

"You have a son," Tamiya says. "Get your shit together. Now call your stupid ass friends. I'll keep looking through Anna's stuff and see if I can find out where she is."

"I think she's at Tylee's," I suggest, in case I can win Tamiya's good favor or at least the slightest fucking glance from her.

"Who is Tylee?" she asks Wyatt, still ignoring me.

"My sister," he says. "She lives nearby. But I asked her and she said Anna wasn't there."

"Were you born before lying was invented?" Tamiya asks.

"Tylee wouldn't lie to me," Wyatt says foolishly.

"Why not?" Tamiya asks, sparing me the misfortune of having to ask that seemingly obvious question. I mumble something about calling Hawk, Steel and Cash before sneaking out to the other room.

.   .   .

I CAN'T HEAR their conversation as I call Hawk up on his personal line. He picks up after a few rings.

"Did you make it out to Wyatt? I have my fucking hands full out in Santa Fe," Hawk says. He sounds out of breath. I want to tell him that we have nothing but good news but Wyatt is a goddamn mess. I don't know how he let shit spiral out of control like this. Anna is a good woman. A *forgiving* woman.

"I made it out there," I reply. "Not like it matters."

"What's the problem? How bad is it?"

"Is there any way you can get your ass further East?" I grunt, casting a glance over my shoulder to make sure neither Tamiya nor Southpaw emerge to listen in on our conversation.

"SO DO I," Hawk grunts. "But I have my hands full. *Trust me.*"

Then he lets out a long, meaningful sigh. Okay. I've known him long enough to know that he's not lying about having his hands full.

"Is it Juliette again?"

Normally, if Hawk is this stressed out it's that woman of his that is far too young for him. I suppose I shouldn't comment on a man's taste in women. I'm not quite in the place for that.

"No," he says. "It's Cash."

"Huh?" I ask. "What the hell is Cash doing out in Santa Fe?"

"Handling business with me and possibly raising hell. He has family problems, I can tell. Just can't tell what they are."

Hawk is paranoid. The only problems the Hollingsworths have are where to invest their money. They all keep on the straight and narrow far more than the rest of us. Tanner played football in college for fuck's sake.

"He would be better use to us out here."

"I know," Hawk says. "Juliette doesn't like him too much either. If she would just stay off the politics, they wouldn't have any problems."

He says that last part in a hushed tone that makes me chuckle.

"Scared to tell her that?"

"Not at all," Hawk says defensively. "She's tied up to our bed as we speak with a ball gag in her mouth."

"Shit."

"Don't tell her I told you that," Hawk says. "But we have time to talk. Steel is out in Illinois. Condom is even closer. He's in St. Louis."

"Fuck. Do I need to deal with his ass right now?" I grumble. "What is he doing out here?"

"Avoiding a warrant."

"Fuck. What did he do?" I ask, although I don't know if I want to. Like the rest of the Sinclairs, Magnum "Condom" Sinclair is a goddamn alcoholic. And you do not want to know how he got that nickname.

"Mess with the wrong woman. What's new," Hawk says. "He owes the club and he doesn't have a family. I have to go check on Juliette. She might be pretty hungry."

Great. I can hear the volume of the conversation between Tamiya and Southpaw getting higher. She's most likely antagonizing him in the most upsetting way possible if I know a thing about Tamiya's stubborn, skinny ass.

"Got it. I have my hands full over here myself."

"How is Wyatt?" Hawk asks, exhaling with even more frustration. I don't want to make Hawk worry, but the truth is the truth.

"In the shittiest condition I've ever seen him."

Considering what happened the last time I was head to head with Wyatt in a wager, this is saying a lot.

"I'll try contacting Anna again. My guess is Tylee spirited her off somewhere."

"That's what I said. Wyatt shut it down."

"It's Tylee. She's manipulative and unhinged. Check again."

"Yes, sir. I'll get Steel down here before we take action."

"Call me if you need anything else," Hawk says. "Bucky might be close by. I'll send him your way too."

My father always told us we should treat Ruger like a brother. But Ruger 'Bucky' Blackwood ain't all the way right in the head. I don't mind working with him for club business, but I don't want him in the same room as Tamiya.

"Do we really need that creepy motherfucker to pick Anna up? You're likely right about Tylee."

"What if I'm not?" Hawk says. "Remember the Blue Blood Knights?"

"This is different. This is domestic. He gambled on Little League games."

Hawk snorts. "Has he lost his mind?" I can tell he's trying not to laugh. I know if he saw Wyatt's condition he wouldn't find anything funny about it, but his best friend has to admit that this low point has been a shocking twist in Wyatt's gambling problem.

"Anna might not forgive him."

"Doesn't matter," I remind him. "He tattooed her. He won't let her go. Smartest thing we can do is help him get her back quickly before shit escalates out of control."

"Exactly why you need Bucky. I'll get him out there. Keep Wyatt from blowing his brains out. We'll get his girl back."

"Let's hope."

Chapter Twenty-Two
Tamiya

I don't want to look Gideon in the eye right now. When he comes back into the living room, I pretend like all my anger is exclusively for Southpaw, a man whose real name is apparently Wyatt Shaw. He doesn't look like a Wyatt. He looks like a screw up. When Gideon comes back in, I'm trying to get his ignorant ass friend off the couch.

"Your wife isn't going to take you back if you smell like raw donkey ass. Get up."

"I can't."

"Get your ass up, white boy."

Gideon clears his throat. He keeps trying to get me to look at him. Dumb motherfucker. I don't want to deal with him right now and he's way too much of an idiot to figure out why. I guess I know why he's so damn eager to help out the drunk asshole plastered to the couch right now.

Southpaw groans and stands to his full, impressive height. He's taller than Gideon, but Gideon is far more attractive. I never saw myself being attracted to men with "fair features", but Gideon's face has a beautiful structure. It's oddly hot when his cheeks turn that dark red color when he's nervous and his brown eyes stand out against the rest of his golden appearance.

On the other hand, Wyatt looks like a terrifying grizzly bear. He has hair all over him and I don't think he's shaved his face in a long time. Ew.

"I'll shower," he says. "But if you don't find me Anna by tonight, I'll sell you to a fucking Mexican..."

I don't even bother cursing out that stupid drunk. He walks past me and disappears, unfortunately leaving me alone with Gideon in this living room. Gideon did a good job with cleaning up this spacious, otherwise modern farmhouse living room, but the stench is absolutely disgusting. I understand the original vision... a gorgeous neutral L-shaped couch. Pampas grass in a vase. A mounted television with a sleek frame that makes it nearly invisible over the fireplace mantle. Unfortunately, the living room *reeks.*

He approaches me and the urge to throw up gets stronger.

"Why the fuck are you pissed off?"

"I didn't realize we were going to chase the ghost of hookups past."

"What the fuck are you talking about?"

"You won his wife in a bet? I watched Sons of Anarchy. I know bikers are a bunch of whores."

Gideon grabs my forearm. I try to pull it away, but he grips me tightly and drags my body against his. I am just about ready to smack the shit out of this violent motherfucker.

"Look at me," he demands, making me want to refuse him even harder. I look at my feet.

"I said look at me, Tamiya."

His tone darkens. *Make me,* I want to tell him. I hear Wyatt turning on the shower upstairs. I keep looking at Gideon's feet although I don't know what the hell I expect him to do.

I finally break and the look on Gideon's face is nothing but pure outrage, but I can't tell why the hell he's so damn offended. I'm the one who has to hear about how he's been with Southpaw's wife and sister.

"You are the only woman I have ever loved in my entire life," he says. "I swear to God."

The expression on his face is so serious, but so unnecessarily angry at the same time. I can't bring myself to look away from his dark, sorrel-brown eyes, especially since he is saying something fucking crazy.

"You don't love me."

"Don't tell me what I feel," he says. "In fact, I need you to put an end to all your disobedience. Tylee was a foolish, one-time thing. And I never slept with Anna, nor did I ever want to. I swear."

I want to believe him so badly. But if you've ever been around a lying ass man, you know they have absolutely mastered that fake sincerity and puppy dog eyes. If Gideon will lie to my face like this, he's a dog all right.

"I don't think you made cupcakes while you were trapped in a damn motel room together," I snap at him. Does this man honestly think I'm stupid?

"You're right," he says angrily. "I spent most of my time outside working on the bike or attending to club business. I'm helping him find Anna because she's his old lady. That's all there is to it."

I yank my arm away from him, still itching to fight him, but Gideon doesn't let me. He grabs my waist and drags me against him, kissing me fiercely and possessively. He bites down on my lower lip so hard that I yelp, but that doesn't stop him from covering my mouth with his and holding me so close that I can hardly breathe.

When he finally pulls away, his face is still dark and disturbed.

"You have no right to be jealous," he says. "I love you, Tamiya. But you're still squirming like a brat, refusing to acknowledge what I just said."

"I'm not a brat. I'm just not letting you manipulate me with words."

The shower shuts off upstairs. I hear Southpaw stomping around like a giant. Gideon squeezes my cheeks and then moves his hands down to my neck. He doesn't squeeze, but he's making it quite clear that he could if he wanted to. If I pushed him to it.

"I love you," he says, looking me dead in the eye with a crazed expression on his face. "That means fuck all the women in my past. That means you are mine, Tamiya. There will never be another woman that holds that place. My father stayed married to my mother for thirty-six years before he passed away. Never had a biker chick so much as suck his dick."

Is that the pinnacle of loyalty? Gideon runs his tongue over his lips slowly. I don't dare interrupt him.

"I will never hurt you or choose another woman over you, Tamiya. As long as I live…"

"Gideon. I tried to kill you," I say to him slowly. "And you… you still killed my sister."

"If I knew she was your sister, I wouldn't have done it," He says, his fingers curling slightly around my throat, like the temptation to squeeze just got a little too high. I can feel the desperation in his hands. Gideon craves an answer from me that I'm not sure I can give. His hands remain loose around my neck.

"I'm sorry," he says, the darkness in his eyes suddenly softened. "I mean it. Her boyfriend was a piece of shit, but… she was just trying to protect someone she loved."

"She's gone forever."

"I know."

His hand falls away. "I know."

Gideon wraps his arms around me, and it's just so genuinely loving that it scares me. I don't know what the hell is happening between us. Why I'm jealous. Why he's saying he loves me. This doesn't seem… right. It's just my body hijacking my common sense. That's the only thing that explains this.

He confirms my suspicions by using his index finger to gently tilt my face up to his this time. I'm so close to Gideon's warm body and he smells just like he did on the highway, but soaked in another layer of his masculine scent from the effort he exerted cleaning up after Southpaw.

I look into his eyes without being told and immediately know what to do next. My breath catches as I raise myself up a couple inches on my toes and kiss Gideon back. My hands catch on his broad shoulders, causing a thump in my chest and a more pressing thump between my legs. His muscles are so broad and his strength just feels so fucking good after so many miles on the run.

I don't want to stop kissing him and I can tell Gideon doesn't want to stop either. He reaches for my pants and slides his fingers past my underwear.

"Stop..." I gasp, because we're standing in the middle of South-paw's living room, he's out of the shower and the front door is open. Gideon doesn't care.

"It's my pussy," he whispers. "I'll get it nice and wet if I want to."

"Do you mind doing that after I find my wife?" Southpaw booms. I yelp and jump away from Gideon who is surprisingly reluctant about getting his damn hands out of my pants now that Southpaw emerged. I didn't hear his gigantic ass coming down the stairs, so my cheeks warm up with humiliation, although Southpaw seems more irritated than bothered.

Gideon gives Southpaw an irritated look himself. "To be honest, I'd rather take her upstairs and finish what I started."

I elbow Gideon hard in the stomach, which he ignores.

"Unless you can finish in ninety seconds, that's out of the question. We're following your lead and going to Tylee's house... once I have a drink."

"Do you want to meet Anna drunk?" I ask innocently. Southpaw gives me a wicked look and runs his tongue along the inside of his cheek to stop himself from saying something — I don't care what, as long as he has the good sense not to say it.

"I thought Blackwood men beat their women into silence," Southpaw grumbles, pushing past me and storming towards the exit like I said something wrong. I give Gideon a look that he had better do something and he returns my look with an expression asking me to "drop it". White men are fucking crazy. They will fight over sports teams but ask you to "drop it" over major disrespect.

The only reason I pay any attention to Gideon's instructions to leave it alone is because I want to get this shit over with. Gideon just dropped a bomb on me, fucked me in a gas station bathroom and made me consider something I never wanted to — a future.

. . .

I'VE BEEN a rolling stone for so long that I don't know if I can settle down. Though I feel like a fool for making all that fuss over the other women and then choking up when he said the words every woman wants to hear from an attractive man... I love you.

It's easy for him to say, but it's not as easy for me. I have more baggage than I know what to do with and the only person I ever even considered talking about guys with was Damara. And I guess my old boss, Rebecca. It's been a while since I've heard from her...

Southpaw is pretty eager to check out Tylee's place again, but I stop the group of us outside in front of the bikes and insist we wait for backup and come up with an actual plan in case I'm wrong. Southpaw complains that he's tired of waiting around so we bribe him with a trip to Taco Bell while we wait for Bucky and Steel to come.

Fifteen minutes after we order our burritos and tacos, a girl opens the restaurant door and Southpaw perks up. This has to be the slowest Taco Bell on planet Earth. Since when does the food here take fifteen whole minutes? Nobody else seems confused by the slow ass food, but the place has the vibe of a mob front.

Southpaw looks happy to see the girl who opens the restaurant door, but she's not the right complexion to be his wife.

"Oske? How did you get here so quickly?"

"That bitch and I broke up," Oske says, walking towards the table and dragging a chair up to the end. "I've been out in Granite City working at a nightclub."

"Doing what?" Southpaw asks gruffly.

"None of your business," the woman who is apparently named Oske says. "Gideon. Who is this woman?" She asks, pointing at me.

"She's trouble," Gideon says. "That's all you need to know."

"Actually, my name is Tamiya."

"Interesting," Oske says. "Well. Wyatt is my cousin. Gideon is... very homophobic."

"Shut the fuck up," Gideon snaps. "Who the fuck called her?" He says, nodding his head in Oske's direction.

"I messaged her about the situation three days ago," Southpaw says.

"Did he tell you that he already checked Tylee's place?" Oske said.

"He's so stupid. Tylee can easily outsmart him. Anna is definitely over there."

"I am not stupid," Southpaw grunts.

Oske sighs. "What should I order? How many more of these losers are we waiting for?"

"Watch your mouth," Gideon says. "I never liked your tone."

"And I never liked your racist ass," Oske says. "So I guess we're even."

She talks to them like she isn't afraid, which instantly puts me at ease. I doubt I could get away with saying this much in front of Gideon, but Oske clearly has Southpaw's protection and some access to his authority. I like the way she carries herself.

Also, she has a fascinating physical appearance. I know it's wrong to stare, but the more I look at her, the more I think she is some type of Native American. I don't know all the specifics, but I know the tribes of the Southwestern United States include the Hopi, the Apache, the Navajo, the Pueblo, and others that I can't pronounce. It would be rude to ask and it's honestly a little rude to stare but... that girl is pretty.

She has a tanned face with freckles, round features and large, dark eyes. Her smile and teeth only add to her exotic beauty. The way she dresses is a little strange, but I guess everyone has their own tastes.

"Get up and order something," Southpaw commands her. "I'm not waiting on your ass."

"Who asked you to wait?" Oske responds before she rolls her eyes and flounces off. Southpaw doesn't look up from his food, which is good because he is seconds away from dripping nasty sauce all over his beard. The second Oske leaves, I feel this desperate sense to get close to her. She knows things. Clearly. But she's not a racist ass biker, which only inspires more questions.

I make an excuse to slip past Gideon so I can intercept Oske while she orders and talk to her. The bikers won't be able to see me around the corner unless one of them gets up. Not likely to happen considering their enthusiasm for the feast in front of them.

"I'm going to the bathroom," I mumble and kiss Gideon on the cheek to make my actions less suspicious.

Chapter Twenty-Three
Reaper

When Tamiya returns to the table, something is off about her. I put my arm around her and kiss her cheek. We haven't discussed the pending clubhouse meeting, but I'm sure it will be a problem. Right now, I don't need more fucking problems. She's acting funny... That makes me suspicious. Especially with a snake like Oske in the room.

Tamiya barely responds and I feel a nervous throbbing in my chest. Oske sits with her order and begins talking about some bullshit with a smug ass smile on her face. I don't trust her as much as Southpaw does. She helped us out a couple times, and I know by some hillbilly fuckery she's part Indian and part Shaw, but I still don't trust her.

My father always said you shouldn't trust Indians. He said they were taught from birth to hate white people and if I'm honest, Oske has a racist look about her. Tamiya seems smitten with her, which instantly makes me suspicious.

Tamiya and Oske at least convince Southpaw to give Tylee's place another chance. Steel and Bucky show up, drawing more attention to our table than I would like. All the employees gather around the cash register staring at us until Southpaw gives them a look that would cause just about anyone to sink into the ground.

"If you hit her hard enough, she won't run," Ruger says, picking some leftover cheese off Southpaw's taco wrapper.

"Excellent advice," Steel says through gritted teeth. "For a goddamn monster."

Tensions rise from the obvious criticism. What the hell is Steel thinking? He knows my idiot cousin is always itching for a fight. He says shit like that on purpose to get people going, just to escalate situations. Motherfucker has no peace of mind. The shitheads keep fucking arguing.

"It's called discipline," Ruger says. "Gideon understands."

Tamiya gives me a look that tells me I had better act confused about my cousin's comment. My other option is to punch him in the goddamn face. But Tamiya's watching. And I don't want her ass pissed off.

"There are other ways to have a conversation aside from smacking someone around," I mumble half-heartedly. I can tell I'm on thin ice with Tamiya and I don't want to piss her off by agreeing with Ruger. He ignores Tamiya's existence entirely and gives me a mean look.

"Some nigger throws you a crumb of pussy and you already turn your back on a brother?"

I can feel Tamiya's body go rigid next to mine. Oske raises her eyebrows and sets her food down. Steel and Southpaw keep eating. But I can't let this go. Ruger and I lock eyes. He knows he fucked up, but he's also a stubborn motherfucker.

"What the fuck did you say?"

"I said what a man who exercises his freedom of speech gets to say," Ruger says, smirking like an asshole as he reaches over to Tamiya's plate and takes the rest of her burrito and shoves it into his mouth. Southpaw and Steel exchange glances.

"Careful," Southpaw mutters, although he knows I'm not going to be careful... I've heard him say it himself.

EVERYBODY KNOWS Gideon is crazier than a coconut after the goddamn war...

. . .

I FLIP the table as I stand up. All hell breaks loose.

"GIDEON!" Tamiya screams, more out of surprise than anything else. I lose control of myself and grab Ruger by the collar, dragging him away from the table and creating massive amounts of chaos as I knock over more chairs and tables. I can hear people screaming, but I can't tell who.

I slam Ruger's back into the wall and throw my fist at his face. I don't know if Tamiya asks me to stop. I don't care. It's one thing to use the word in private, but intentionally disrespecting my woman is out of the fucking question. I won't stand by and tolerate that shit. Not a goddamn chance.

Ruger groans as his head smashes against the wall. My fist hits his stomach so hard, I knock the wind out of him. I swear I hear the word "police", but I don't know where the word is coming from. Ruger tries to fling a limp fist at my face. Wyatt screams at me, but I can't stop myself.

"Don't be goddamn disrespectful," I snarl at Ruger as I slam his head against the wall again. I let up on the grasp I have on his neck. He lets out a loud groan and finally gets his fucking eyes open and puts up a decent fight back. I might have surprised him, but he's not weak.

Ruger slams his fist into my face. I spin him around and slam him into Southpaw who pushes him back into me.

"Drag his ass outside," Southpaw says.

I SPEND way too long not keeping track of Tamiya. Even with blood pouring out of his stupid fucking face, Ruger is hard to handle. I drag his ass outside of the Taco Bell and shove him onto the ground.

"That's enough," Southpaw growls. I stop because after all my time in the army, I have an instinctive response to that sort of command. But that doesn't stop my desire to beat the fuck out of the man on the ground.

"The cops are on their way," Southpaw says. "We don't have time to discuss the plan."

He throws a dirty look my way like that's my fault somehow.

"Let's get the fuck out of here and head to Tylee's place."

I GLANCE around manic for Tamiya and see her standing next to Oske. I don't like them being close. I hurry over to Tamiya and throw my arm over her shoulders.

"Everything okay?" she says.

"Yes."

BUT SHE DOESN'T SOUND okay.

"ARE YOU SURE?"

"I'm sure."

"Did she say something to you?"

"JUST DROP IT, GIDEON. PLEASE."

I DON'T HAVE MUCH of a choice given our circumstances. If I want us to head out West and get back to some peace and quiet, we'll have to hurry the hell up with the bullshit going down over here.

Tamiya gets on the back of the bike. She clings to me more tightly than before. Something is definitely up with her and considering how little I trust Oske, I sense she opened her mouth and said some shit about me that pissed Tamiya off.

She won't say that she loves me, but she acts all jealous when there's even a mention of another woman. Shit makes me anxious to find Anna more than ever. One look at Anna, and Tamiya will see for herself that there is absolutely no chemistry between me and Southpaw's old lady.

She's not my type. I prefer messy, unhinged women like Tamiya who spend most of their waking hours trying to kill me. At least I know I'm fucked up. She nestles comfortably on the back of my bike. Steel leads us to Tylee's and I follow.

Oske rides with Ruger, who refuses First-Aid and keeps the dried blood caked to his fucked up face. Southpaw leads the two of them a couple miles away from Tylee's house so he can remain on call. If Anna or Tylee sees him directly, they might shoot. We're going out ahead to find his wife and clear the scene – make sure Southpaw gets out without a bullet. Stay in the club long enough, you find out bikers have a strange effect on women. I don't know what it is but we get guns drawn on us more than the regular man. I've seen it myself.

Tamiya is quiet and wraps her arms around her body when she gets off the bike. She doesn't make any of her usual insightful comments about Tylee's place. Steel gets off his bike and gives her a once over as we stand in the driveway.

"So what do y'all think? She has her stashed in the basement or down at the lake house somewhere?"

"Does she normally park outside or in that garage?" Tamiya asks, pointing to Tylee's two-car garage.

"Couldn't tell you," Steel says to her. "But she would always side with a woman in a fight. It's her nature. Probably best we send a woman to talk to her."

"I don't know her," Tamiya says, glancing at me like she expects me to rescue her. Judging by how she's been acting ever since Taco Bell, I'm surprised she's looking at me at all.

"We didn't bring a woman just to look pretty. Unless you suck dick too."

"Shut the hell up, Steel. I tore up Ruger's face and I have no problem doing the same to you."

Steel glances over Tamiya again.

"She's a hot piece of ass."

I can feel burning around my ears from the way he's talking about her, but Tamiya throws me a sharp look and right now I don't want to piss her off more than necessary. She storms away from Steel towards the front door and pushes on the doorbell.

IT'S NOT Tylee who answers the door, but another red-headed woman. Steel speaks before I do.

"Kylie Hollingsworth?"

HER FACE HARDENS IMMEDIATELY as her eyes travel across the three of us. The last time either Steel or I saw Kylie Hollingsworth, she was a little girl. She isn't that much younger than us, but Don Hollingsworth keeps a tight hold on his daughters, especially considering what their mother, Annabel Hollingsworth, was like growing up. We aren't allowed to speak of that, but if it weren't for Don keeping his woman under lock and key, she might have been pregnant for half of Texas.

"I don't know who you are."

Of course she doesn't remember us. Steel and I exchange glances. I nod. I'll take the lead. Or at least I think I will until Tamiya sticks her hand out.

"Hi, I'm Anna's sister. I heard about the trouble she's having with her shitty ass husband. I picked up those two bastards at a gas station. You won't have any problems with them."

I can tell that Kylie is skeptical. But Tamiya is black and Kylie isn't exactly an expert on race...

"They're Rebel Barbarians," Kylie says quietly. She glances at our patches.

"Where is Southpaw?" Kylie asks once she gets a good look at our names.

"Nowhere near here," Tamiya says, lying with surprising ease.

. . .

"TYLEE'S GONE for the next week. If you're Anna's sister, I'm sure she'll want to see you. She hasn't left the basement since Tylee left."

Steel and I make an effort to push past Tamiya so we can get in the house. Fuck manners. We have what we need, don't we? Kylie gets all fierce in the doorway and stretches her arms out like she has no intentions of letting us past.

"I think it's best if Anna only sees her sister. I don't trust either of you."

NEITHER STEEL or myself can find it in us to argue with her. Steel pulls out an e-cigarette, immediately starting up my own cravings for nicotine. Ever since my time in the Army, smoking always calmed me down. I switched over to more modern products to make things easier on my lungs after all the shit that went down over there that fucked me up.

Never could shake the habit entirely.

TAMIYA WALKS INTO THE HOUSE, giving me one last look as she disappears. I still feel that tightness in my chest. Something is *wrong*. I just don't know what the hell it is.

"CALL SOUTHPAW," I tell Steel once he has enough puffs to get his ass nice and relaxed. "I bet Anna's in that house and I have a feeling we have more trouble heading our way."

"What kind of trouble?"

"I don't know. I just have an instinct for it."

CHAPTER TWENTY-FOUR
TAMIYA

I'm spinning over in my head what to do. First, I learn that Reaper will be going to some crazy ass club meeting that sounds like a haven of drugs, sex, alcohol and violence. Then, I have this situation with Oske and what she wants me to do.

Maybe I shouldn't trust her but... through my years investigating, I have good instincts about people. She sounded genuine. It's not just that – Oske sounded scared.

BUT WHAT SHE wants me to do is goddamn crazy and could definitely get me killed. I can't see Reaper reacting well to this.

You have to make it happen the second you get back to Tucumcari. That's what Oske said.

AND WHAT DOES this woman want me to do to help the club? She wants me to kidnap a baby. Not just any baby. Steel's niece. It feels... *wrong.*

. . .

"You have to trust me," Oske said. "They can't know because... *there's a traitor amongst the Barbarians...*"

What she wants seems fucking crazy. I have a hard time believing that the leader of the Rebel Barbarians would want me – a person they barely know and trust – to kidnap a baby. I have to find a way out of this. I can feel it. Or maybe... I have to trust Reaper.

"Gideon will want to help."

"Are you stupid?" Oske snapped. "I told you... You can't trust the other bikers."

"I don't understand."

"You're a private investigator. I thought you were smart."

The more I talk to Oske, the more I see why Gideon doesn't like her. I don't exactly have a problem with her, but she's blunt in a way that seems excessive considering she's asking me to commit a felony.

"This is crazy. You can't expect me to just take a baby across state lines."

"Wyatt is looking for a leak in information," she whispered. "And if you don't do it, he wants me to tell you that he's going to drive up to Denver himself and kill Rebecca, burning her business to the ground and having several bikers piss on her corpse."

Oske says this so matter-of-factly that it sends chills down my spine. Clearly, she's quoting directly. From everything I know about Southpaw, he's exactly the type to both threaten something so heinous and possibly follow through with it. Gideon killed people and he has a way milder temper than the unhinged dark-haired psychopath we just dragged out of that big ass house.

I don't want Rebecca caught up in anything, but it doesn't feel right lying to Gideon.

The worst part is, he can tell I'm keeping a secret.

. . .

ONCE KYLIE LETS me into the house and shows me Anna's secret location where she has Wyatt Jr. sitting in a playpen, getting her out is easier than I thought. She seems surprised to see me and my charade about being her sister quickly falls apart. Anna shoos Kylie out of the room, even if she obviously knows I'm not her damn sister.

"You're the girl Wyatt brought to Gidoen," she says, shrugging when I give her a confused look. "There aren't that many black women involved with the club."

THE CLUB? More like a gang of deranged outlaws. But I bite my tongue. This woman is married to the craziest of those damn outlaws, so she must have plenty of heat in her. I don't want to cross her at all.

I confirm her suspicions that I'm the woman and she begins questioning me like she planned this entire thing. I guess she has a lot of questions. I try my best to answer them honestly, since they're mostly about things that happened a long time ago. Eventually, Wyatt gurgles and tries to get her attention the way kids do when they hear their parent talking to someone who isn't them for too long.

She looks over at him and Anna's face drops immediately.

"He looks exactly like Wyatt," she says. "Well... The caramel macchiato version of him, at least."

She's right about the baby looking just like her husband. They have the same jawline, similar facial features and he has green eyes. His hair is a short, tightly-coiled messy afro, but I can see him becoming as much of a caveman as his father when he grows up.

My stomach drops. The baby Oske wants me to kidnap is a little girl. I can't see the point in doing something that fucking crazy. Oske's explanation hardly makes any sense. Her threat on the other hand felt very fucking real.

"Wyatt misses you."

"Wyatt's an asshole."

.   .   .

SIGH. You don't know how many times I've been here as a private investigator. Women sometimes get more upset when they find out their husband isn't cheating. *He's just unhappy.* Being a private investigator sometimes means just helping people patch their shit up. Anna and Wyatt are devastatingly easy to fix.

"It's not about the gambling. It's about the types of people that are going to kill a man over toddler baseball."

AFTER SEVERAL HOURS, Anna agrees to talk to Wyatt. I feel like I'm intruding watching the first moments they agree to see each other without fighting. The second she looks at him, I see how much this woman loves this man written all over her face. Loving someone that much scares the shit out of me.

Southpaw's face is even worse. I hate seeing him in a way that humanizes him, especially since he's the reason I ended up permanently in Reaper's custody – and with a lot of bruises along the way. He just looks so heartbroken – like the only thing in the world that could fix him is having this woman in his arms. Anna runs to him and he holds her close. My chest makes a funny knot.

I don't know if Reaper would do that for me.

A NAGGING VOICE at the back of my head knows he would. And considering our history, that makes everything so much more confusing. Luckily for me, I don't have much time to ponder the Reaper situation. There is too much for me to plan and consider.

BY THE NEXT MORNING, we're on our way back to Texas. Before she sprung her little kidnapping plot on me, Oske tricked me into giving her my phone number. As Reaper and I ride back to his condo, she texts me the entire trip. I can only reply when we stop for gas, but her messages include a detailed plan, including a location where she expects me to take the baby.

It just doesn't feel right.

BUT GETTING Rebecca burned to a crisp and pissed on doesn't feel right either.

IN SITUATIONS LIKE THIS, it's best that I follow my instincts – and trust no one. The only problem with that is I have to ride back to Texas clinging for dear life to the one person I was just learning to trust. I don't want to leave him out of this, but I'm too scared not to...

ONCE WE GET to his place, Reaper has a dark and sour expression.

"I know there's something wrong with you," he says, his cheeks red. "It's because of what I said. You don't feel the same way."

Guilt twists in my stomach. It's not that. I don't know what the hell I feel for this man. Right now, all I feel like is that I need to calm him down. I need to feel like shit is okay between the two of us because very soon... it's not going to be okay at all.

"Of course I feel the same way."

This is the worst time I could tell him. He'll never believe me once I disappear and do what Oske commanded me. She must have a good reason. I felt that instant instinctive bond with her that tells me... this will be okay. I try not to think about how Reaper will react. *This is for his own good.*

I never enjoyed lying and never thought I was a particularly good liar. Lies can be necessary, but I got into private investigating because I believe the truth is more powerful. Even if it fucks you up completely the way it did with me and Gideon.

"How could you?" he says. "After what I did?"

"Because I've done fucked up shit too. And because... I know you have a good heart."

He chuckles. "How can you say that when I smack the shit out of you? I thought that made me a goddamn unrepentant monster."

Does he have to make this even more difficult than it is already?

My closeness to Gideon makes everything that's about to happen even more difficult. I can feel the complicated mixture of emotions for him whirling in my chest. I shouldn't have this much chemistry with him. It's not fair. And at this point, this is so much more than chemistry.

"You haven't done that in a while," I tell him. "And you're getting better. Because you know if you don't, I'll slit your throat. Eventually."

"Sure you will, baby," he whispers, kissing the top of my head and pulling me close to him. I can feel the energy growing hot between us. I love and hate it. He's so pale, and his golden hair just makes him look so goddamn white. I never thought I'd end up with a guy who looked like Gideon. Shit, I never thought I would end up with anyone at all.

"I don't want you to leave," he whispers. "I mean it. Maybe God brought you into my life so I could make right what I did."

He reaches for my t-shirt, plastered to my chest from our long ride back West, and peels it off of me. I don't respond with words. I let Gideon kiss my neck as a soft and very unwilling moan escapes my lips. That sound makes him pull me even closer and Gideon holds me immobilized in his arms.

"I'll take care of you, Tamiya," he whispers, trailing impossibly soft kisses from my lips to my neck. I want to believe him. I have proof he isn't lying so far, which is more than any guy who came before him ever managed to do...

I squirm in Gideon's grasp as if an effort to escape can force him to prove that he really fucking means it when he says he wants to keep me here. This part of our sexual dance feels especially cruel considering what I'm going to do, but I can't stop myself from acting this way with Gideon.

I crave the side of him that turns into a beast and takes whatever the hell he wants from me with unrepentant recklessness. It feels so fucking good to be his... and it's much easier to admit that with my clothes off. He kisses me relentlessly as he takes the rest of my clothes off and then hoists me off the ground effortlessly.

He doesn't seem to mind my "skinny ass" when he has to carry me to the bedroom. I wrap my legs around him and throw my arms around his neck. Gideon stops walking me to the bedroom, visibly shocked by how much I seem to want him.

"What the fuck is going on with you today?"

"Nothing."

"Mixed fucking messages," he whispers, staring into my eyes so deeply that I can't help but feel completely exposed. My stomach jumps into my throat and I have to remind myself that just because we're close and just because we're connected doesn't make that man a mind reader.

"I love you," I whisper. "It just feels... strange."

"I know," he whispers. "I have never felt this addicted to a woman's pussy..."

He slides his hands between my legs and plays with my clit all the way to the bedroom. By the time Gideon gets me into the bed we've been sharing, I'm ready to cum and buck my hips up to meet him while he hovers over me fully clothed.

I need those damn clothes off and I need to feel this man. He chuckles as I fuss with his clothes, taking sick pleasure in my desperation for him.

"Take it easy, dirty girl," he whispers. "You're gonna get this big white dick soon enough..."

REAPER MOVES his head between my legs and hikes my thighs up so he can drag me closer to him and fully control the pace of his tongue against my bare pussy lips. He is so fucking good at this that my toes curl the second he gently tastes my outer lips.

"I think that sweet ass pussy would look good with a piercing," he whispers, running his tongue over my clit before I can respond and protest what is absolutely never fucking happening.

He wraps his lips around my clit and sucks on it slowly before his tongue returns to work and then he just loses himself eating me out like never before. I think it's because of what I said. I love you. He wanted to hear that so fucking badly. Gideon's tongue moves in slow repeated motions from my clit all the way to my back door, making me desperate to cum and getting my butthole so wet that all I can think about is the slick lubrication back there.

Gasping and desperate for more of Gideon's tongue so I can finish, I grab onto his insanely soft blond hair and bring him closer. He doesn't need more guidance than that before he drives his tongue into me with more intensity, hitting all my pleasure spots one after the other so when I cum, I explode.

The sound I make is the sluttiest sound to ever come out of my mouth. Gideon loves it. A lot. He keeps eating me out until I cum again and only when I'm a shaking mess on the bed does he take his clothes off and press the head of his pierced dick to my entrance.

I'm so wet and eager for him that just my slow breathing draws his dick inside me with barely any movement from Gideon's part. He grabs my cheeks and forces me to look him in the eye as he slides inside me slowly. It's so fucking hot I almost cum immediately. His dick pulses with heat and he feels so damn big that I don't know how he isn't ready to finish right away.

"I love you," he whispers into my ear once he buries himself in me to the hilt. "I love you so goddamn much…"

I KISS him back instead of replying. Guilt sears through me, causing more pain than Gideon's barbells rubbing against my inner walls and stretching me wide to take his dick. This time, he makes everything ten times more painful by taking my arms and pinning them over my head as he fucks me slowly into the bed.

He enjoys every instance of deep penetration, keeping his eyes locked on mine as he pounds me into the bed. I shudder with each deep thrust and arch my hips up, desperate to cum again. He makes me so goddamn greedy…

"I love your pussy, dirty girl," he whispers. "You feel so fucking good."

. . .

WHEN HE CAN'T TAKE it anymore, I can feel the energy in Gideon's body shift. His muscles grow tense and his breathing slows down. His eyes damn near roll to the back of his head as he groans and finishes inside me. That powerful jolt of excitement and fear makes me wrap my legs around him and pull him close to me.

"Fuck," he groans as his weight collapses on mine. "I love you bad enough to tattoo you... I never thought I'd say that..."

Before I can ask him any questions, he kisses me long enough that he gets hard again and we fuck three more times before we fall asleep.

I KNOW what I'm going to do but...

I DON'T WANT to leave.

NOT AFTER I just said I loved him.

GIDEON FALLS RIGHT ASLEEP because he has the club meeting coming up and even if he said he could be a little late, he'll want to head out there soon. It's not so easy for me to sleep.

I toss and turn and every once in a while, I watch him sleeping. That beautiful blond hair sticks out everywhere and his jawline is sharp enough to cut a fucking tree.

I STARE AT HIM, but I don't sleep. I *can't.* Not when I'm about to betray the man I love.

Chapter Twenty-Five
Juliette

BACK IN SANTA FE

HUNTER AWAY AT REBEL BARBARIANS CLUB MEETING...

He's really gone. I roll over onto Hunter's side of the bed and he isn't there... It's just me and our baby, the precious little girl who changed everything. *Mackenzie Rose Sinclair.* My mom's favorite flower was a rose, so I really wanted that to be her middle name. Hunter and I picked her first name together. The name means *fire-born,* which certainly fits her circumstances, since Hunter and I conceived her in a firestorm of lust and primal urges. Mostly his.

Mackenzie coos and I get out of bed for our morning routine together. Once she hears me moving, her cooing gets louder as she realizes breakfast is coming her way. My nipples are cracked and in constant pain from breastfeeding, but it feels good to have that special connected moment with my little girl early in the morning – even when I'm so exhausted I feel like a zombie.

I pick her up out of her crib and feed her before getting Mackenzie out of her dirty diaper and giving her a bath. After bath time, I dress her in a cute, white baby onesie with printed strawberries on it and strap her to my chest in a sling before heading into the kitchen to get myself some breakfast and start my day right.

Tylee calls right on time after I make my green smoothie. I suspect Hunter has her keeping watch on me so I don't escape, but I don't know where exactly he thinks I'm going to go with our two month old baby. I would never do anything to put her in harm's way.

"Good morning, cousin-in-law," Tylee says, concocting a familial term to describe our relationship that I have never heard before.

"Good morning," I reply with a yawn. "How are you?"

"ARE YOU READY FOR THIS?" Tylee asks.

"Yeah. Sure."

I HAVE no idea what she's going to say and honestly? I was not ready. Because Tylee nearly blows my eardrums out.

"I'M PREGNANT," she yells. "I DID IT. I'M PREGNANT!"

THEN SHE JUST SCREAMS OUT OF sheer joy. I hold my phone an arm's length away from my ear, but the scream is enough to upset Mackenzie's spirit and she starts letting out short whines while kicking her legs out in frustration.

"Mackenzie and I are very excited for you," I reply, putting the phone back to my ear. "Does Isaac know?"

"No!" she says. "I can't tell him until after the meeting. I can't believe this, Juliette. I've been trying to get pregnant since I was eighteen. This is a miracle. A miracle!"

"I'm happy for you. Seriously, Tylee."

"I'll call you back," Tylee says. "There's someone at the door."

"Who?"

"I don't know. Be right back!"

. . .

SHE HANGS up without further explanation and my phone buzzes again with a text from Quin. Ever since the baby, I've been in touch with her daily and I've been *desperate* to get her to come out to Santa Fe. It's expensive, and Quin has a lot going on, so I don't expect her to say yes, but her seven a.m. text message surprises me.

QUIN: Can I still come to Santa Fe?
   Juliette: Of course! When?
   Quin: This weekend.

DAMN. That's quick.

JULIETTE: Is something wrong?

QUIN ISN'T the type of person who normally makes last minute plans and considering how far away she is from Santa Fe, her urgency surprises me.

QUIN: Yes.
   Juliette: Call?

BUT QUIN DOESN'T RESPOND and when I send back question marks, she still doesn't respond. I decide to wait a bit for her response while spending the morning with Mackenzie. I work on my latest colored pencil art piece in our living room before suiting up Mackenzie for a walk in the park. I slick her hair back under a hat to protect her light tan skin from the sun and put baby sunscreen on all her vulnerable areas.

She doesn't like the sticky texture but with lots of hugs and kisses, we get through the process and I put her back in the sling on my chest to take her outside.

Hunter has chilled out about a lot of his more paranoid rules lately, and the park near the apartment complex is part of our nice, fancy neighborhood. Women under 120 lbs jog around at night. How dangerous can it be? Plus, Mackenzie loves walks and she loves Santa Fe as much as I do.

I LOVE the sense of freedom I get being outside on my own. Even if I might seem crazy for talking to a baby, I share everything with Mackenzie, describing the streets to her and telling her all my ideas for the big beautiful life she's going to have. I must be lost in my own world because the sound of motorcycles gets lost in the rest of the noise. It takes me a long time to realize someone is following us.

Too long. I left the park and took a long detour to go home so Mackenzie and I could get more fresh air before I notice our stalker. They could have been following us for a while. Crap. I have my phone on me, but I don't know who I can call since most of the bikers are out in Tucumcari at the new club house for the meeting.

Mackenzie doesn't notice anything is wrong and I want to keep it that way. We're close to our apartment, but I don't want to lead the stalker straight to where we live. I need somewhere public and safe to hide – like a coffee shop or a busy boutique. It's so early that most galleries aren't even open. I move faster. The biker doesn't know I noticed them yet, but they'll figure it out soon.

I'm on a residential street, a couple blocks away from anywhere safe and there aren't that many people walking around. Mackenzie is so peaceful. I hold her head against my chest and turn right. The biker follows me. I see a stoop I can duck behind and I hustle, glancing over my shoulder quickly before I get out of sight.

My hustling and the Santa Fe heat already has me out of breath. Mackenzie wakes up. I don't hear the bike engine anymore, which doesn't make me feel better. I don't know if I should go back the way I came, or keep heading this way where I can loop around to our apartment.

"Hey baby," I whisper. "We're fine… Everything is fine and your dad is not going to lock me in a prison until the end of time."

Mackenzie gurgles like she doesn't even believe me. I give her head a quick kiss and inch to the edge of the stoop so I can peer around it. I take a quick look, but I don't see a bike. Telling myself I just missed it, I duck low and look around the corner of the stoop again. No parked motorcycles and no outlaw bikers. *Shit.*

I didn't get a good look at the type, so I can't even text someone the make or model of the vehicle. I reach for my phone and send Tylee a text message.

JULIETTE: Someone is following me. Gonzales. Canyon Rd.

I HOPE Tylee picks up that those are the cross streets. She doesn't reply, so I quickly send the same text to Hawk. I can't stay hidden behind this stoop for long. I assume the bikers must be on foot since I can't hear the bikes anymore. Holding Mackenzie's head against my chest, I glance around the stoop again and with no one following me, I keep going ahead.

But when I get to the end of the street and turn, I run straight into someone. I gasp loudly as my arms shield Mackenzie from the impact. Flashes of awareness jump into my mind as my body slams against the stranger's. *Leather. Faceless. Too big.*

I stumble back, ready to turn on my heel and sprint in the other direction, but a hand clamps around mine. I look at my captor's "face", but there's nothing but a sheet of black glass reflecting my terror. Their motorcycle helmet obscures their identity completely.

· · ·

SOMETHING TAKES OVER ME.

BLIND RAGE and the desire to protect Mackenzie turns me into an animal.

SHE'S QUIET, like she knows I'm about to lose my mind. I can almost hear my heart pounding, like motorcycle boots thumping against desert sand. The next sound out of my mouth is feral. I've never yelled like that before. I kick my attacker in the crotch as hard as I can. The stranger groans loudly, dropping my hand, and I run for my life.

I've never run this fast before, and I know it isn't very fast. I hold Mackenzie against my chest tightly. I can't believe I got away, but now I'm running blind and fast through the streets which seem uncharacteristically empty. I glance behind me, which proves to be a huge mistake.

The biker stretches their arm out and nearly grabs me again. I feel the whoosh against my neck and I'm just happy they didn't get a hold of my hair. Shit, shit, shit… I look across the street I have to cross and I swear nothing is coming when I step out, but at the last second, I see a flash of red.

I SCREAM Mackenzie's name and hold her against my chest. I hear a thud and logically, I know it's my body hitting the car, but there isn't much consciousness left in me. It just happens so quickly.

"MACKENZIE!". The thud. Then blackness.

CHAPTER TWENTY-SIX
REAPER

When I wake up, I have a smile on my face. Best sex of my life. That's what last night was. I didn't realize how much better sex would be when you are head over heels in love with the woman you're doing it with. Might be a harsh thought, but lucky for me, dad is dead and mom is behind bars, so I don't have to deal with the race thing until later.

But once I get my senses about me – not longer than a minute – I get that army-sense that something is wrong.

"TAMIYA!"

If there's trouble in this house, there's one fucking place it's coming from. When I don't hear her respond instantly, my heart drops into my stomach.

I get out of bed and walk to the kitchen with my dick swinging, which is how you know it's fucking serious. Only a disturbed man walks into his kitchen early in the morning with his ass and dick out.

She's not there. No signs of breakfast. No signs of coffee. No signs of her skinny ass anywhere.

What the fuck?

. . .

THERE'S a note on the counter top.

MY HEART SINKS into my stomach. I rush over and read it. Then, I get pissed off. *This woman is out of her fucking mind.*

I CAN FEEL myself losing my shit while reading what the fuck she's up to. My head spins.

GIDEON,

I'M sorry I didn't tell you, but I didn't know what to do. This doesn't feel right, but that woman said you were in danger and that I couldn't trust anyone.

I'm going to drive to Juliette Sinclair's house and kidnap her baby. I have to be honest with you, this doesn't feel like the right thing to do, but my back is against the wall and I don't know who I can trust.

It would kill me if anything happened to you.

I DON'T WANT you to die because I refused your boss or his commands.

The thing is, I don't trust Oske the same way Southpaw allegedly doesn't trust the bikers. When I get the baby, I'll make sure Juliette can get her daughter back, make it seem believable that they actually caught me, and then I'll be gone.

I don't want you to try to find me and I'm sorry if anything happens to the bike.

WE HAD FUN, Gideon. But we don't belong together. I tried to make it work, but what happened with Oske is a sign that I'm meant to be on the run.

. . .

I WILL ALWAYS REMEMBER YOU.

– TAMIYA.

MY WHOLE WORD GOES RED. I haven't felt pure rage like this in so long, the last time I did I was probably a teenager kicking the shit out of Ruger. My hands shake I'm so fucking mad. I call Southpaw. No response. I run through as many of the club phone numbers as I can, but none of them pick up.

What the fuck? There's no way Tamiya did some crazy shit like this. Has she lost her fucking mind?

I'M ALWAYS the one who runs at the words "I love you"...

THERE'S no fucking way she did this. I slam my phone down and trash the house. I want to say I blacked out, but I didn't. I knew exactly what the fuck I was doing. She's everywhere in this place. She's the one who made this house in Tucumcari feel like a home and not just a functional living space near the clubhouse.

How could she do this? How the *fuck* could Tamiya do this. Broken furniture litters the floor. I shattered glass from a window. Broke every fucking plate. There are blankets and papers everywhere. Money. Shotgun shells. Disassembled weapons. Trash.

But she's gone.

SHE'S FUCKING GONE.

. . .

AND SHE COULD GET herself killed doing this shit.

THERE'S ONLY one person I haven't called yet and she's the last fucking person I want to involve in this. But if Tamiya did something stupid, she's the most likely one Juliette will call. *Shit*. Our club meeting is soon, so Isaac has his entire family out West road tripping up and down the old Route 66 highway until the meeting.

Fuck.

I HAVE to call Tylee Sinclair. I can already imagine her glaring at her phone with disgust, like I've done her wrong just by calling her. But it doesn't fucking matter.

I NEED MY WOMAN BACK. Thankfully, Tylee answers. I can hear my own breathing. I sound like an angry, outraged animal.

"It's Gideon."

My voice sounds strained. Different. I can feel my blood boiling. Pressure. Rage. It wants to come out so fucking badly and honestly, Tylee is the perfect outlet. *Where the hell is Tamiya?*

I have to try to stay sane, even if I already feel like I've lost my mind. A million terrifying thoughts run through my head. The most worrying being this: *What if she never comes back.*

"Shit must be bad if you're calling me," Tylee says.

She's too calm, which means that she doesn't know what's happening yet. Maybe she isn't with Juliette...

"I don't have time for this, Tylee. We have a goddamn emergency on our hands," .

I sound different. Like I'm on enough drugs to knock out an elephant. It's the rage coursing through me, which I'm chasing down with enough liquor to punish the shit out of Tamiya when I finally get my hands on her.

"I haven't said anything. What the fuck do you want?" Tylee says, dropping whatever minimal pretenses of politeness she had in the first place.

The rage pushes up against my skin and Tylee's rude ass comment swirls around in my head. I know I could stop myself, but the hatred and anger just spill out of me and I call Tamiya a *word* that I fucking shouldn't. That breaks me up inside the second I say it.

"Nigger girl escaped from my house and I think she might have done a kidnapping."

Tylee's reaction hits me immediately. *You fucking asshole.* It's worse than being an asshole.

"Christ, Reaper!" Tylee says. Her voice changes and gets louder. "You can't just run around using the n-word whenever you like when you might be broadcasting it to the entire world."

I know I'm wrong, but I can't help feeling defensive. My rage is too blinding. Too all-consuming. I can feel sorry when I get my hands on Tamiya's crazy ass again. I try to push my embarrassment and shame away, but I can feel Tamiya's disapproval seeping through the phone.

What kind of asshole says that about the woman he loves? I nearly double over, leaning against the counter, desperate to say something normal and productive, instead of angry and hateful. I need her back. I just need her back.

"Call her whatever you want. I was asleep and didn't notice... She's heading to Santa Fe. You have to find her."

"What bitch?" Tylee says, losing what little patience she might have had. "Get your ass over here and stop wasting my time. Because we have a missing baby over here and if your racist ass knows what happened, you'd better get over here and fix it!"

SHIT. Tylee hangs up. Just when I'm about to move on and drive over to her, Southpaw calls. Like my life couldn't get any worse.

"I NEED you at the clubhouse. Now," Southpaw says. *Great. Just what I need.*

Chapter Twenty-Seven
Juliette

I regain consciousness and launch straight into a full blown panic. The first word to come out of my mouth is my daughter's name as my head flashes with visions of all the horrific things that could have happened to her. *What if she flew out of my arms and then...?*

"MACKENZIE!" I scream, whipping my head around and clutching at my chest, where I don't feel her warm body. When I sit straight up, my eyes snap open, but wherever I am is pitch black. My boobs ache because it's been hours since I've fed her if it's dark out. *Where is she?*

Terror grips me immediately and my heart feels like it's rattling erratically around my chest. I feel a hand on my shoulder and nearly scream again, but the hand moves quickly over my mouth, blocking my scream.

Tylee's voice emerges from the dark. "It's okay, Juliette. I got you out of there. But the biker got away..."

My head hurts. Tylee takes her hand away from my mouth now that she's sure I won't scream. Her fingers interlace with my braids as she pushes them away from my cheeks. It's hard to get air into my lungs as I attempt to respond to her.

"What biker?" I say. "Where's Mackenzie?"

I can't think about anything except my daughter.

"Shh," Tylee says. "Don't worry. Just calm down. Breathe."

TYLEE CONTINUES SPEAKING in her calm, gentle voice, but it bothers me that she doesn't come right out and answer my question.

"I was behind the car that hit you," Tylee says in a calm voice. "Earlier when we spoke, I noticed someone stalking my house. I left my phone behind and snuck out, and came straight to Santa Fe. I was worried about you."

"Where's Mackenzie?"

"Did you see the biker's face?" Tylee asks, her calm suddenly giving way to a trembling, nervous worry. "It's very important, Juliette. Right before I stopped my car, I saw you looking straight at them..."

"Where's Mackenzie?"

I can't hide my impatience this time. Tylee's hand falls away and her voice sounds tight and distant.

"I'm sorry, Juliette."

THE PAIN IS like a smooth but sharp knife sliding through my flesh, starting in my abdomen and pushing all the way through up to my throat, searing every inch of my internal organs on the way up. I can't even scream. A strangled noise comes from my lungs.

"What do you mean you're sorry? Where is my child? Where's my baby girl?"

"THE BIKER TOOK HER," Tylee says, her trembling voice turning into full blown tears. "I left you on the ground and I ran. I swear to you, Juliette, I ran like hell but they put her on the bike and..."

Tylee throws her arms around me and while a part of me wants to sit in complete denial and pretend that Tylee's lying, Mackenzie is just in the other room, I know this is real. I can feel my daughter's absence in the instinctive way that I don't think I could have ever understood before having a kid of my own. I let Tylee hold me as we both sob, but I'm shattered completely.

"I CAN'T GET in touch with any of the Sinclairs while they're in Tucumcari, so I sent Lafayette. Where he's leaving from to the clubhouse is a five hour drive, so he'll get there in the middle of the night. Don't worry, Hunter will come."

I don't even bother to ask who Lafayette is, but I've never heard that name before.

"No," I whisper. "No…"

IT'S NOT that I don't want to see him. It's just that… he'll never forgive me for this. How could he? If the roles were switched and Hunter got our weeks old daughter kidnapped by a dangerous biker, I can't say I would jump to forgiveness so quickly. I wouldn't want to see him at all.

Tylee hugs me again. "This wasn't your fault. It wasn't."

"Who would do this? I thought… I thought we were done with this."

"If I knew, we would get right in my car and go after them," Tylee says. "Trust me."

THEN, Tylee's phone rings. She pulls it out of her pocket and then wrinkles her nose in disgust.

"IT'S GIDEON."

"Reaper?" I ask to confirm what seems like an unlikely situation. Tylee nods and answers the phone.

EVERYONE KNOWS Tylee and Reaper hate each other. I can't keep track of all the advanced biker lore, but whenever they're near each other, the hatred is palpable. Tylee won't explain herself, and frankly, I stay out of biker business whenever it doesn't affect me. I have enough problems.

"Shit must be bad if you're calling me."

Tylee puts the phone on speaker because she's shady like that, especially when it comes to Reaper. I hear Gideon's voice crackling over from the other end.

"I don't have time for this, Tylee. We have a goddamn emergency on our hands," Reaper says. He sounds drunk or high, which considering what I've heard about the Rebel Barbarians clubhouse, makes a lot of sense.

"I haven't said anything. What the fuck do you want?" Tylee says, dropping whatever minimal pretenses of politeness she had in the first place.

"Nigger girl escaped from my condo and I think she might have done a kidnapping."

"Christ, Reaper!" Tylee says, smashing the buttons on her phone dramatically until it goes off speaker phone. "You can't just run around using the n-word whenever you like when you might be broadcasting it to the entire world."

I sidle up next to Tylee and put my ear next to the phone. She's shady by nature, so she doesn't even shoo me off.

Reaper continues. "Call her whatever you want. I was asleep for once in my fucking life and didn't notice my goddamn alarm going off. The bitch escaped her binds and my tracker says she went straight for Santa Fe..."

"What bitch?" Tylee says, losing what little patience she might have had. "Get your ass over here and stop wasting my time. Because we have a missing baby over here and if your racist ass knows what happened, you'd better get over here and fix it!"

Tylee hangs up emphatically and then looks at me.

"I'm sorry for his language."

"It's fine," I grumble. I don't have time to take every ignorant person on earth to task for their language. Do I think it's a good thing that Reaper drops the n-word, or that any of the bikers do? No. But if I'm not within arms' reach to slap the shit out of them, I have to quietly judge and then let it go. Maybe it's not healthy, but it's how I kept my peace of mind living in the middle of nowhere all those years as one of the few black people around.

Tylee shakes her head. "No. It's not fine. He's too damn ignorant. Life has a way of sorting people out. Don't worry."

"WHY WOULD THIS PERSON TAKE MACKENZIE?"

"I don't know," Tylee says. "But if Reaper has a woman captive who knows enough to come out here and find you... it makes me wonder what else she knows."

Every biker has a different relationship with their old lady. I have no idea what happens between Tylee and Ghost, but sometimes I wonder if she knows more about club business than she lets on. Hawk doesn't have a confessional style of handling business. But Tylee grew up in this life – I didn't – so maybe her man has different ideas of what she will put up with.

"We should go after her."

This possible crazy person took my daughter. I can't think straight and even if I could, I would be thinking the same damn thing.

"No way," Tylee says. "I'm following club protocol and laying low. I don't want Ghost or your crazy ass man to whoop me for putting you in trouble."

I understand that Tylee is several years older than me, but I don't want her thinking I need protecting to this extent. I had a baby and turned twenty over the past year. I've seen things she wouldn't believe and... I did technically commit arson. While I may not be a hardened criminal, I'm far from soft.

"It's my daughter, Tylee. You're pregnant. You can't honestly tell me you would sit here if someone kidnapped your daughter."

Tylee gives me a sympathetic look. "I wouldn't. I know I wouldn't. But the Sinclairs are different. If Hawk is anything like Ghost, he'll bruise your ass purple for disobeying him on this type of thing."

"I would let him do that a thousand times if it meant getting Mackenzie back faster," I explain to her. I can tell I'm close to convincing Tylee, so I stay quiet and just look at her, hoping my forlorn maternal expression will touch her. She's pregnant, so she must be currently experiencing the mixture of hormones and the shift in consciousness that happens when you realize how important it is to bring life into the world for the first time.

"You're crazy," Tylee says, shaking her head. "We don't even know who took her."

"We know where Reaper's place is. We could get out there quickly."

I don't know how close we are to Reaper's place, but it's better to get a headstart than to sit on our asses doing nothing. I don't think I could live with myself if I just sat there and did nothing. Tylee keeps looking at me like I'm crazy, but not like she's given up on me entirely.

Tylee laughs. "Yeah, not in my car."

"We can take a motorcycle," I suggest. I barely know where we are, but if we're anywhere near a Rebel Barbarian, we have to have access to a motorcycle. Judging by Tylee's suspicious silence, she *does* have access to one.

"My husband would *kill* me if I took his baby. He just bought a barely used 2024 Indian Chief off some biker who needed the money for surgery," Tylee says. "It's the only bike that he doesn't have torn apart right now."

"Perfect."

"You don't understand, Juliette. If anything happens to that bike, my husband will slit my throat."

"You're pregnant and he's your husband. He'll understand that you did this for a good cause. Plus... Hunter won't let him do that."

She scoffs. "Do you genuinely think Hawk can kick my husband's ass? No offense sweetheart, but my husband is about as big as a grizzly bear with a gut like a sumo wrestler."

Hunter is muscular in comparison to Isaac, but Tylee is right about the size difference. If Isaac sat on Hunter, he could break him in half.

"What about Southpaw? He'll get the entire Shaw clan to protect you and your unborn child. *Please,* Tylee. My baby is out there."

She stares at me for a few seconds and then sighs.

"If I don't help you, I know you will find a way to steal the keys and run off on your own."

"I plead the fifth."

Tylee's lips purse into a thin line. She spends enough time around troublemakers to know that I'll do exactly what she thinks.

"I can't help you steal my husband's bike and escape to the middle of nowhere, Juliette. I can't."

SHE PAUSES FOR A BEAT. I just keep staring at her and hoping my guilt trip works.

"YOU ARE IMPOSSIBLE," Tylee says. "I can't help you, but I'll look the other way. And I'll leave a pistol on the counter. Two grand. A cell phone. Keep that location on. Don't do anything I wouldn't do."

Chapter Twenty-Eight
Tamiya

I heard Juliette's footsteps coming down the hallway. I've been in this motel long enough that I know there isn't anyone else on this floor and only one person could be rumbling down that hallway with that much fury in her steps. I know now the baby girl is named Mackenzie, and I set her in the middle of the motel mattress on a fresh towel so I can answer the door and hopefully avoid getting shot in the face.

Once I got to the motel, I changed out of the biker leather and into clothes you would expect to see on a normal black woman – jeans and a t-shirt. I hate that the only t-shirt I could find before I left smells like Gideon and has a white skull on the back. *I'm going to miss him.*

Before Juliette finds me, I swing the motel door open. She gasps and points the pistol at me that was hidden behind her back. At least she doesn't shoot. I immediately throw my hands up just in case.

"Juliette Sinclair. I'm so sorry. I have your daughter and she is completely safe. If you come in here… I can explain."

Juliette does not look like a woman open to discussion. I can feel my nerves acting up, but I tell myself to stay calm.

"Look. You're with a biker, right? You know they aren't perfect. Well… Gideon Blackwood killed my sister, okay? Then your boss kidnaps me and sticks my ass with him in Texas and... my life has been turned upside down."

"I can put you out of your misery after you give me my baby back," Juliette says, keeping her gun trained on me as she creeps slowly past me into the bedroom. Honestly, she clearly doesn't know what she's doing with the gun and I could have easily disarmed her ass. She's pretty short too. But I let her get to her baby. I caused enough problems here and possibly some trauma.

"What do you know about Oske?"

"What about her?" Juliette says, barely giving a fuck about her muzzle control now that she has her baby easily in her line of sight. Makes me wonder if that thing even has ammo in it. Before I follow my instincts to snatch the gun away from Juliette, she sets it on the dresser and picks up Mackenzie. Her mommy instincts kick in immediately and she smells Mackenzie's diaper before looking over her shoulder at me.

"You changed her?"

"Yes. I didn't want to hurt her, I swear. There's something going on with the club and I don't know what it is."

Juliette holds Mackenzie to her chest, bouncing her up and down. My stomach twists in a knot just watching them. Considering what Reaper and I have been up to the past few months, it wouldn't be that crazy if I ended up getting pregnant. Not like I should be thinking about having Reaper's baby, considering what I'm about to do.

"What do you mean?"

"Oske told me that I *had* to kidnap your baby. That Southpaw wanted me to do it because he had 'eyes on me' and was looking for a mole. She threatened me and I was worried if I didn't do it... she would get someone else to do it. But I'm sorry, Juliette. I think I should go."

The faster I leave, the better. I don't need Gideon tracking me down. It's for the best that everything ends between us. He won't forgive this. Not after he exposed his heart to me.

"Where is Oske?"

"I have no idea. I didn't trust anyone. I assumed you would track me down, but I don't know who else is coming and who knows about this."

"I doubt Wyatt would have you kidnap my baby."

"I don't know the guy, okay? And what I do know about him involves him asking Gideon to fuck me to keep me quiet, his degenerate gambling addiction, a drinking problem, and his wife left him with their baby."

Juliette nods along with me, but she doesn't seem surprised in the slightest.

"He was clean for three months. I warned Anna it would take longer than that."

"I think betting on Little League was the last straw for her. But it doesn't matter. They're back together now."

"Just in time for the club meeting," Juliette says, groaning as she sits Mackenzie on her hip. I feel that uncomfortable knot tighten in my stomach. I don't want to call it envy, but it's like I'm wishing for something I never thought I wanted. "Listen, I know Oske, but I can't say for sure she wouldn't do something like this. I don't think she would hurt me but... She definitely has secrets."

"How would that relate to kidnapping your baby?"

"Sowing seeds of discord in the club. Before you got here, they didn't always get along," Juliette says. "Maybe someone wants them to go back to the way they were."

"What? Total fucking anarchy?" I mutter.

Juliette scowls and I bite my tongue. It's not like the baby understands the swear words, but I guess I hear her point.

"I don't know," she says. "But you don't have to run away. I'll help explain everything and while they're at their meeting... we can figure out the Oske situation. My friend Quin might be coming to town soon... We can hang out."

She looks at me with wide, light-brown eyes. This girl is one of the most light-skinned black people I've seen. She just *almost* looks mixed race, although you can tell she isn't. Her pretty round face and the motherly way she's holding Mackenzie almost tempt me to stay.

Wouldn't it be nice if life was that simple? I don't really believe I can stay here, though. I want to believe it. But the more I stare at Juliette and the baby and think of Reaper saying "I love you"... the more I want to run away.

"I have to get away from Reaper," I say to her, lowering my voice so she assumes the worst. I know it's wrong for me to play on her emotions like that, but the only thing running through my head is self-preservation.

Juliette's eyes grow wide.

"Did he hurt you?"

"Not badly. But... we're bad for each other."

I'M NOT good for Gideon. I piss him off. I drive him crazy. I make him say and do things that he wouldn't normally do. He didn't know who he was when he killed my sister, but I know that he loves me and I'm still willing to do something that I know will hurt him. What type of person does that make me?

"Are you sure you don't want to stay here and work things out with him? If Reaper is anything like Hunter, he will have made assurances that you wouldn't get away."

"I can keep Gideon off my tail," I answer confidently. Though I have to be honest, I don't feel confident at all.

"Will you at least tell me where you're going?" Juliette asks me. "I'm not going to give you too much credit, but you took better care of Mackenzie than our last babysitter."

Again, there's that pang in my chest at her mention of being a good mom and just watching how Juliette cares about her daughter. She's a part of that world too, strangely enough. That club of degenerates has a soft side to it and that soft side is standing right in front of me, tempting me away from doing the right thing. I need to run away from Gideon Blackwood, not become part of his world.

I can't be his old lady. *I can't.*

. . .

"I'LL TELL you when I get there if you give me your phone number," I tell Juliette, hoping I can throw her off for a while.

"Promise?"

"I promise."

"You had better get a head start," Juliette says. "For all you know, Gideon could be tracking you."

She gives me her phone number on a piece of paper and I stick it into my bra.

I DON'T THINK she's onto something when it comes to Gideon tracking me, though. That man is a hobby mechanic. The rest of his tactics have been blunt instruments. I'm not worried about Gideon tracking me. Once I disappear... I'll be gone. He'll hate me for a while, but he's a tall, hot, blond white man. Some biker chick will be trying to get into his pants by the end of the week.

Even if I have doubts about Juliette's advice, I'm not trying to make enemies. I already kidnapped this woman's baby. I nod and thank her for the recommendation.

"How would I know if he has a tracker?"

"I don't know," she says. "Check your phone location, maybe. Or the bike."

"Thanks, Juliette," I tell her. "I promise, I'll call you when I get there."

I DON'T KNOW if I mean it, but there's a part of me that likes this young mother and wishes I could be friends with her.

I'M JUST ALWAYS MEANT to be on the run...

DRIVING from the motel to Denver takes all night, but when I get there, Rebecca Knight's car is parked in the driveway of the AirBnB address, just like she promised. I grin. It's been a long time since I've seen Rebecca and our relationship has definitely transformed into more of a friendship since I've last seen her.

I text her once I'm outside and she swings the door open.

218

"I CAN'T BELIEVE you're here," she says, throwing her arms around me. "And you won't *believe* what I found out."

Chapter Twenty-Nine
Reaper

Southpaw gives us permission to go after Tamiya. I don't know what the fuck she was thinking, but that's not the problem Wyatt is focused on right now...

Oske put her up to this?

I can see his mind turning over what to do as we mount our bicycles and I activate the second secret tracker I put in every one of my vehicles... It's not like I don't trust her. It's just that... she's a handful and I learned fast to sleep with one eye open around Tamiya.

I didn't realize it would get this bad. But this shit... it's a worst case scenario. *Why the fuck would she do something like this?*

At least I prepared for her skinny ass to get into this type of trouble at some point. Tamiya was a private investigator, so I suspected that if she ever stole one of my bikes, she would search for an AirTag or something like that. I gave her a decoy that would give her false confidence if she ever escaped.

What I actually did is a little bit more complicated. I was an Army Ranger, and I'm not as stupid as she thinks.

Tamiya thinks I'm a "hobby mechanic" which she muttered under her breath several times while we were together, but I know how to rig up a GPS, a battery, an old iPhone and a couple copper wires to create a tracker that I soldered to an interior part of the bike. Makes me feel safer about my bike and safer about Tamiya.

I can't explain why the fuck she took off to Southpaw. I don't have any answers for *that.*

WHATEVER THE FUCK she's up to... she should have told me.

I guess it's my fault she doesn't trust me. I'm not the best guy and all the love in the world doesn't make up for it in her mind. I deserve it.

I lost my shit on the phone to Tylee and fucked up. I never really thought about using the n-word until it fell out of my mouth. Until I said it about a woman who I love. I feel sick to my stomach. I know I'm a villain. As sick as I am, I'm still getting on the back of this bike to drag her ass back here.

But I know I'm fucked up and if I expect Tamiya to stay with me instead of continuously running away... I'll have to be a better man.

WITH DAD GONE, I lost any reason to think of being a good man. I did whatever the fuck I wanted and just thought about money, the club... no fucking future. With Tamiya, I can think about the future. And I know her messed up skinny ass is just like me. She thinks she can hide from her problems or run away from them but I love her too much to let that happen.

EVEN IF I'M not good enough to be with her. I'll work out what to do about that once I catch up with her.

WE FOLLOW her route as best as we can along the highways, and her car stops when we stop two hours into our journey. In Denver. Shit. Wyatt is a couple minutes behind me, so by the time he gets to the stop, I'll have to tell him that Tamiya's ass escaped all the way to Denver and we're only days away from the club meeting...

·   ·   ·

MAYBE IT'S BETTER if I go after her alone. I fill the bike up with gas and hit my vape while I wait for the others to catch up. When I talk about a drive to Denver, it isn't hard to get permission to head up there on my own.

"What the fuck happened between the two of you?" Wyatt asks. "That woman is an angel, so if she fucked you over for Oske, you must have done something."

"Have you considered that the Indian bitch is the problem?"

"Yes," Wyatt snarls. "I *have* considered that. The second we get done with our meeting, I'll find her. Oske doesn't have any money and she has vices. I'll find out why the fuck she put Tamiya up to this."

"Because you don't teach her any goddamn respect."

I shouldn't push Wyatt like this. But I'm pissed off that Oske scared the shit out of Tamiya so much that she would take off like this. If he had any fucking control over Oske, she wouldn't be a goddamn problem.

I'M lucky that he doesn't take any offense or if he does, he doesn't think it's worth it for us to argue about this. I know I shouldn't push him.

"Listen, Gideon. Go up to Denver. Have Ruger conduct a proxy vote for you and once you get Tamiya and bring her back to Texas, we can question her about Oske and better yet, get all these damn women in a room together for questioning."

"What other women are you talking about?"

"Tylee. Juliette. Anna. All of them. I'm sick of them running things around here, causing nothing but goddamn mayhem."

"I'll get Tamiya back. I promise."

"MAKE SURE THAT YOU DO," he says, downright glaring at me like it's my fault she took off. "She's a good woman, Reaper. Don't screw that up."

THE LITTLE DOT tracking Tamiya hasn't moved since she got to Denver. If I don't stop, I can get to her in a few hours. I say goodbye to the boys and drink a Monster Energy drink before I get back on the bike and ready to get that woman back in my arms where she belongs. It's the longest ride of my life and the closer I get to Denver, the more I have to wonder exactly *how* I'm going to get Tamiya to come back to New Mexico with me.

I get to Denver at 3:46 a.m. and park my bike outside the address where Tamiya's tracker led me. She has my spare bike parked outside next to a black Ford Taurus and a busted up Toyota from the nineties. No lights are on. I move my bike across the street and lean against it vaping until 5 a.m.

With no movement from the house, I walk to find some coffee nearby. It's Denver, can't be that hard to find a McDonalds where I can get some coffee. Tamiya would complain that I refuse to pay $4 for an "actually good" cup of coffee, but I like McDonald's just fine...

I get back to the house with my coffee at around 5:23 a.m. and there's still no movement. Nothing happens until 6:20 a.m. when a black woman walks outside of the house to the mailbox. She barely registers that I'm sitting across the street watching the house. The woman looks like Tamiya, but she's fat and Tamiya couldn't hold onto any weight if she tried. Not like she eats a damn fucking thing.

The woman eventually notices me, wrinkles her nose and runs back inside. *Shit.* Well, if Tamiya's in there, she'll either be running out the back door to escape or running out the front door to shoot me in the head.

I can't let that happen. I walk across the street and knock on the front door. I don't have a plan in my head. All I know is that I'm not letting Tamiya get away from me like this. I knock a few times and nobody responds.

"Tamiya! I know you're in there..."

Nothing. Then I hear footsteps and women's voices muttering in hushed tones. I pound my fists on the door again.

"I'm not afraid to break the door down. Tamiya... *Please...*"

I don't think she's going to open the door, so when the door swings open, I just stand there with my mouth hanging open like a dumb ass trout. It's not Tamiya standing there, though.

"Where's Tamiya?"

The woman looks me up and down. She's taller than Tamiya and has a much larger frame. Sweatpants. Dark circles under her eyes. Copper hair that hasn't been brushed in days and mascara smudged over the freckles on her cheeks.

"Tamiya's asleep and I'm guessing she doesn't want to see you," the woman says, followed by a yawn.

I DON'T CARE if she wants to see me. I push past the woman in the doorway, not bothering to get her name or share mine.

"HEY!" She yells as I step into the small house. "THIS IS ILLE-GAL! DAMARA! GET MY GUN!"

Damara? *What the hell is going on here?*

I hear shuffling and hazard a guess about which of three doors in front of me might be Tamiya's bedroom. Before I can choose, the third door swings open and Tamiya stands in the doorway, half asleep and wearing *my* oversized t-shirt over her skinny ass body.

"Fuck. Shit." she says when she sees me. "What the hell are you going here?"

The copper-haired woman steps between us.

"Is that him?" she asks.

"That's Gideon, Rebecca," Tamiya says, her eyes stuck on mine. "He's not going to hurt us."

"He just broke in," Rebecca says just as Damara returns holding the gun like she's never held one before. *Her* presence is the only thing that can take my attention off Tamiya. When I look at her, Tamiya seems to read my mind. "You didn't kill her, Gideon. I don't know who you killed but... it wasn't my sister."

I DON'T KNOW what the fuck to say.

SOMETIMES YOU WISH you could bring back the people you killed. Especially if you aren't sure you had the right to kill them. I'm stunned. Immobile. But still emotionless. This can't be right...

Tamiya senses my shock, but nobody moves. I'm too smart to move. I don't want to die in this damn living room, just after I learn there might be some redemption for my soul in the end. Tamiya might not leave me...

Rebecca takes the gun from Damara, allowing a wave of relief to settle over the room as someone more responsible takes hold of the gun.

"Don't worry," Tamiya says. "They're trustworthy."

"I haven't committed any crimes," I say flatly.

The women in the room exchange glances, but as long as they don't say anything, I don't feel particularly worried about their knowing looks.

"Rebecca didn't give up looking and she found evidence that Damara might have taken a boat from the coast of Florida to some island nobody has ever heard of."

"People have heard of Dominica," Damara says. "They just mistake it for the Dominican Republic, which worked to keep me hidden for years."

"I'm good at what I do," Rebecca says. "Maybe I just need cases that give me faith in humanity instead of taking it away."

Damara keeps staring at me, even if I return my gaze to Tamiya, trying to figure out the smartest and fastest way I can close the distance between us and get my arms around her. She takes one step out of her room which brings me marginally closer to that goal.

"Didn't he still kill someone?"

"Yes," Tamiya says, keeping her eyes on me. "But he didn't kill you."

SHE RUNS across the room and for some strange fucking reason, Tamiya throws her arms around me and hugs me. I don't know what the hell is going on and I doubt I will ever completely understand women. But her tits are pressed against my chest. And she's warm. And this crazy fucking woman who kidnapped a baby and ran away to Denver is finally back in my arms.

I hold her tightly. Not just because I miss her so goddamn much or because her feminine scent mixed with what remains of mine on my t-shirt gets me rock hard in an instant.

"I love you, Tamiya. I hate how much I love you."

Her fingers sink into my hair. She calls my blond hair "wispy" when she plays with it. I love the way her fingers feel against my scalp as she indulges herself in the texture of my hair with delighted fascina-tion. I pull away from her slightly, and look down at her.

My dick jumps in my pants. This skinny pain in the ass does things to me that no other woman has. I keep my hands on her hips. Every ounce of pain I felt losing her comes rushing back to me followed by hot shame for the word I uttered on the phone to Tylee Sinclair.

I called her that. This beautiful, loving, soft woman, whose life I nearly destroyed. My breath catches in my throat and I wonder if I deserve to love her. She touches my lips and I nearly fold as emotions surge in my chest. You don't feel like this in the military. It's counter-productive to your survival to let shit hit you like this. It's much easier to be numb.

"What's wrong?" She asks.

"All I do is hurt you. That's why you had to run away from me."

Her eyes are so goddamn wide and beautiful. I can't keep talking. I know we have to, but I know what I say to Tamiya right now could ruin everything. I don't want that to happen either.

"I ran away because I lied to you, Gideon. I kidnapped a baby. I betrayed your club... I don't even know who I betrayed. All I know is that I make trouble in your world."

"You're my trouble," I say, my grasp on her hips tightening. "Good trouble."

Tamiya's eyes look into mine and guilt shoots straight through me again. Kissing her again won't make it better. Not without me telling her the truth.

"When you were gone, I did something bad..."

Her face falls and my heart breaks immediately just watching her look at me with that much disappointment. I want this woman's admiration and love more than I want anything else.

"What did you do?"

"If he cheated, I'll rip his balls off," Rebecca says. I try not to let it bother me that we have an audience. It doesn't matter who surrounds us because once I look into Tamiya's eyes, the world fades into an invisible blur and she's all I can see.

"I wouldn't fuck around on you. I just... I slipped up and cussed on the phone. Called you something to Tylee and..."

I feel too goddamn guilty to keep looking into Tamiya's eyes. But I can't expect her to come back to Texas with me unless we both put all our shit out on the table.

"Oh shit," Damara says after a few seconds of silence. She figured it out. Rebecca makes a little sound and then I just say it.

"I may have used the n-word talking to Tylee."

Tamiya breaks away from my grasp. I don't think I have the strength to look her in the eye, but I know I deserve every bit of hatred and loathing she rains down on me. Pure disappointment. When I look up at her face, it's almost expressionless. I watch her try to hide her hurt and I want to take it away.

"I'm sorry."

"Why are you telling me?" She responds stiffly.

"Because I love you. Because I'm missing the club meeting to drive hundreds of miles out here to Denver to bring you back. But I want you to choose me, Tamiya. I want you to be with me."

"You want me to be with a guy who called me the n-word?"

"I want you to be with a man who would kill everyone in this room to be with you."

"That nigga crazy," Damara mutters, hustling to the kitchen shortly after my threat to 'get a glass of water'. Rebecca stays watching both of us. She's clearly protective over Tamiya.

"Gideon. No killing people."

"Then what do you need from me, Tamiya? I want to be a better man. I don't want to hurt you. Since Wyatt dropped you on my doorstep, you have been the biggest challenge since I became a Ranger."

She's close enough that I can touch her again, but I don't know who closed the distance between us and I don't know if I have a right to touch her. It doesn't feel like I should. But she's so close. And I want her. My hands reach for her hips again. Tamiya's tense, but she doesn't move away.

"What the hell is our life going to look like, Gideon?"

"Whatever the fuck you want," I whisper. Now that I'm looking at her again. Holding her. I can imagine her forgiveness. I can imagine myself working for it. Doing anything for it. When a man knows, he just knows. And I know this woman is mine.

"Okay," Tamiya says, nodding slowly. "Well, right now I'm a bit occupied."

I try not to let her feel my frustration, but Tamiya has always had a special way of sensing my emotions and doing her goddamn best to get under my skin.

"Occupied?"

"I want to rebrand and start a new company," Rebecca says. "My dad gave me a $50,000 gift for finishing two months of rehab."

"So what? You want to live in Denver?" I ask Tamiya. I can already feel my world closing in around me at the idea. I don't want to be surrounded by that many obnoxiously happy liberals stoned out of their goddamn minds.

Tamiya looks from me to Rebecca.

．　．　．

"OR WE START IN TEXAS."

REBECCA SHRUGS. "Are there hot guys in Texas?"
Damara calls from the kitchen. "Yes, there are!"

Chapter Thirty
Tamiya

I didn't think I would follow Gideon back to Texas. I didn't think *anything* that happened when I promised to meet Rebecca would happen. She found Damara. Naturally, that begs the question... *who was the woman who was shot?* Damara left her ex-boyfriend three days before Reaper shot him. He had been cheating on her with a sixteen-year-old and she was sick of getting made a fool of by some "trick ass white boy". Her words.

Apparently, she had gone to the police, but all of them were in his new church group and didn't believe her or care about the illegal relationships he was conducting with various underage girls. *Creepy.* Damara's best explanation for Reaper's crime was, "Maybe he shot the side bitch. I'm not complaining!"

If I hadn't spent the past few years hunting down the man who I thought killed her, I would agree with her. What if whoever he killed had a family? What if that person tracks him down the way I did?

Damara had an answer for *that* too. "How many bitches out there actually have the intelligence to conduct that type of investigation?"

. . .

Damara convinces Gideon to let her take his bike back to Texas so we can ride together.

"I rode with a gang of racists far scarier than your skinny ass."

"Since when am I skinny?" Reaper snaps. "Tamiya's the skinny ass around here…"

Despite their arguing, he gives in, and it's definitely because he doesn't trust what I'll do once I get on the back of that bike. With Rebecca inside packing up, somehow more ready than I am to spontaneously move to Texas, and Damara starting up her bike, I lean against Gideon's and watch him get ready for a long ride.

He has his rituals. Tucking in his dog tags. Hitting his vape a few extra times. Messaging the twins. Messaging Ruger. Taking his rings off and zipping them inside his jacket. Gideon hits his vape one last time before handing me a helmet. He hasn't been able to look at me for very long since his little confession inside.

"Hey," I say to him, trying to force some connection out of him.

"Did I do something wrong?"

"No. I just… You know I love you, right Gideon?"

There it is. He looks at me and instantly, I feel that gush. That undeniable warmth I always felt with him. I know he's hurt and I know he hurt me. Trust me, hearing that a man you love would even *think* about referring to you that way is beyond gut-wrenching.

"Yes. But I don't deserve it."

"You have to stop thinking like that if we're going to be together. Neither of us are perfect. We're going to screw up. I just… I need you to understand why it's wrong."

"I do."

"Good."

"Hate is ugly, Tamiya. I know that."

"Good."

"But it's inside me."

"I know."

"Then how the hell can you love me?"

He's so close that I want to rip his clothes off and head back inside instead of standing here having this conversation. How the hell can I explain why I love him? How can I explain that I loved him before I even knew the truth about Damara? That I was willing to love him when I believed the worst about him.

That I still love him now.

I don't get it anymore than he gets it. I press my hand to his chest. Our eyes meet. I can feel his heart rate getting faster as I touch him.

"Because..."

"I just think," he whispers. "I'll be working my whole life to be good enough for you and that's what I want to do."

I want to answer him, but no words manage to form. There's just something unreasonably stunning about him that forces me into silence. He has a gorgeous face. Sharp jawline. Hair that's so goddamn golden and soft... I'd rather kiss him than talk.

"Okay," I whisper finally, after what feels like an eternity of staring into Gideon's eyes like we're in a corny movie. "Then I guess I'd better stick around."

"I'll track you across the country if I have to," Gideon whispers, running his thumb over my lips and sending a shiver straight between my legs. He gets me so goddamn horny that it's impossible to think.

I move closer to him, hoping for another kiss, hoping for something more. He can see it in my eyes and the smirk crossing Gideon's face tells me that he's about to give in to my desires. I lean in expectantly and his lips meet mine. He's the perfect kisser right now. Everything that I need...

We kiss so long that Damara revs the engine loudly and zooms off without us. Reaper sets the helmets down and grabs my cheeks without a care in the world. I let him hold me and kiss me until our lips are numb. This time, when we look at each other, I feel better. Ready.

"You know I'm going to marry your skinny ass, right?"

I smile at him.

"And..." he says, reaching around to touch my butt. "I'm giving you a nice tattoo right on your ass... so no man will ever touch you again..."

Before I can protest, Gideon squeezes my butt cheeks and drags my body against his for another kiss. He plops me up on the bike seat and we make out until Rebecca comes outside to see if there's a problem with the bike.

"Nope," Gideon calls out to her. "Just enjoying the shit out of her lips."

REBECCA WATCHES us makeout for a while before walking back inside.

Gideon helps get my helmet on and joins me on the bike. I settle my body close to his and get ready for a long ride back to Texas.

HE SWEARS I don't have to worry about "the Oske situation", but right now, that's not all I worry about.

WHAT IF SOMEONE else comes after him? The thought must have at least crossed Gideon's mind. That man would rather keep his worries to himself and implode than let anyone inside his head. Except me. I rest my head on Gideon's back and promise that when we get home, we'll figure it all out together.

HOME.

· · ·

I HAVEN'T HAD a place to call *home* in a while and it feels weird.

WEIRD, but good.

CHAPTER THIRTY-ONE
CASH

The second I walk into Hunter's place, I feel squeamish. Nothing wrong with the place. It's a nice house in Santa Fe, it's just that Juliette's art makes me deeply uncomfortable. He calls out to me to come straight to the kitchen for the two of us to discuss business. Important business, according to him.

I'm just happy that I don't have to get involved in another one of Southpaw's gambling situations. The man never met a game he wouldn't bet on. Part of you has to admire a man who has balls of steel. Another part of you has to wonder what kind of idiot is dumb enough to bet all the money they have on Little League games.

Since Hunter is sober, I bring my own liquor.

"Where is Juliette?" I ask him.

He rolls his eyes. "She's out with this friend of hers. Quin."

"She has time for friends with the baby?"

"That's what I said," Hunter grunts, sipping on Dr. Pepper. "She's a pain in my ass. I need a distraction and there's a great opportunity coming up."

"Clean money?"

He nods. "Yes, sir. Clean money."

"Okay."

Doesn't make too much of a difference to me, but it's much easier to work a job laundering clean money right about now. Our family has been through enough recently without one of us heading off to prison. Cody has enough problems out in Dallas with the IRS up his ass for five years of allegedly underpaid taxes.

"I s'pose I could use a little cash," I tell Hunter.

He smirks. "None of y'all ever turn down an opportunity to make money."

"What have you got?"

He pulls out a binder of pretty legit looking documents. I glance through them, but it doesn't take me long to figure out what he wants us to get invested in.

"This might be legal, but it's goddamn dangerous, Hunter. And un-Christian."

"When the fuck was the last time you went to church?"

"My mama is going to make my life a living hell if I invest in a titty bar."

"It's not just a titty bar," Hunter says. "We're also gonna sell shrimp."

"What does your old lady think about that idea?" I ask him.

"She hates it," he says. "That's why I need you to run it."

I laugh. Hunter ought to get back to drinking if these are the brilliant thoughts he comes up with outside of liquor's influence.

"I'm not running a titty bar."

"Fine," Hunter says. "Then get some lazy ass Hollingsworth to come up here from Texas and run it for us. I don't give a shit. Fact of the matter is, I crunched the numbers and the last three around here… all the girls got deported."

Hunter gives me the most serious look. This 'legal' business venture is already beginning to sound like far too much trouble.

"Is there a reason you want to get into this business?"

"Why the fuck else?" He snaps. "Money."

I shift uncomfortably in my seat. Yes, money. The Hollingsworth family has always had enough of it since investing in gas stations along the old Route 66 highway and our whiskey distillery that produces

Hollingsworth whiskey and other products, not like that ever stopped any of us from looking for the opportunity for more. I just didn't think Hunter Sinclair was hurting for cash.

"Didn't think you needed any."

He gives me a dark look and then lowers his voice as if his old lady might pop out from around the corner at any minute.

"I lent Wyatt $100,000 and Juliette thinks I have the money to buy her dream home sitting in an account somewhere."

"A strip club isn't going to get you $100 grand quickly."

Hunter's face darkens again. "I know."

"I see."

"You don't have to be involved in the other business."

"Drugs are risky," I respond, perfectly interpreting Hunter's insinuation. Running drugs out of your own club is the perfect combination of risky and smart, but it's the kind of business you can get away with in your twenties. I don't know if Hunter really wants to risk jail with his wife and baby at home.

"I know," he says, taking a sip of Dr. Pepper that looks almost wistful. "But Juliette's pregnant again. And she's having twins."

Fuck.

I DON'T HAVE to say the cuss word out loud. My face says it all. That's the thing about being born red, you never get the privilege of hiding your emotions. My cheeks are always quick to match the color of my hair.

Hunter tries to hide his emotions, although I can see how complicated this is for him. Bringing twins into the world on top of Mackenzie might be tough if he keeps up the habit of bailing out Southpaw's stupid ass.

"What if we come up with a better idea?"

"A legal idea?"

"I said a better idea," I reply. "Not a legal one."

. . .

The apartment door opens and it's clear that Juliette is home. I can hear her talking from the doorway along with a baby babbling along in an attempt to match the rhythm and cadence of her mother's speech. Hunter presses a finger to his lips, but I don't need to be told to keep club business away from an old lady.

I rise to my feet out of politeness, and Juliette turns the corner, not just holding Mackenzie, but with a woman. Holy shit, look at the ass on that woman. And the tits. She's full-figured all right. The entire room fades around me, if I'm honest.

I just see this woman standing next to Juliette and become fixated with her instantaneously.

"Hello, ma'am. I'm Tanner."

Juliette steps between us. "Don't look at her. Don't talk to her."

That makes me want to look and talk to her even more... Unlike me, this gorgeous woman has some type of obedience for Juliette's command. I view it as a suggestion that I have every intention of ignoring completely.

Quin looks like she has good pussy. Women that big usually do. There is something about a plus-sized woman who is somewhere in the super-plus-sized range that does it for me. Quin gets my dick hard instantly. I don't even mind that Juliette can tell.

"*Hunter,*" she says sternly. "Are you going to intervene or let him keep acting like a pervert?"

"Can you relax, Juliette? He's introducing himself."

That sexy ass chocolate cupcake with extra frosting steps aside from Juliette and I can tell immediately that everything about my appearance impresses her. That doesn't surprise me. I have meticulously built my body since I was sixteen-years-old.

I obsess over everything I eat and how I spend every minute of my day. I find a woman like this one... fasc*inating.* The race thing doesn't bother me. I know the rules. Screw black women, don't marry them. My father understood that sometimes a man has dark urges.

None of those urges are as dark as the ones that strike me in the presence of this voluptuous woman. I don't even care about her name. I just want her clothes off, my tongue in her pussy and my face squeezed between thick ass thighs.

"My name is Quin."

Juliette glares at me as I take Quin's hand. This is not the time for a normal handshake. I take her hand and kiss it. Fuck. She smells like an Oreo milkshake. I can't take my eyes off her, but her eyes dart away quickly.

"Okay, we're getting out of here," Juliette says, glaring at me. "Stay *far* away from the studio. We're discussing women business."

Hunter gives her a look that I don't quite catch. Juliette ignores him and walks off with Quin in tow. Her friend moves a lot more slowly than Juliette. I can't tell if it's because she's less athletic, less angry, or because she wishes she could stay in the kitchen with me. I don't bother hiding the fact that I'm watching her ass as she walks away.

Once they're out of earshot, Hunter chastises me like he's some fucking priest.

"You don't have to stare at her like you want to eat her."

"I want to do a little more than eat her."

He scoffs. "That's what you think. That chick is seventy shades of fucked up."

"She must be what... three hundred pounds?"

"Who gives a fuck?" Hunter says, sipping on his soda. "We're here to talk business, not pussy."

"Can't talk business until I talk pussy."

He knows I have the upper hand here and he hates it.

"There's nothing to talk about. She spent the past three years stuck in a bed. Juliette says she barely recognizes the chick."

"She's gorgeous."

"She's fucked up. Don't even think about it, Cash."

"Why not?"

Hunter looks around like someone might come popping out around the corner.

"For one thing, she's black."

"So is Juliette," I say in a normal speaking tone. I'm not afraid of shit.

"Yeah, but she's light and well... I don't care about that stuff. Your mama is gonna hit the roof if you show up with a woman like Quin to Thanksgiving."

"I'm not going to bring her to Thanksgiving. I'm going to stuff her like a Thanksgiving–"

"Please. Spare me."

"What's wrong with her?"

"Nothing."

"You said she was fucked up."

"Oh. That. It's not important."

"Great. Then I can still sleep with her."

"She's Juliette's best friend, Tanner. So you can't."

I DON'T like Hunter's attitude. He used to be more of a go-getter.

"IT'S BEEN at least a month since I've been with someone."

"That is a normal amount of time to be single."

"Not for me. Women crave my dick."

"Fuck, listen. I don't care what the fuck you do. But if you touch her and Juliette asks me to put a bullet in your head, I'm gonna listen to my old lady without question."

"Okay. We can talk business now that I have your explicit permission."

"Not what the fuck happened."

·　·　·

I HAVE to calm him down. Hunter doesn't stand a chance of stopping me once I set my mind on something, and it will be best for both of us if we don't argue about the chocolate cupcake his old lady just dragged into the back room.

240

I'LL BE BACK for her later.

Chapter Thirty-Two
Reaper

"What do you mean Cash kidnapped someone?" I groan. "Listen… I don't have time for this shit. Tamiya and I have big news…"

Why the fuck can I never get a good night's sleep anymore? Tamiya and I have been keeping this news private until we're sure everything will be okay with the baby. I'm ready to tell the club and she's ready to tell Damara and Rebecca.

Not like I wanted to make the fucking announcement at two in the morning. Tamiya hears me on the phone and moves her legs against mine a bit. I freeze when her cold ass feet touch mine. If she had a little weight on her, she wouldn't be so cold all the time.

With a baby on the way, I'll have to start giving her ass deep fried everything. I wrap an arm around her and pull her close. She'll wake up if I'm on the phone soon enough.

Southpaw growls back at me. "Do you think I'm happy about having to do this? I sent his ass on a mission to find Oske, instead he kidnaps a potential criminal from Hawk's condo and takes her to… I don't know where."

"Is it really that important we find them? Maybe she ran away with him. If she's a potential criminal."

Tamiya wakes up. I glance down at her to see her gigantic brown eyes staring at me questioningly. She can have an unnerving way of looking at a man sometimes. I feel guilty of something I haven't even done yet.

She puts her hand on my chest, making everything just a little better. I'm doing everything in my power to make sure the boss doesn't drag me out of bed. From what I heard, the club meeting was a shit-show. They elected the rest of the board members, but that peaceful election preceded a gambling-related brawl instigated by Steel of all fucking people.

I'm glad I was with Tamiya instead.

"JULIETTE IS LOSING her fucking mind. Hawk wants to make her feel better..."

"Then he should give her some goddamn dick instead of waking our asses up in the middle of the night."

Southpaw sighs. "I told him that. Anna said I was an asshole."

I can hear Anna in the background. "I still think you're an asshole. Juliette is scared. Her best friend went missing with a 6'6" redhead. It's giving Lucifer."

Southpaw grunts. I don't blame him for his frustration. Anna doesn't mind being a handful and a half.

Tamiya's hand trails down my chest and my dick sprouts a semi before she even gets to the waistband of my boxers.

"Listen... I'll tell Hawk you're leaving tonight so just... don't tell him any different until I figure out what to do."

"Tell him to give his wife some dick and stop waking me up in the middle of the night."

"I'm not gonna tell him that."

"It's *Tanner Hollingsworth.* What's the worst that he could do to some chick?"

We pause.

.   .   .

We both know.

We grew up with Tanner. We know he's not all the way right in the head, quite frankly.

The silence is palpable.

"I'm not getting out of bed," I say firmly. And it's not just because Tamiya has her hand wrapped around my dick, although that definitely plays a role.

"Fine," Wyatt growls. "Stay quiet. I'll deal with the Sinclairs tomorrow."

"We don't need this, Wyatt," I remind him. "You still have that crazy Indian on the loose."

"I know," he says, clearly annoyed that I keep bringing up Oske. She has been unreasonably difficult to find, greatly frustrating all of us. Rebecca and Tamiya are working on tracking her down in their free time, but they have real *paying* clients to deal with most of the day.

"We don't need more problems," I remind Wyatt. "We're just gonna have to trust Tanner won't hurt the girl..."

"I don't know if I'm willing to make that bet," Wyatt replies.

"G'night."

I hang up abruptly because Tamiya advanced her techniques, moving my boxers all the way off so she can get her lips around the head of my dick. I want to chastise her for doing some shit like that while I'm on the phone handling club business but... her mouth feels so fucking good.

"You are a dirty girl..." I groan as she takes the full length of my dick all the way down her throat. She flicks the piercing across the tip and I nearly cum from the slightest brush from her perfect tongue. Her mouth is so wet, so fucking soft... I want to cum inside it badly.

"I love you baby," I whisper when Tamiya tightens her suction on my cock and gives me the best head I've ever woken up to at two in the morning. She is so goddamn good at this...

BEFORE I FINISH, I know I have to have her. I stop Tamiya from sucking my dick and pull her on top of me. She's so light that it's easy to get her on top. She spreads her thighs apart and I watch my dick disappear into her gorgeous black pussy slowly as she sits on top of me.

I love watching her ride my dick. Once I'm all the way inside her, Tamiya moves her hips, taking me deeper, enjoying the hell out of my cock without any inhibitions. Her small breasts bounce with each thrust into her pussy and her dark brown nipples get impossibly harder and darker as she gets closer to finishing.

Her pussy gets tight around my dick as I reach down to rub her clit so I can watch her finish on top of me. Tamiya's breathing slows down and she starts moaning when she gets close.

"Cum for me, baby... Cum for me..."

I grab her ass as she moves her hips so I can feel her smooth, soft butt cheeks jiggling as she rides me. I can feel myself getting closer with her. She leans forward to kiss me and as her nipples graze my chest and her soft lips touch mine, I lose every ounce of control. My balls tighten against my body and I pull her closer to me as I groan and finish.

I can feel her cumming along with me and I pull my woman's soft, dark-skinned body against mine. I still feel that pit of guilt in my stomach sometimes for what type of person I've been. But I love this woman and I love that she makes me want to be better.

"Don't move," I whisper. "I love feeling your pussy around my dick."

"I wasn't planning on it," Tamiya whispers, playing with my hair again and kissing me.

"Good. We're already up... might as well go for round two in a bit."

Tamiya nods and moves her hips a little like she's trying to get me hard again.

"Fuck, you feel good," I whisper as my dick stirs to life again.

"I love you, baby," Tamiya says, kissing my neck and my chest, making it even easier for my arousal to return.

"I love you too, dirty girl. I love every last inch of your skinny ass..."

THE END

Click here to order Biker's Ritual
Cash & Quin's Story
bit.ly/barbarians4

Click here to get a text message from Jamila Jasper when the next book drops:
bit.ly/textjamila

Character Glossary

The Four Families

The Sinclairs
The Shaws
The Blackwoods
The Hollingsworths

The Shaw Family

Harlan Shaw, HARLEY, Club President – married to Renée, who he had two daughters with until Renée died in 1994. Harlan's daughters from his first marriage are Kelsey and Tylee. Harlan remarried Deborah Hollingsworth, who became his old lady and they had four children together: Ethan, Wyatt, Stacy, & Owen.

Renée Shaw, Harley's first old lady – Tylee & Kelsey's mother who died in 1994.

Deborah Hollingsworth Shaw, Harley's Old Lady – married to Harlan Shaw. She had two children with Harley while he was married to Renée Shaw (Ethan and Wyatt). After Renée's passing, Deborah and Harley married.

Tylee Shaw Sinclair, b. 1990 – Harlan and Renée's daughter. Works for the family, fell in love with Isaac Sinclair.

Kelsey Shaw, b. 1993 – Harlan and Renée's daughter. She works for the club and lives on her own in a small trailer ten miles off Route 66 in a small Missouri town.

Ethan Shaw, BEAR, b. 1989, Officer – Harley's eldest son. The angry one.

Wyatt Shaw, SOUTHPAW, b. 1991, Jr. Officer – Harley's second son, the main character of the book *Biker's Surrogate*. His old lady, Anna Shaw, recently married him and they have a beautiful baby together.

Anna Shaw, Southpaw's old lady b. 1993 – Anna, a former nurse, encountered the Rebel Barbarians during an escape from a creepy suitor and fell into Southpaw's clutches. Their initial meeting was filled with confusing emotions, but eventually, Anna chose Southpaw.

Owen Shaw, SCRAP, b. 1996, Officer – Harley's youngest son. The patient one.

Stacy Shaw, b. 2000 – The youngest of the Shaw daughters, she still lives with Deborah Hollingsworth.

Claude Shaw, ROTTIE, *club member* – Harley's brother.

Michael Shaw, KEY, *club member* – Harley's brother.

The Sinclair Family

Randall Sinclair, RANDY, Club Vice President, b. 1956 – Club Vice President and patriarch of the Sinclair family. He is Harley's best friend who served in Afghanistan in 1991. He had twin boys, Ryder and Hunter after his service in the first Gulf War. He served along with Lyle Blackwood.

Karen H. Sinclair, b. 1979 – Karen Hollingsworth married Randy when they were very young and she had twin boys after his service in the first Gulf War. Karen had a past as a biker chick, defying her father's wishes to ride with the various club members.

The twins...

Ryder Sinclair, STEEL, Officer, b. 1992 – Hawk's twin brother is currently serving time in *Lansing Correctional Facility* in Kansas.

Hunter Sinclair, HAWK, Jr. Officer, b. 1992 – main character of *Biker's Servant,* Wyatt's best friend from high school and his right hand man. He possibly has a problem with alcohol.

Barrett Sinclair, BENCH, Officer, b. 1967 – Randall's brother and fellow club member. He has one divorce under his belt from Selma Sinclair, but remains in a contentious marriage with his second wife, Caitlin Sinclair.

Selma Sinclair, b. 1969 – divorced from Barrett Sinclair. Isaac Sinclair's mother. Tylee's mother-in-law (who hates Tylee's red hair). She was Barrett's high school sweetheart and remains bitter about their divorce. She hates Caitlin for stealing her man.

Isaac Sinclair, GHOST, b. 1986 – married to Tylee Shaw Sinclair.

Caitlin Sinclair, Barrett's old lady, b. 1975 – Magnum's mother and Barrett's old lady and current wife. He marries Caitlin after divorcing Selma when Isaac was 10-years-old.

Magnum Sinclair, CONDOM, Officer, b. 1992 – Caitlin and Barrett's son. Hawk's cousin. He owns an apartment building in Santa Fe.

The Blackwood Family

Lyle Blackwood, DOC, Enforcer, b. 1958-2023 – Religious Gulf War veteran who distrusts Wyatt Shaw.

Brexlynn Shaw Blackwood, Doc's old lady, b. 1968 – Claude Shaw's sister, Harley's cousin. She is bitter and doesn't like Harley very much. Religious. She is currently in prison for conspiracy to commit murder.

The twins

Jairus Blackwood, BISHOP, Officer b. 1992 – Gideon's older brothers live in Montana on a ranch and only come down to Texas for the quarterly meetings and club business in the summer.

Jotham Blackwood, PINS, Officer b. 1992 – Gideon's older brothers live in Montana on a ranch and only come down to Texas for the quarterly meetings and club business in the summer.

The other siblings

Gideon Blackwood, REAPER, Jr. Officer, b. 1994 – Religious and violent contender for the throne of the Rebel Barbarians motorcycle club. Ex army ranger.

Tobias Blackwood, PRIEST, Officer b. 2000 – currently in prison for aggravated assault. Runs the prison's weekly worship session. Sells weed. Called Priest because he didn't have sex until he was 22 years old, the week before he got initiated and went to federal prison.

Ruth Blackwood, b. 2006 - Lyle's precious youngest daughter. She is the family's biggest rebel, currently attempting to enlist in the Air Force.

Doc's nephew... adopted into the family

Ruger Blackwood, BUCKY, new member, b. 2004 – Lyle's nephew. Loyal to Lyle. Collects hunting knives. Socially awkward.

The Hollingsworth Family

The Hollingsworth family extends across all of Route 66 but the Hollingsworth family home sits in Lubbock, TX. Due to extensive real estate dealings, several members of the Hollingsworth family own property at the end of the old Route 66 highway in Santa Monica, California.

When it's time for their story, you will learn more. Consider the tall, strapping red-heads to be shrouded in mystery, obsessed with money, and hell-raisers like the other Barbarians.

Don Hollingsworth, died in the Amarillo clubhouse fire – Tanner's father died in the Amarillo clubhouse fire. He was the Hollingsworth family patriarch and left behind an enormous trust which various family members and other individuals stake claims to throughout the series.

Annabel Hollingsworth, b. – Don's wife and 'old lady' Annabel is proud of her Southern heritage, including all the dark and dirty parts of her family's past. After her husband's death, she avoids most dealings with the Rebel Barbarians and focuses instead on her family and ensuring healthy marriages amongst the young Hollingsworths.

Tanner Hollingsworth, CASH, b. 1991 - The eldest son of Don & Annabel, Tanner runs the majority of the family businesses in Texas & California. While the Hollingsworth family is known for their distillery and liquor production, they have diverse investments across the Southwestern United States. Tanner alone owns over 800 acres of land across the Southwestern United States.

Kylie Hollingsworth, b. 1999 - Tanner's younger sister. She manages the distillery in Southern Missouri and is currently unmarried.

The Blue Blood Knights

A gang of outlaw bikers who were cast out from their original brotherhood. All members of the Blue Blood Knights are former cops who were disgraced for various reasons or who chose to live on the wrong side of the law...

Afterword

Thank you for reading Gideon & Tamiya's story.

Did you make it to the end? Thank you so much if you did. I truly appreciate it. This was a wild story with a character that most would consider to be completely irredeemable. From Book #1, I knew I would have to give Gideon his own story. Tamiya is a character that came to me later. I wanted to give her a **very real reason** to hate Gideon and connecting her to his big secret just felt right.

The two of them fit so well together.

Our next story will have a less complicated plot for the bikers, but will get extremely tense for Quin and Cash Hollingsworth.

Get ready for this action packed, smut-filled adventure that focuses more on the internal dynamic between Cash/Quin with a NEW secret and NEW villain revealed that the club will have to deal with in the future books.

Fans of characters like Anna, Juliette, Tamiya and even Rebecca Knight will want to stay tuned for their favorite characters reappearing in Book #4 and future books.

If you enjoyed *Mafia Surrogate,* the nanny/boss dynamic that plays out between Quin and Cash will shake you up.

Cash is a different demon entirely with a dick that will blow your mind. What? This is the Afterword. I'm keeping it real with y'all.

I really miss the sexual dynamic between Rian/Heavyn but what is exploding off the page with Book #4 has ended up so much darker and deeper.

There will be **at least five books** in this series and the fifth book will take us back to the Sinclair family. Steel — Hawk's twin brother — will get a love story that will blow your mind.

Some preview chapters from his book and teasers will be included in Book #4. You *seriously* don't want to miss out.

I started a tradition in the afterword of sharing some recommendations with you and hopefully I can do that today…

If you enjoyed the dynamic between Tamiya/Gideon, I have a few books with a similar dynamic.

Despicable is a dark college bully romance with a tall/dominant blond male lead who is 6'6" tall and very muscular. The black female lead in that book is one of my favorites of all time — Amina Hewitt from Texas.

I absolutely *love* the dynamic between Seb/Angie in *Pretty Little Monster*, so that might be another book if you enjoy Southern white men, rock stars and secret baby romance books.

Teasing The Tyrant has a mischievous female lead and a messed up alcoholic male lead, so you might enjoy their fights and fucks too…

The next book will have even more family, even more biker lore, and honestly, I can see myself writing *so* many books in the series, that I would *love* to keep going with that continued support from you…

I have books planned for most of the current members and lots of possible members we can bring to life as the series continues.

What do you think? Are you enjoying the series so far? If you *are* enjoying the series and made it through this personal letter — thank you! I would truly appreciate if you left a review on this book and put a 🐍 emoji in the review so I know you read the afterword… It will be our little secret. 🙈

My final word on the upcoming book?

There will be plenty of dark romance themes and more about our previous couples.

The next chapters will be live on Patreon first.

Click here to learn more about my behind the scenes community: www.patreon.com/jamilajasper

I cannot thank you enough for being there on my journey.

If you made it to the end of this author's note especially, double thank you.

I hope the wait for the next book doesn't drive you insane.

Forever grateful,

Jamila

About Jamila Jasper

The hotter and darker the romance, the better.

That's the Jamila Jasper promise.

If you enjoy sizzling multicultural romance stories that dare to *go there* you'll enjoy any Jamila Jasper title you pick up.

Open-minded readers who appreciate **shamelessly sexy romance novels** featuring black women of all shapes and sizes paired with smokin' hot white men are welcome.

Sign up for her e-mail list here to receive one of these FREE hot stories, exclusive offers and an update of Jamila's publication schedule: bit.ly/jamilajasperromance

Get text message updates on new books:
https://slkt.io/gxzM

Extremely Important Links

ALL BOOKS BY JAMILA JASPER
https://linktr.ee/JamilaJasper
SIGN UP FOR EMAIL UPDATES
Bit.ly/jamilajasperromance
SOCIAL MEDIA LINKS
https://www.jamilajasperromance.com/
GET MERCH
https://www.redbubble.com/people/jamilajasper/shop
GET FREEBIE (VIA TEXT)
https://slkt.io/qMk8
READ SERIAL (NEW CHAPTERS WEEKLY)
www.patreon.com/jamilajasper

JAMILA JASPER

Diverse Romance For Black Women

MORE JAMILA JASPER ROMANCE

<u>**Pick your poison...**</u>

Delicious interracial romance novels for all tastes. Long novels, short stories, audiobooks and more.

Hit the link to experience my full catalog.

FULL CATALOG BY JAMILA JASPER:

https://linktr.ee/JamilaJasper

Mafia Playmate
(PREVIEW)

https://bit.ly/bostonirishmafia1

Boston Irish Mafia Romance Series

Mafia Playmate

Mafia Property

Mafia Surrogate

Mafia Possession

Mafia Stalker

Click here for the complete collection:

www.jamilajasperromance.com/catalog

Content Awareness

Read this passage if you require content warnings for sensitive material. I do not give detailed content warnings that will spoil the plot, but be aware of this note.

This is a mafia romance story with dark themes including potentially triggering content of **all** varieties, violence, frank discussions and language surrounding bedroom scenes and race.
All characters in this story are 18+
Sensitive readers, be cautioned about some of the detailed romantic material in this dark but ***extremely hot romance novel.***

Description

A large pink box arrives on Aiden's doorstep with a woman inside.
His mail-order bride arrives in her birthday suit and tied up in knots
with a pretty pink silk ribbon.

Aiden never requested a dark-skinned beauty...
His family would never approve of such an impure connection.

Who is this woman? What does she want?
A note in the box reveals the truth...
**The woman in the box - *Valentina* - is a gift from an anonymous
sender who wants something dark and twisted in return.**

Chapter One
Aiden

You have one job in the Murray family. You grow up, you get your marks, you listen to Pa, you marry a nice Irish girl, preferably a blond or a redhead with lighter features.
You do what Padraig Murray asks.
You pray everyday and you keep your rosary wrapped in your pocket. You stay loyal. You keep our bloodline strong.

Pa demands a meeting with me now that I'm back in the city. He claims it's important, but it can't be that important if he wants to meet me during the Red Sox game. It feels good to be home. There's something special about Boston, but maybe that's just it – paradise is wherever our family is.

After Pa, I'll go home and see Roscoe, my Rottweiler. Then get my shit together and call my younger brother Darragh to check in on his training and find out if Rian's around. Over the weekend, I'll head to Leominster to visit Callum and then Sunday after church, stop by to see Ma and Odhran. I brought a gift home with me for Tegan, Rian's daughter, and I can't wait to see my niece's face light up when I give it to her.

If there's one thing I don't miss about being home, it's a never ending list of shit to do.

I meet my father at our usual casual meeting spot, Mulligan's, a place where we aren't afraid to celebrate Irish pride. A place where you can catch the Red Sox game and no one can catch your conversation. *It's as much home as anywhere else.*

I spot my father hunched over the bar from the street, his face illuminated by a warm orange bulb as he watches the pre-game announcer talk. I prefer football to baseball, but Pa bets on all their games, so he likes to keep his eye on the Red Sox each season.

When Pa calls, you answer, and he's desperate to know about the affair with the Italians – what the fuck happened, have I found the renegade cousins who pissed off the Italians, and whether I've killed them yet. *I haven't.*

It's all bad news and my ass is on the line if I don't find a way to sort out all the shit that happened in Long Island. At least we're guaranteed peace with the vicious Italians. *Those greaseballs aren't any better than the blacks. 'Trust 'em as far as you can throw them', Pa told me. But for now, we have peace and that's what matters. At least to me.*

I enter Mulligan's and the conversations fall to a hush. *Aiden Murray's back.* I clear my throat and the conversations continue. But there are more phones pulled out than before and two guys sitting in the back leave. I don't hate the reputation I have. Most of the bar fights I earned this cutthroat reputation in were Darragh's fault, but that doesn't change what people say about me.

Darragh, my younger brother, can still throw his weight around in the ring, but he got his practice here, in this fucking place. Our last fight here was over a girl. Darragh kicked some Puerto Rican's ass and a few of our boys jumped him outside... I don't know what happened to the guy after.

My father slides a twenty-dollar bill across the bar to the bartender, Finnegan O'Malley, a one-eared ex-hitman, who in turn fills up two glass pints of amber Sam Adams. Pa's already several drinks ahead of me. *Great. The news can't be that bad then.*

I pull out a bar stool next to my father, who barely acknowledges me, although he must've caught me entering the bar through the reflection on the glass behind the bartender. He shoves one of the pints across the bar towards me. He knows I prefer Guinness, but I don't mind starting with this. I can see my dad's reflection in the glass. He looks older than I remember. He's pushing 70, so I shouldn't be surprised by the large streaks of gray through his slick hair which was once blond, but changed color throughout his life, settling on a dark chocolate brown, like Rian's.

I glance at the television to check the score, but the game hasn't even started yet. I can smell the alcohol coming off of him already.

"You can have a Guinness after you drink this," he says. "I heard you did good work with the Italians."

He sounds raspy, but calm. My tension dissipates. This is just a normal, father-son meeting. Nothing to worry about.

"I didn't find Eoin or Robert. Haven't heard fuck since they all screwed with Vicari," I say as I take a sip of my beer.

"Maybe the Italians killed them," he says. "They're a violent, vicious group of people."

"Yeah."

Like we're ones to talk. Pa's done with his Sam Adams already and waits patiently for me to catch up, as if I could catch up to a man who's been drinking for an hour. At forty, it's not so easy for me to keep up with long nights of drinking. I don't know how he does it.

He waits for me to have a few more sips, his eyes glued to the television. Chris Sale throws the first pitch. It doesn't go so well. My father glances down at his glass and sighs. "It's going to be a long night."

"That bad this season?" I grunt, glancing up at the Detroit batter sliding into second.

I've been too busy to keep up with baseball. My father grunts. Yeah, it has been that bad.

"Any other news?" I ask him, finishing off the Sam Adams. Dad grunts and snaps his fingers for the bartender, Finnegan. The buff, tattooed bartender hustles over as dad orders two Guinnesses without opening his mouth. Bad news if he's drinking Guinness.

"Cops got Rian last week. They're charging him with manslaughter."

Manslaughter?

"What did he do?"

"What the fuck do you think he did?" Dad responds calmly. "He killed somebody, they caught him. That boy's not careful enough and I have to pay to get his ass out of trouble. Maybe some prison time would do him good."

"That's what you said the first three times," I grunt. Sale throws a good pitch and my father's face visibly brightens.

"If it weren't for Tegan, I'd let him spend a few extra years behind bars," Dad confesses. "Your mother won't let me do that to his daughter."

"What's going to happen to her?"

"I don't know," my father says. "No one has seen the kid in a week."

"What?" I growl, sipping at my beer and hoping this is my father's idea of a joke since he sounds dangerously unconcerned.

"What do you mean no one's seen her? Is she with her ma?"

My father shrugs.

Rian's notoriously bad taste in women landed him with a child he should have never brought into the world. She's a sweet girl, but doomed by a mobster father and a whore mother.

Her ma doesn't live in Boston anymore. She wants nothing to do with Rian.

"Where does he say she is?"

"Last time he saw her was the night he got arrested," Pa says before taking a sip of his beer.

"What about the cops? Did they give her to his lawyer or something?"

I don't have a single paternal instinct in my body, but my mind courses with worry over Tegan, despite my father's calmness.

"She'll turn up," he says, pouring more alcohol down his throat.

Fuck, Rian. My brother must be an even worse parent than our father. His daughter's missing and he's behind bars and there's no one else to look for her except…

"I can find out where she is. Once I get Roscoe and take care of–

"It would serve him right if something happened to her," my father says coldly. "Her mother isn't Irish. He keeps fucking up. I'm tired of cleaning up his messes. Now *drink*. This is not why I asked you here."

I bristle at his comment, but it's just Padraig Murray. This is who he's always been and my brother should have had the good sense to keep his dick in his pants. I made it to forty without fathering bastards all over Boston. Rian should have been more careful. I drink a few more sips, but I can't let this go. *Who else will worry about the fucking kid if not me?*

"How the hell did Rian let this happen? Can I talk to him?"

"Best that none of us talk to him. The cops listen to everything. I can get messages into the prison and messages out, but I don't want you talking to him."

"Fine," I grunt, finishing off my first round of Guinness and ordering us another. I try to pay, but my father stops me and then finally answers my other question.

"Your idiot brother trusted a woman," he says. "He wants a mother for that little girl so badly, that he's willing to do anything. He's willing to kill for a woman who doesn't deserve him."

"I didn't know he had a woman," I grumble.

"*Had* is correct," Pa says. "She's dead."

I wish I could tell you a chill ran through me, or I had some other human response to my father's announcement. I don't need a university degree to understand what he's implying. Rian had a woman, she got him locked up, so my father had her killed.

"Will that affect his case?"

"No," Pa says. "It was very clean."

"Who?"

"None of your business, Aiden. You worry about your shit, I'll worry about your brother."

I want to feel sorry for Rian, but he deserves it for crossing our father. This is what happens when he pisses off Padraig Murray. More problems for all of us.

"How much time is he facing?"

"Three years since he's been in jail before. I tried to get that stupid motherfucker to get his life together, but your brother just wants to be a fuck up."

"Who's the lawyer?"

"Someone from Nigel & Bancroft."

At least he isn't cheaping out like he did for Rian's first case. I don't want to push my father's buttons, and despite his outward calm, he must be furious at Rian for drawing more attention to us, but Rian has his uses.

"It's Rian," I remind him. "Crazy fucking Rian. We need him out soon. There are some jobs only Rian has the balls to handle."

Padraig snorts. "He takes after my father. Too proud and too violent for his own good."

We created the monster Rian Murray is. He's our responsibility.

"He needs another woman."

"He needs a woman who isn't a fucking spic," my father spits. "At least the child looks white."

"What about this previous woman? What'd she look like?"

"It doesn't matter," he grunts. "She's dead. Now drink. We have more important things to talk about than your idiot brother and his shitty taste in women."

I drink because Pa commands it. I do everything he commands and have since I was a child. I have the burns and scars to remind me of what happens when you disobey my father. At first, I hated him for what he did to me, but to keep an organization like ours together, you need to inspire fear.

YOU HAVE to be cruel to survive – that's just how the world works. I can't let Tegan go. The second I see Darragh, I'll ask about her and track her down.

· · ·

I DRINK SO I don't lose my temper. He doesn't give a fuck about Tegan. No one does. Maybe he's wrong and one of my sisters took her in. But who would do that? Evie's saddled with her drunkard husband and two unruly kids of her own – Katie and Patrick. Kiara's off at university and Maeve's sixteen, too young to have any involvement.

"I need to tell you something important," my father says somberly, as if there could be something more important than my missing niece right now. I'm burning with desire to leave, but if I get up without my father's dismissal, he'll hurt me. Or someone I care about. Not like there are many of those people yet. It's foolish to get close to people in this life.

"Then tell me."

If he notices my tightening tone, my father doesn't acknowledge it.

"There's a plot against my life. I don't know who. I don't know why but... there's someone out there trying to kill me," my father says, the faded tattoos on his knuckles even more wrinkled than I last remember. He's getting older, but aside from his physical appearance, he shows no signs of slowing down. If anything, he's desperate to prove himself more. If he wasn't ordering more killings than necessary, maybe Rian wouldn't be locked up.

I don't want to dismiss his concerns as paranoid, but he's the leader of our family. There's always a plot against his life. It comes with the territory. My father doesn't have to worry because he has us. *Family.*

"Fuck that," I grunt. "No one would be stupid enough to try to kill you. April 2013, four days after the bombing. An entire decade ago. That's the last time anyone tried."

I was thirty back then, old enough to be the one who ended that war before it started. Back then, we only killed when necessary. I got five tattoos that year, one for each kill. Each a painful release, each representing a necessary act to keep my family safe.

My father smirks and keeps drinking. He shrugs. "That's what I thought. But I'm serious. This time is different. This time the bastards might just get me. I'm getting old, Aiden. Most guys in our line of work don't make it this far."

"What happened?" I grunt, urging my increasingly drunken father to get to the point. His cheeks blaze tomato red with alcohol and his blue eyes swim with tears, again brought on by drinking rather than any emotion. He grunts and knocks his biggest gold ring against the bar's surface contemplatively.

If anyone tried to kill him, surely Darragh would have mentioned it. He's responsible for keeping our father alive.

"I feel it in my bones," Pa replies. "Someone wants to destroy our family."

"Yes," I grumble. "Our cousins. But they're gone and if they were anywhere near this city, we would have heard about it."

"I don't know. Something big is coming for us. I feel it."

"We can make decisions based on feelings now?"

"Cut the shit, kid. You know my instincts are good because you're like me. You can smell shit before it hits the toilet bowl."

"I'm home. If anyone tries to kill you, they'll have to get through me, Darragh, and Callum."

My father smirks. "My boys. I'm proud of all of you. Except Rian. He's a piece of shit."

Ah, Padraig. Honest as fuck, especially when he's drunk.

He might not be proud of Rian, but he still loves my brother enough to spring for decent lawyers and to make sure Tegan goes to the best day school in Boston. Once she's old enough, she'll go to Milton or Dana Hall, or another nice private school where she can meet someone to untarnish her sullied blood, that is as long as I can find her. If Rian's behind bars, she could be anywhere. Hopefully not with her mom's people.

She belongs with us, even if Rian made mistakes. She looks like us and that's good enough to cover up his shameful behavior. I don't know what Rian was thinking with that Puerto Rican chick. Tegan's mother was low class.

Let's hope my brother's behavior doesn't come back to haunt all of us. Let's hope his daughter is safe, sound asleep somewhere and protected.

"Thanks, Pa," I mutter, uncomfortable with even this much emotional closeness between us. I love my father, but trusting him too much is dangerous. Rian found out the hard way that it isn't worth it to defy our family beliefs, and it definitely isn't fucking worth it to screw around with the wrong women.

"And Aiden? I need you to hurry the fuck up and find a wife. I'm getting old and I want to retire, but I need a family man to lead this family. You're the oldest. Why the fuck can't you keep a woman? Do I have to send you back to Galway?"

He wants a real answer.

"Not interested in chasing after girls, dad. All they want to do is take your money and ask where the fuck you're going. I've had enough."

"That old dog won't take care of you when you get old."

"Neither will some Boston snob who could take my ass to the cleaners in a divorce."

He laughs, which is the best reaction I can hope for. He quickly moves along to talking about the game and his plans for the business, and then asks me questions about Long Island. They're a mess out there, but doing better under John Vicari's leadership. We're developing a few buildings together and are prepared to make a lot of money in the real estate game. John does cleaner business than his father. Too bad the old man died of a heart attack... that's the word anyway.

"I need you to find a nice girl," my father reminds me once he's almost blackout drunk. He can barely keep his head up. *Great.* I'm not dragging his ass outta here tonight. If he wants to get so wasted he can't sit up straight, I'll leave him for Finnegan.

"We have this conversation every time we talk."

"This time, I'm serious. I want to retire. I don't want you bringing home no spics either like the Duffy boys."

"Fuck's sake, Pa. You can't talk like that around here anymore."

"I can say whatever the fuck I want. I want Irish children. Irish fucking children and I need you to have a wife so I can retire."

"Retire any old fucking day you want," I growl. "It'll be good for you to stop worrying about who I fuck or marry or the fate of the fucking family."

"The fate of the family matters," he says, taking another sip of his newest glass of beer before rubbing condensation off the sides with his napkin.

"I'm too old to have kids," I growl. "I'm too old to get tied down. You and mom were lucky you even found each other."

That's bullshit and we both know it. They stay together because they're Catholic, because back in the eighties, my dad killed someone for her father and won my mother like a prize. He also put a baby in her quickly and then kept her pregnant. There's nothing romantic about their love story or marriage in the Murray family.

"If you can't find a girl, I'll find one."

"The last girl you found me was a crazy fucking redhead who wanted to bring Roscoe Jr. into the bedroom. No thanks."

My father shrugs. "She was white. Do you know how hard it is to find a white girl around here who hasn't been fucking ruined by some fucking Puerto Rican or black guy?"

"What do you want from me, Pa?"

I know what I want. I want an end to this conversation, and I want my father to give me a fucking break about women and dating. All the Irish and Catholic women in Boston know to stay away from us, and the ones who don't learn their lesson pretty fucking quickly.

"Find a nice white girl with big tits and blond hair and get her pregnant so I know you're fucking serious about family. That's what I want."

"Give me time."

He continues, getting to what I suspect was the original point he wanted to make before the liquor got to him. "And get your ass to the site in Back Bay tomorrow bright and early."

"Why?"

This is the first I'm hearing about something wrong at the Back Bay construction site. I know something's wrong because my father doesn't do anything bright and early unless there's a problem to solve.

"You'll find out tomorrow. You just got back. Go home. Pet the dog. Your mom's tired of walking that big fuck. He nearly knocked her over near Harvard Square."

"How is mom?"

"Pissed off."

"Why?"

"Eh. Upset about another woman. It's nothing."

It's nothing. Dad just got his second mistress pregnant and even if we all know about it, we're all supposed to pretend it's no big deal that our elderly father knocked up a Irish teenager who he supposedly hired to clean the construction company office.

I hate how he treats our mother. What's the point of having a family or a woman if you hurt her? There's no getting through to him, but I have to try for my mother's sake.

"You treat her better, pa. Seriously. She needs you."

He grunts. "Get your ass home kid and get a white girl pregnant."

"Thanks, dad."

"If you can't find one, I'll find a good Irish girl who needs a green card and bring her over to you!"

My father is the last person I want picking my romantic partners. I mutter something to him about cutting back on liquor, then I pat my father on the back and leave the bar. This is the closest we've felt in years, but there's still a wall between us and there always will be. I felt closer to him when I was younger, when it was easier for me to justify the life I led. I know I'm a screw up, I know I don't belong anywhere near a woman or a family or any of the fucking things my father wants from me.

He knows it's wrong to bring a kid into this life, but he did it anyway. He knows that we're villains, but he doesn't care. Fuck, I don't care either, I suppose. I'd just rather not ruin a perfectly good woman.

I drive out of the city listening to rock classics on the radio. Just as I turn down my street – I live at the end of a cul-de-sac – I notice the large box on my front step. There are only five large houses at the end of this cul-de-sac, all of us with wide open well-maintained lawns around traditional New England colonial houses.

The box on my front step is fucking enormous – and I don't remember ordering anything for delivery. My hand moves swiftly to the pistol under my seat. I feel no fear as I reach for the gun and slip a mag out of my pocket. I feel ready.

Leaving the city for any amount of time always carries a risk, especially since I didn't exactly leave the place with a house sitter. The last time my teen brother Odhran house-sat, he trashed the place and had a threesome in my bed. I hop out of my black GMC Sierra with the gun under my coat and approach the box slowly, glancing furtively over my shoulder for anyone who might have eyes on me.

The box has holes in it. It's large. Pink. Wrapped in a bow. I reach for the bottom of the box and try to lift it. *Fuck.* It's heavy. I drop the box and I swear I hear a sound coming from inside it. *Is that possible?* I try to peek through the holes but it's too fucking dark and something's telling me opening this box will be a shitshow. It has to weigh about a hundred pounds. Maybe more. I'm no weakling, but it still takes a measure of back strength to lift a box that fucking heavy.

I open my front door and greet Roscoe Jr., my rottweiler, as he bounds towards the door to greet me. His coat looks shiny, the nub of his docked tail wags back and forth. Pa's choice, not mine. He runs up to the box and sniffs at it a bit.

There's definitely something in there and it gets his attention because Roscoe utters a low bark.

"Roscoe, go lie down."

Once he heads off to his bed, I throw my doors open wider and eye the giant box to decide how to carry the fuckin' thing. I would call Rian if his stupid ass wasn't in jail. I could call Callum, but he's still hung up on some fucking girl and won't answer my calls because I won't sugarcoat my opinion of him. Then there's Darragh... He's probably twice as drunk as Padraig. Not a good option either.

I'll have to carry the box myself. I stretch a little and then grab the edges of the box and grunt as I carry it a few feet inside my doorway. I set the box down more gently. *Is there something alive in there?* If it were an animal, I suspect Roscoe would be barking from his spot in the house, but he's laying down as I commanded, gazing at me curiously and wagging his tail.

He's probably wondering why I'm not taking him for a walk since

I'm back. *At least he didn't bite the sitter this time.* I close my front doors and then search for an opening on the giant pink box. Finding none, I start with the ribbon and peel it away. The box comes up to my waist. It's *enormous.*

If it didn't weigh a hundred fucking pounds, I would assume it's a novelty gift or something extra special from one of my brothers. Which of my piece of shit brothers would get me a welcome home gift? It's not like either of them are here with a six pack of Guinness right now...

I peel the top of the box open and there's another box inside it, also pink. I open the second box and stumble backwards as I expose the contents. I don't mean to act like a fucking idiot, but I nearly fall over, because this is the last thing I expected to find on my doorstep. I just got back to Boston... How long has that box been out there?

HOLY FUCK, why isn't she screaming?

I GAIN control of myself and approach the box again, heart pounding because my second assumption is that the human female in the box might be dead and that's the reason she hasn't made a sound. The sick thought twists my stomach into an unyielding knot.

I slowly approach the box again, ignoring my heavy breathing, focusing instead on taking in as much information as possible about the situation. I move the flaps of the box open and stare at the woman's face.. Suddenly, her eyes snap open before swiveling around and looking me directly in the eye..

Holy fuck, this woman is alive.

"What the fuck is this?" I grunt to myself. Not to myself. I'm not alone. I dry swallow and run my fingers through my hair. She's black. Someone tied up a black woman in a pink ribbon, wrapped her up like a gift and put her in a box on my doorstep. This has to be a sick joke.

I'm almost too scared to reach into the box and touch her, but I have to touch her to get her out of the fucking box. Whoever this woman is, she ran into the wrong fucking people and ended up in the wrong living room.

I have tattoos and vows of loyalty to prove how I feel about people like her. "Don't worry. I'll get you out of there."

I don't know why I'm bothering with comfort. I reach into the box and grab her at the base of her spine before hoisting her out of the box and gently setting her on the ground. My stomach lurches. This is some sick, twisted shit. Whoever did this to her stripped this woman naked, bared every inch of her dark skin, the color of Arabica coffee, and wrapped her in a pink ribbon, contorting her limbs and running the ribbon over her bare breasts, between her thighs and in loops around her body so she's wrapped up like a chocolate present.

My body has an unconscious, primal reaction. I could unwrap her like the present she's been wrapped up to be, but I need answers quickly.

She has a gag in her mouth, a round white ball that keeps her lips spread open and hooks at the back. Her eyes roam around the room in terror as I reach into my pocket for my knife. I've killed people with this knife and now I'm using it to save someone.

Her skin prickles with goosebumps as I touch her. I apologize, but I need to brace myself against her to get her free. I press the serrated edge to the ribbon and make the first cut.

I cut her legs free. She groans as her legs fall in a curled heap. She cries out and tries to jerk them again, but however long she's been in that position was far too long for her to have full control of her legs and hips.

"Don't move," I remind her. I touch her skin again and my stomach lurches. Fuck, her skin is so dark. I look pale as fuck touching her and even putting my hands on her drives guilt through me. She's black. She's the wrong kind of person. I run my tongue piercing over my lower lip as I focus on all the parts of the ribbon I have to cut free.

When I have her limbs mostly free, she rolls onto her side, groaning in pain as her arms and legs curl in an awkward and splayed mess next to her. Even her wrists bend at an unnatural angle. I know she's alive, but the woman still looks dead.

I swallow slowly. What the absolute fuck is this?

"I'll take the gag out, but you can't spit or bite or do anything of that nature. Do you understand?"

She stares at me, but she can't say anything. I approach her mouth slowly and reach around her to find the clasp of her ball gag. I unhook it and take it out of her mouth. She groans again and winces in visible pain as she attempts to close her jaw. She slowly moves her hand to her face and rubs her cheek, groaning.

I crouch next to her, staring at her in awe, knowing that I shouldn't but am completely incapable of taking my eyes off the naked woman in front of me. If her nudity makes her uncomfortable, that hasn't sunk in yet. My cock stiffens inappropriately in my pants and I clasp my hands in front of my dick, refusing to take my eyes off her.

Her breasts are small, but they protrude forward in tiny, dark orbs with nipples that are even darker than her extremely dark skin. Holy fuck, I didn't know nipples came that dark. My eyes widen inappropriately and I pray she doesn't notice my leering. Who sent this woman to me and what exactly did they send her for?

Christ, Aiden. Get a grip. You're staring at her crotch now and it's obvious.

She's waxed completely and my gaze snaps to the bare, dark brown lips. I wonder what this strange woman conceals between those lower lips and what color her flesh is between those thin, toned legs. I clear my throat.

"Who are you?"

"Read the card with the gift," she manages to say, with a raspy voice and an accent I can't place.

"I asked you a question."

"Read the card with the gift," she repeats.

I raise an eyebrow and walk towards the box. There's a large card at the bottom, about 8 x 10 inches, printed on thick paper. I pull it out of the box and read the note, muttering it out loud to myself. *What the fuck is this?*

Dear Mr. Murray,

We hope you enjoy your object. Your task is simple. Use the object wisely. Have unprotected sex with the object and film a 4K quality video.

Compress the video file and send it to the email address below.

The object may be initially unwilling but both of you will face strong motivation to comply. The object understands that documentation of her existence belongs to us and if she fails to comply enthusiastically, we will destroy her identity.

If we do not receive the video within one week of today's date, you will both lose what's most important to you.

Tegan Murray counts on you to succeed. We have possession of the girl and you would be wise to listen to our orders if you or your family want to see her safe.

Do not call Padraig Murray. Do not call anyone else, or you will both suffer.

It takes less than a second to fire a bullet.

You must comply. When you're finished with said object, it is yours to keep.

Sincerely,

Your Benefactors

OA

"WHAT IS THIS SICK SHIT?" I growl, throwing the card back into the box, causing the woman still kneeling on the ground to flinch. My heart thuds.

These people have Tegan and this woman might know where she is and who they are. I won't be a part of this sick fucking game.

CHAPTER TWO
VALENTINA

"You have to do what they say," I say to him. "*Please.*"

It's not what I want to say, but these were my instructions if I wanted to survive. I never saw the people who put me in the box, but I heard their instructions and their threats clearly.

My throat burns raw as I attempt to plead with the man in front of me, hoping that he'll spare me. *He's involved with the people who took you. He's dangerous.*

The more I talk, the quicker he'll piece the truth about me together. I don't want this man to know *anything* about me. My voice. It's bad enough that he's seeing me naked. It's bad enough that he's about to take a part of me that I never wanted to give to strangers, that I always wanted to *mean* something.

I want to keep a piece of myself to myself. I've never had that privilege before. I won't have it tonight. He's an utter stranger to me and a terrifying one at that.

The gigantic blond man glowers at me, his blue eyes enough to melt me in place. He's 6'4", his hair looks slightly unkempt. Black ink swirls around his pale skin in a variety of Celtic knots, cursive Bible verses and symbols that I don't understand. *Lots of tattoos. He must be a gangster. Something like that.*

I hate that I'm naked, but I'm glad that I'm free. There was nothing but pain in that box. The drugs helped at first, but they didn't last thirty-six hours. That's how long it took to get here from Idaho. Technically, the drive takes twenty-five hours, but I tried to measure time – I have a good sense of it because of the piano – and I know they took thirty six.

There's no getting out of this. Maybe this one won't be as wicked as the first.

"Who are you?" the man growls at me. "Who did this and what the fuck do you have to do with this?"

His anger sends a surge of terror through me as his face reddens with frustration. He has absolute control over this situation and he knows it. I can't afford to freeze and make it worse by proving to him what he already knows – I'm vulnerable, weak and utterly at his mercy.

I position myself to cover my breasts as much as possible as well as my *other* parts, but he's already seen every bit of me. Modesty is entirely pointless.

"My name is Valentina," I rasp out, my voice getting stronger as I tell him my name.

"Is that your real name?" he growls, stepping forward and towering over me.

I'll never know if I had another name. I've been called Valentina since I was a little girl. Sometimes Val, but never anything else. I must've had a life before, but I don't remember any of it. All I remember is Pulsifer. He was my father, my abuser, my everything. I wouldn't call this freedom, but there's still a weight lifted because this is the closest I've ever come to leaving the governor's mansion.

The blond man is even taller than I thought he was. I'm more vulnerable naked and despite wanting to stand up for myself, I shrink back from him.

"Yes," I say as firmly as I can manage.

"Who sent you? Because I'll be damned if I screw around with a n–"

He stops himself, but my skin feels a flush of outrage and humiliation as his lips hover over the n-word. I want to hit him, but I don't know what type of man my new master is yet. A racist. That part I understand. He's not the first racist I've had to deal with. He might be the richest though. *He lives in a mansion.*

"Who sent you?" He roars. His face reddens as he screams and his creepy blue eyes look bloodshot. I shouldn't cross him, but I stopped giving a fuck about what happens to me a long time ago. I've already experienced the worst.

"I don't know. All I know is they want you to do what's on that note."

I don't want that. I have to go through with it, but I definitely don't start off wanting that monster anywhere near me.

"No," he growls, his jaw tightening. "I... This is fucking ridiculous. Tell me who sent you, woman."

His anger mounts and my fear intensifies. I'm no stranger to racism, but for the word to nearly fly off the tip of his tongue like that. *How can someone who looks like that be so ugly inside?*

He reaches into his jacket and I know he's reaching for a gun before he pulls it out. The men who sent me here weren't any better than the man who received me as a gift. My throat tightens and I try not to lose control of my bladder as he pulls the pistol out of his jacket and points it straight at me.

Men are all the same and they're all violent disgusting pigs who will put a bullet in an innocent woman's head if she gets in their way. They'll use us up and spit us out and there isn't a man alive capable of real love...

"If you shoot me, you'll die," I state plainly, trying to sound like I have control of the situation. I'm not lying, but I'm also not stupid enough to mean that as a threat either. "And whoever you love enough for them to threaten will die too."

"I don't give a fuck," he snarls. "Who sent you?"

I don't believe that he doesn't care. I sense a crack in this man beneath his outrage. His anger cloaks his genuine concern. If he wanted to kill me, he would have done it already.

"Do I look like I was in control of the situation? You have their instructions. Are you going to do it or not?" I say to him sharply. Talking to him like this could be dangerous, but he doesn't react to my strengthening voice or sharp tone.

"Am I going to rape you?" He growls, lowering the gun. "Is that what you're fucking asking me?"

He has a thick accent which I can finally place. *Boston.* I'm in Boston, or close enough to Boston that men sound like Matt Damon in *Good Will Hunting.* I don't know anyone in Boston, but maybe that's for the best since I don't know any good people. Never have.

I don't respond to him. He reads the card to himself again and mutters a long string of curse words. I'm already naked and despite his apparent hesitation, the man hasn't offered me clothes. He doesn't know if he's going to do it yet, but I do.

HE'S GOING to have sex with me.

"YOU HAVE TO FOLLOW THE INSTRUCTIONS," I say to the terrifying blond man pleadingly. He still hasn't told me his name and I don't know if he will. He might worry I'll go to the police. "At least according to them." Hopefully he thinks of another solution since he's clearly some type of gangster.

I've been through enough shit to know that the police don't care about women like me. The police have *never* cared.

"This is a crock of shit," he hisses, spittle flying from his mouth as his face reddens with pure vitriol. "I have *never...*"

He glares at me like I'm responsible for this. Every inch of my body aches and I have little patience for this bastard acting like I'm the fucking problem.

"Never what?"

He glowers. "I've never been with... I don't... I don't fuck black women."

His voice drips with disgust, but I don't mind because I find this man's racism equally repulsive. He's more bothered by my race than the fact that I arrived on his doorstep naked, wrapped in ribbons, and sent to him in a box.

"You have to follow their instructions. I don't know what happens to you if you don't, but I know what happens to me."

I'll be lost to my past forever.

"Who fucking sent you?"

"I don't know."

I should have expected his next actions. He's a sicko, because the people who sent me only send gifts to sickos. My boss... My *old* boss was probably worse than this man. He was certainly much uglier, but all cruel men are the same.

He quickly racks a bullet in the chamber before re-leveling the gun to my face so I am forced to stare directly down the barrel.

"Kneel," he commands without wavering. I can see in his eyes that he's capable of shooting me. He runs his long pink tongue over his lips. He has a piercing through his tongue, a giant gold knob with a Celtic knot in the center. *What the fuck?*

My knees ache and I can't stop myself from groaning as I obey him. I have no choice but to listen to him despite the pain shooting through me. My stomach turns and if I'd eaten anything in the past 48 hours, it would've come up on this rich white man's hardwood floor.

My head lolls forward and I struggle not to cry out as more pain surges through my legs.

"Who sent you?"

"I don't know," I answer truthfully. If I had those answers, I would disappear in the middle of the night and find some way to get my real identity from the people who own me, or I suppose owned me before him.

"You must've come from somewhere," he says, his finger hovering near the trigger. It never occurred to me that he could do worse than hurt me, that he could kill me. *But he might. The men who did this to me never considered that.*

"My master sold me."

"What the fuck?" he snarls. "What the fuck does that mean?"

"I grew up... I grew up in a house with an older man. He sold me when I turned twenty-five."

"Sold you to who?"

"I never saw. I just know... I know what kind of company he keeps."

"Who was your master?"

"Governor of Idaho. Ezekiel Pulsipher," I respond as calmly as possible, even if just saying his name brings back flashes of horrific memories that still torment me every night. Who needs sleep, right?

"I don't know who the fuck that is," he spits. My chest swells with odd satisfaction that there's a corner of the universe not entirely ruled by Ezekiel.

In any other situation, his confusion would have been confusing. Old Zeke was a king in his universe and I wasn't the only girl in his harem. *He owned me since I was six years old. I don't want to tell this criminal about that, but I wouldn't feel sorry if this psychopath turned on my old master. I wouldn't feel sorry if these modern slave owners met this monster.*

I glare at him. I'm not here to give him an explanation. He's not the victim here, I am, and judging by his accent and other cues slowly coming into view, I'm on the other side of the country with no identification, no proof of who I am...Nobody knows I'm here.

It doesn't matter that I'm alone, I have to survive. I don't know what life will be like on this side of the country, but this is the best chance I've had to escape my entire life. *I can fool this white man. I know I can.*

"Why would someone do this?" He snarls.

"Maybe you're a criminal. Maybe they want revenge," I offer, perhaps pushing him too much with my attitude. His body tenses when I say the word *criminal.* Men. They think they're so careful with their emotions, but they get careless when they're underestimating you. Men get careless when they think they have the upper hand.

"I can't do what they want," he says, keeping the gun fixed at my head. This does little to warm me to him. "I can't screw... If my father found out... he would paint the sidewalk with your brains."

Charming. Now I have a definitive answer about the extent of this man's criminality.

He sets the gun on the table behind him and re-reads the card for the third time. His face turns several shades of red.

"This is sick," he spits, glowering at me with familiar, racially motivated revulsion. In most situations, I can't actually know if a man is racist. I have proof about this man.

"You have to. Whoever sent me paid a lot of money. You messed with powerful people," I tell him. "And they have someone you love and if you don't do this–

"I haven't messed with anyone," the man growls, interrupting me. "Get up."

I thought the pain shooting through me would knock me unconscious, but I had too much pride to ask him for relief. I slowly rise, my limbs barely cooperating. I look and feel ashy. I hate that I missed my routine. Spend a any amount of time in a box and you will miss the most damning prison you had before. My body still aches.

He looks me in the eye and I'm too scared not to meet this man's gaze. He's a predator and showing a predator fear gives them permission to pounce.

"My name is Aiden."

Aiden. I shouldn't care what his name is, but hearing it makes me consider him differently. The name sounds forceful and as rooted in his heritage as his Celtic tattoos.

"Great," I reply softly, unclear about what to do with the information.

He clears his throat and speaks again, "I thought you should know before we..."

"So you changed your mind?"

I shake before my body knows I'm shaking. This has happened before. Men have *taken* my body several times. Ezekiel *owned* me and believe me, he made good use of his property. Aiden. The name sounds Irish, but the man standing in front of me is All-American. He's 6'4" tall with *very* pale blond hair, but a thick crop of it. It's nice to see a man who isn't bald and who clearly works out. He's very muscular and the gun is out of the way, which sets me at ease.

"I don't know who sent you, woman. But I intend to find out. Seems like the best fuckin' way to do that is follow their instructions."

I knew it.

Aiden reaches for me and I fight my gut reaction to flinch. I don't want him to know how much I fear him. I want him to worry that I'll stab him in his sleep. I want him to feel like he's risking his life every time he rapes me.

Aiden puts his hand on my shoulder. I expected his touch to be rough, but it's very soft.

"Do they have anyone you love?"

I don't want to tell him, but his blue eyes harden and I sense that I'd better tell the truth if I want him to get this over with. His hand cups my shoulder too gently for me to describe. After the sharp angles and the pain of having my body squeezed into a box, his softness is surreal.

"I... I don't know."

"I don't want to hurt you. I won't rape you."

"If you don't have—

"I know," he growls. "But I won't hurt you. You have to consent. I..."

"I belong to you," I tell him, refusing to look away from him. I want him to gaze into my eyes and see a human being. A part of me desperately wants to shame him. It's hard to stare into those eyes and not feel something. He has intense and expressive eyes.

"No," he whispers. "You belong to yourself and once this is over, I'll have to let you go."

I fight back laughter. He won't let me go. I know men like Aiden better than he can even understand. I've lived my entire life in a world of pain and depravity.

"They'll hurt you if you don't do it. Surely my life isn't as important as yours."

"You're right," he growls. "But I've never fucked one of your kind and I don't intend to rape you either. That's not *my* thing."

He says it with the implication that he knows someone who prefers rape. And there he goes with the race talk again. *One of my kind...*

"You have to do it."

"Then agree to my terms."

"Terms."

I don't phrase it as a question and I don't want to sound too eager either.

"I'll give you money."

"So I won't be a slave, I'll be a prostitute."

His face reddens. "I'll send you away. You said they have someone you love. So you have a family?"

"No. I don't."

His hand drops from my shoulder and I glance down at his crotch. Despite Aiden's assurances that going through with this is the furthest thing from his mind, his dick bulges from his jeans. The bulge sends a deep surge of discomfort through me and my head swims.

There's no escape. All my smart-mouthed comments and my internal pleas that I might be able to survive this... I have to go through with it.

"What do you want, then?"

"A place to rest my head for a few nights. Time to get on my feet."

"Done."

He clears his throat. "I'll film it on my phone. I just... I've never..."

Aiden suddenly leans forward and kisses me. His lips surprise me with how soft they are when they first make contact. I want to scream, but it's a good kiss that draws me into Aiden's world instantly. His smell consumes me. His fingers claw at my cheeks as he holds me suddenly and keeps me still so he can kiss me.

Before Aiden, kisses felt like... cottage cheese. I want to push him away but the kiss is too fucking good for me to break away from it. I don't want to upset him, anyway. When he breaks away, his cheeks are red.

"I'm fucking dirty," he says and the revulsion in his voice tells me that he means it.

He doesn't look like he hated the kiss despite the words coming out of his mouth. He leans forward again and kisses me. This time, he spreads my lips apart and slides his tongue into my mouth. The piercing teases my tongue, sending a shiver straight through me. It's better than the first kiss and I kiss him back. He's the first man I've ever kissed back, the first man who has kissed me well enough for me to even try.

Men have done so many horrible things to me in my life and not one of them has kissed me properly. Aiden pulls away again and he pushes hair out of my face.

"We'll do this in my bedroom. Go upstairs. Third door on the left. Shower first."

Shower first. I don't like his tone, but I can't exactly blame him for it. I've been trapped in a box for several hours in a row and I probably smell exactly like it. At least he isn't pointing a gun at me anymore, and doesn't kiss me like a gross, perverted old man. He kisses me like... he would be a good lover.

That's another experience I've never had, another sad truth about my life that I never want to dwell on.

It hurts to walk up the stairs, but my body revels in the most freedom I've had in days. I almost want to race up the stairs to get to the bathroom quicker, but I walk patiently to the top and follow Aiden's instructions to find his bedroom. I can hear Aiden talking to his dog, telling him to stay on his bed for the next little while while he's busy. His house smells new, even if it's an old colonial that has probably been around since Boston's founding.

The bedroom is *extremely* neat. The floor smells clean and as my bare feet touch it, I feel like Aiden's right to wrinkle his nose at me. I'm the dirty one. *But he's sexually aggressive, and a racist one at that.* I can hear him following me up the stairs. He walks slowly, but he has a heavy gait. That may come in handy later if he tries to sneak into bed with me when I want to sleep. If I need to fight him off. That type of thing.

I had to fight off Pulsifer sometimes. That got easier as I got older. Aiden's a lot bigger than some decrepit governor of Idaho.

I find the bathroom door open and I walk inside. He has a clawfoot tub that could hold seven people. Judging by the perverts Pulsifer normally deals with, Aiden probably has had seven people in this tub at once. It sickens me to think what other secrets he could have. I flinch as he appears behind me. For a man with a heavy gait, he can apparently walk quietly when necessary.

"Get into the shower. Take your time. I'll set up the camera."

He sounds nervous, which makes me nervous. I imagine him being completely cruel. A monster would be crude and quick. Monsters *really* want you to cry. Aiden doesn't have any of those traits. He glances at my breasts, his cheeks redden and he swears under his breath.

"I can handle the shower," I say to him. He stares at me for a few seconds before leaving the doorway. I relish this alone time. I'm too grateful for my survival to think about escape. I wish I could tell you otherwise, but this is the truth. I grew up being passed around America's dirty underworld. Escape stopped being a real consideration when I turned eighteen and realized this was my destiny – permanent sexual slavery.

I clean myself as best as I can and try to ignore the numb feeling spreading over my body as I anticipate Aiden's actions. Most men are very rough. You can close your eyes and do your best to block out the pain, but nothing stops the dirty feeling of being powerless and having another person use you like an object.

Once I'm clean and have spent as much time in the shower as I think I can get away with, I step out and grab one of the insanely fluffy white towels hanging from the rack. As soon as I put it on my skin, the luxurious warmth spreads through me and the towel is so soft that I get a momentary feeling of safety.

I've carved out a life for myself despite my circumstances. I don't want anyone to feel sorry for me. I've learned how to play the piano. All the men who owned me had books that I enjoyed reading. I write poetry too, though none of it is good enough to share. Who would read my poems, anyway? Certainly not this blond hunk of muscle. His brain is probably the size of a pea.

He returns to the doorway and scowls as he watches me dry

myself, reminding me that he's oversized and perpetually disgusted by me. I'm not shy about him seeing my body. He's seen it all anyway and he's going to have sex with me on camera, so there isn't a point in pretense.

"I took a vow that I would never touch a woman of another color," Aiden growls, sounding angry with me, like it's my fault that I'm black and he's racist.

I don't respond to him.

"I don't know if I can get hard," he says. "You might have to work to get me off."

I purse my lips. I have to ignore his suggestion that I'm too ugly to arouse him. White men. I try not to generalize them, but it doesn't help that all the men who have hurt me have had brilliant blue eyes, just like Aiden's. He has more of a pretty boy look, but he still has those cruel blue eyes.

"Have you done this before?"

"Yes."

I'll respond to his direct questions, but other than that, I have nothing to say. It's not like he cares.

"I'm sorry."

I give him a curious look, but I don't say anything. It's smarter not to say anything.

"If it helps, I'll make it good for you," he says in a gruff and gravely voice.

Don't bother. I want to say something cutting, but I don't want to anger him. Violence and sex are intertwined in the male brain, especially men like Aiden, a giant clearly used to getting what he wants.

This time, not responding to him provokes cheek redness. White men are always turning red when their feelings are about to take over. I brace myself for another racist comment.

"Whoever sent you must know my family. They must know about our beliefs and I want you to be clear about mine. I know my history and my heritage. I believe firmly in the superiority of my people over all others. This will not change because I stuck my cock in you," Aiden says, his voice trembling with rage as he stares at me.

I drop the towel. I'd rather him finish this than continue listening to his racist tirades.

I don't flinch, even if I want to. His words cut me deep, but Aiden, for all his complaints, still reacts like a man. His gaze drops decisively to my breasts and his teeth instinctively sink into his lower lip. His supposedly difficult to rouse cock bulges forward in his pants. *It doesn't look like he's struggling to get hard at all.*

He's even redder than before and his left hand clenches into an angry fist. I hope he's not the hitting sort. Those are always harder to deal with.

"Get on your knees," he commands, asserting power over me as my naked body renders him powerless to continue his racist little speech. I don't defy him. Despite my complete disgust with Aiden, pleasing him represents my best chance at survival, so I consent to his commands.

Any position on my knees still hurts. If Aiden cares, he doesn't show it. He walks towards me and crudely thrusts his hips into my face. His trousers smell like cigarettes and beer. His pants pockets bulge with car keys and a few other objects I can't identify. A simple, brown belt cinches over his dark blue denim.

His thighs are thick and muscular, barely held back by his pants. My heart quickens as he shifts his stance to his left side, cocking his hip. I glance down at his shoes. Brown boots. The tips are probably steel, so I don't want to do or say anything that could provoke him to kick me. I'm in enough pain as it is.

"The camera's over there," he says. "We'll have to move. I just wanted to see if you would obey me."

He leans forward and kisses the top of my head. *He's fucked up. It aches down here on my knees and I'll have to get up again.*

Aiden commands me to my feet and I follow him back out into his bedroom. He shows me where he has his cellphone set up on a bookshelf right in front of Sun Tzu's *The Art of War* and an extremely tattered copy of *The Holy Bible*.

"Kneel there," he commands, pointing to a spot in front of the lens. "It's already recording."

I obey him and quietly kneel before Aiden, facing away from the camera. He walks into the frame and commands me again, "Look up at me. I want to see your face."

When I gaze at him, he frowns with that mixture of revulsion and disapproval I already recognize as his gut reaction to me. Despite his cruel facial expression, he's still hard. I can still see the bulge in his jeans and it's terrifyingly huge the closer he gets to me.

"I don't cum from getting head," he says. "But I doubt you can arouse me without it. Take my dick out."

He's so full of shit. This man has the biggest erection I've ever seen. *He doubts I can arouse him? Something is making him unbelievably stiff and there's no one else in the room but me.*

Taking my time to remove his cock from his jeans is the only way I can postpone it. I've seen dicks before, and most of them are completely unpleasant to look at. Many of the ones I've seen are shorter than my pinky finger. The governor called some of the world's most depraved men his friends.

Aiden remains resolutely planted in place, glowering down at me as I unbuckle his belt and then slip the jean button through the loop before unzipping his pants. Because of his muscular butt, I can't rely on his jeans to fall off on their own. I hook my fingers through the back, making contact with Aiden's ass as I pull the jeans down. As I ease his jeans over his ass, I can't help but notice how deliciously round and muscular his ass feels. My hands fight the urge to cup his firm glutes and focus on the required task - getting his dick out of his jeans.

His breath catches as the jeans slide down, revealing an equally toned and muscular pair of thighs. He has tattoos everywhere, but the thigh tattoos are the most alarming. *Choose death.* He has a skull, several Celtic knots, Bible verses, and intricate designs woven together in a tapestry of a criminal's life.

A pair of crisp white boxer briefs cling to Aiden's thighs. More details of his bulging cock become apparent to me. The monster curves slightly in his briefs, the thick head oozing fluid that creates a wet spot where the tip touches the fabric.

The elastic waistband of his boxer briefs sticks to his hips and as I remove his underwear, I expose more tattoos and worse. He has scars and partially healed wounds all over his body, not to mention more muscles. He's the most muscular man I've ever seen this close and it feels wrong to notice.

All the men who fucked me were ugly and cruel with bodies and tongues that failed to arouse me. This man might be a sick mother-fucker but at least he's handsome. It's a small comfort, but I've never touched a man with such well-defined muscles, and the least I can do is appreciate it.

His cock springs free and juts forward with all the arousal Aiden claims he doesn't feel. His body doesn't lie. I haven't even touched him yet, but his cock already protrudes with pure enthusiasm. Once I get the briefs over his ass, they remain taut and stretched around his thighs.

I can't help but stare at Aiden's dick. I've never seen one as big as this. His dick is nearly the length of my forearm and it's thick, with a dusky pink color. The tip reddens immensely, like he's sore from how hard he is. *His dick is so red.* Tufts of trimmed dirty blond hair cover the base of his cock and his shaft is so heavy, his erection leans to one side.

Clear fluid oozes from the tip.

"Don't just stare at it. The camera's rolling."

He probably doesn't mean to be insensitive. He's nervous about this too. It's not like he wants me in this position. I grasp the base of Aiden's cock to hold it up and he makes an uncomfortable grunting sound. He pulses with heat and saliva pools in the corners of my mouth against my will.

He's huge. I run my tongue over my lips so I can get them wet enough to stretch around Aiden. I lean forward and he grunts, nearly jerking back.

"I can't..."

I grasp his shaft tighter. It's too late to back out of this. Before Aiden can pull away from me and deny both of us a chance at survival and escape, I run my tongue over the head of his cock and lick up every drop of the clear fluid emerging from the tip. Aiden's next groan sounds more like an uncontrollable moan of pleasure.

Pleasing him is good. Pleasing him will bring this to a quicker end and I'll have a much greater chance at survival if I please him. The thought occurred to me that once my use has run out, he'll kill me, but I can't dwell on that. If pleasuring this man ensures my survival, it's what I'll do.

I tighten my lips around the smooth, bulging head of Aiden's big cock. He makes an ungodly pleasurable groan as I get his dick head wet with my spit and prepare myself to take the length of that enormous thing down my throat. If I gag, he could hurt me. I have to make him like it. We're being filmed, aren't we?

I tighten my lips more and get Aiden's dick even wetter. His next groan is even louder than the first and he touches the top of my head instinctively before remembering himself and jerking his hand away from me.

Men enjoy having lips around their cocks, but this man really likes it judging by the moans coming out of his mouth. I flatten my tongue along the underside of Aiden's shaft and then slide the full length of his dick into my mouth.

Tears prickle in the corners of my eyes as I stuff every inch of Aiden's dick in my mouth. He groans with pleasure again and I tighten my lips around the base of his cock as I feel the tip tickling the back of my throat, threatening my gag reflex to erupt. I squeeze my eyes shut and focus on breathing slowly through my nose.

As the tip of Aiden's cock touches the back of my throat, he moves his hips slowly with one thrust, and then he erupts. His climax happens so quickly that we're both equally surprised. The tears threatening to pierce the corners of my lids fall freely down my cheeks. I make a gagging sound as Aiden pumps thick ropes of cum into my throat.

The first warm gush fills my mouth and as Aiden tries to remove his cock from the sticky deposit of fluid between my lips, even more spills from the tip and he leaves my lips, face and mouth a mess of cum as he stumbles away and gains his composure after a few steps, making the conscious choice to put as much space between us as possible. There's surprise evident on his face, especially his eyes. *They're terrifying.*

I cough once and try to swallow the cum in my mouth, but that does nothing to remove the thick ropes coating my face and lips.

"Fuck," he says. "I've never..."

"I'm fine..." I whisper, leaning forward, trying to wipe the cum off my face and not wanting to look Aiden in the eye out of pure humiliation. I look ridiculous, I'm crying and there's cum all over me. I worry he won't go through with the instructions on the card. Then what? I'd rather stay here, thousands of miles away from the governor than to *ever* return. If Aiden doesn't finish this, I don't know who might come looking for him.

Aiden crosses the room, standing straight in front of me with his cock hanging limp. My body tenses with uncertainty. I can't predict how he'll react. He crouches in front of me, forcing me to gaze at him with concern. *Is he going to hit me?*

We're face to face and Aiden takes his finger, places it beneath my chin and turns my face so I'm staring him right in the eye. We're still on camera, but it doesn't feel like it. This moment is just for the two of us.

"That was the best head of my life," he whispers. "Once we make this fuck tape, I'll pay you back for that with my tongue. I owe you."

The touch of his finger and the intense blue gaze feel romantic, but Aiden's words emerge with a business tone. There's no romance here. I nod slowly and he rises to his feet.

"Get up," Aiden commands. "Get on the bed and face the camera."

He won't look at me as he commands me this time. I don't want him to look too closely. He's seen more than I would show a stranger, if I ever had control of my life enough to make the choice not to. I avoid gazing into the camera lens directly, but I obey Aiden and position myself in all fours on the bed.

I feel lewd on display like this. I tilt my head downward so my hair falls down over my shoulders to cover my breasts from the camera's view. It's not exactly modesty, but it's the closest I can manage given the circumstances.

I glance over at Aiden through my peripheral vision. He's hard again, with barely any time between this and his previous orgasm. The way he spoke about his ability to cum, I expected a man with some type of sexual dysfunction, not a seconds-long refractory period.

My throat tightens as I imagine my body stretching to accommodate that thing. I nearly choked on Aiden's dick in my mouth. That enormous thing could make me bleed if he isn't careful.

"Arch your back," Aiden whispers. "I want to see your ass."

It might be my imagination, but I swear his voice shakes like he believes the words emerging from his mouth represent the worst taboo. He approaches the bed slowly with that gigantic cock jutting from his hips.

"I've never filmed something like this," he murmurs as he draws closer. Aiden presses his large hand to my lower back tentatively. His hand is so fucking warm. His warmth spreads through me and I squeeze my thighs together to avoid any biological reactions to his touch.

I can't control my response to him. Aiden moves his hand down my lower back over my ass cheeks, his palm curving around my soft cheek. He makes a low growling sound in the back of his throat as he touches the inside of my thigh and discovers my wetness.

"That will make it much easier," he murmurs in response to my wetness. I think that'll be it, but Aiden slides his finger through my juices, swirling his index finger in slow circles through the juices on one thigh before moving to another. "But this is the only time. I don't fuck around with black women. Understood?"

I don't answer him. I just nod. If I'm going to have sex with this racist, I want to get it over with quickly. Judging from what happened before, maybe this won't last long. That's my best hope.

Click here to order Mafia Playmate:

https://bit.ly/bostonirishmafia1

Patreon

13 SEASONS OF SERIAL CHAPTERS

NEW preview chapters published WEEKLY on my Patreon.

Read all 6 seasons of *Unfuckable* (Ben & Libby's story)...

Unfuckable

For a small monthly fee, you get exclusive access to over 375 chapters of my first completed bwwm dark and spicy serial romance, as well as the spin-off serial...

DESPICABLE

The second serial, despicable has 300 chapters available for all Patreon subscribers to access instantly and... we officially have a **third completed spin-off bwwm romance series.**

And yes you get access to all of this at the $5/month tier with more benefits at more pricey tiers.

The third serial is about Clover + Thomas. Thomas has a shocking connection to a character in the second serial and Clover is an all-new African American female lead.

This series has three *very long* "seasons" of chapters, the length of five full-length novels all-together.

You will probably have over three months of binge-reading before catching up to current content, making this one of the most 'bang for your buck' author Patreon subscriptions out there.

Don't take my word for it.
Check the post history:
www.patreon.com/jamilajasper

PATREON HAS MORE THAN THE ONGOING SERIAL…

INSTANT ACCESS

- NEW merchandise tiers with **t-shirts, totes, mugs,** stickers and MORE!
- **FREE paperback** with all new tiers
- **FREE short story audiobooks** and audiobook samples when they're ready

- #FirstDraftLeaks of Prologues and first chapters **weeks** before I hit publish
- Behind the scenes notes
- Polls and story contribution
- Comments & LIVELY community discussion with likeminded interracial romance readers.

LEARN MORE ABOUT SUPPORTING A DIVERSE ROMANCE AUTHOR

www.patreon.com/jamilajasper

Thank You Kindly

Thank you to all my readers, new and old for your support with this new year.

I look forward to making 2023 an INCREDIBLE year for inter-racial romance novels. I want to thank you all for joining along on the journey.

www.patreon.com/jamilajasper

Thank you to my most supportive readers — my Patreon subscribers!:

Queen Ke

Jamie C

KimW

Warrior_pprincess

SavageSam

Roslyn H.

Katrina

LMSYT

Lainey R.

Naomi

GrumpyMillenial

Jay

Asia A.

Angela D.

Danyelle C.

WakeupMakeup Slay

Jocelyn F.

Nikki O.

Cdublu

Carla

Jonathan

Kelly

Jessica

Jasmine

DARSHELL

Dawn

Tiabuena3

Leigh

Yvonne

Ashlee

Crystal

Marshybabyyy

Shout

Quaniquequia

TK

Kayla

Shronda C.

Ma-Eyongerie

Kayla

Chantell

Kheiara

ophelia

Vickie

Cass

Kamil

Kaela

Love

Miryam

Charlene
Summer
Lola
Eryn
DD Davis
Symone
Deborah
Beatrice
Valescha
Khadija
makhalaab
Kaya
Glitter Garden
SavageSam
sybil arroyo
Ncsportsfan79
Jessica G.
Danielle
Yola
Joslin
Alexciz
Stacia
Ayanna
Asia
Hailey
Kaya
Nikki
Naomi O.
Jessica J
Chakiya
Noelle
kourtnee
Martha
Nikki Valentina
xjkpop

Valeria

BlkBae

SweetS

Msteeq

Rhonda

Darrah

Killa

Shavon

Misty

India

Kassandra

Imani

Nala

Chantell

Benvinda

Roger

Lexi B

Zapphire

Vbrooks

Tasha G

Kiera

Valencia

Stacy

YANITZA

Texansgurl76

Emma

Tinette

Jenny

Mariah

Nale

Tanisha

Trenita

Shelle

dulcemaria413

Shanice

Letarsha
Tania
Neeka
Julia
Linda
Lisa
Jiannie
Jillian
Tameka
Asia
Scarlette
Olwyn
R W
Fayefaefee
Brianna
Tiffany
Katie
Diamond
Kera
Tia
Love Reading
Dominique
Sheria
Jennifer
Georgette
Monique
Wendolyn
King Turtle22
Jessica
Nic M.
JustChill
DJC
Atira
TheeLastHokage
Yvonne

Chrissy

Janelle

Rian

LaRonda

LaRonda

Deanna

dlawson382

Jasmine

Haley

Belinda

Sercee

Yvonne

Jadelock

Farah

Tamiya

Quin

J.Payton

Geek Girl

Ashley

Rubi

Pilar

Sandra

Jurnee

Anni

Shannet

Joneesa

GlitzyHydra

Amanda

Barbara

Brianna

Jamica

Lyons

MARY ANN

Marketia

SarahD

LoverofHawaiiHearts

ceblue

Yolanda

MonaGirl Lewis

Dianna

Mary

amna

Nysha

fayola

Ty

Abria

Shyra

Andi-Mariee

Jamila

Naee's World

KEISHA

Jennett

Fredericka

Candece

Chante

Pholuv

Lydia A

Sabrina

JM

Jackie

Mo

Natrilly83

Ashaunte

Tolu

Margaret

Wendolyn

Lori

Dionne

ZLB

Kristina

Nicol

ELBERT

A. Harris

Jesi

Brenda

Desiree

Angela

Frances

LaShan

Only1ToniD

Debbie T.

Tiffanie

April L

shawnte

Kay

Lisema

Yvonne F

Natasha

Colleen

Julia

Amy

Jacklyn

Shyan R

Kiana B

Pearl

Javonda

Sheron

Maxine

Dash

Alicia

margaret

Love2Read

Juliette

Monica

Sandhya

MaryC
Trinity
Brittany
June
Ashleigh
Nene
Nene
Deborah
Nikki M
Dee
TyKira
Kimmey
Laytoya
Shel W
Arlene
Judith
Mary
Shanida
Rachel
Damzel
Ahnjala
Kenya
momo
BJ
Akeshia
Melissa
Tiffany
sherbear
Nini J
Curtresa
REGGIE A.
Ashley
Mia
Tink138110
Phia

Sharon
Charlotte
Assiatu C
Regina
Romanda
Catherine
Gaynor
BF
Perpetua
Tasha G
Henri Ann
sara
skkent
Rosalyn
Danielle
Deborah J
Kirsten
ANA
Taylor R.
Charlene
Louanna
Michelle
Tamika
Lauren
RoHyde
Natasha
Shekynah
Cassie
AnnaBooms
Keitheena
Nick R
Gennifer M
Rayna
Anton
Jaleda

Kimvodkna
JaTonn
Jazmine
Anoushka
Raynischa
Audrey
Valeria
Courtney
Donna
Patrisha
Jenetha
LaKisha J.
Ayana
Taylor
Christy
Monica
FreyaJo
GRACE
Kisha
Christine
Alexandra
Amber
Natasha
Stephanie
LaKisha
kristylove7
Cynthea
DENICE
Latoya
monifacd .
Doneishia
Mariah
Gerry
Yolanda T
Yolanda P

Susan D

Phyllis H

Alisa K

Daveena K

Desiree S

Kimberly B

Robin B

Gary S

Stephanie MG

Georgette A

Kathy

Marty

JanetDaniels

Megan

Shelle

Delores

Janet

Lydia

Phyllis

Freda

Charlott R

Join the Patreon Community.